I0663427

TOTHARS

BONDED BILLIONAIRE SHAPESHIFTERS
BOOK 2

D G IRELAND

ARTISTIC ORIGINS

CONTENTS

BOOKS BY DG IRELAND

Nonfiction	
The Puppy Baby Book	Mastering Your Money (2022)
Puppy Adoption and Beyond	Writers Preparation Handbook
Mastering Your Money (2008)	What's Breaking Your Budget
Online Classes	
Writers Preparation Handbook	How to Format Word Docs Like A Pro
Cozy Mysteries	**Sci-Fi-Fantasy**
The Alcott Family Adventures	**The Thol Series**
Hot Chocolate	Prophecy of Thol
Bitter Chocolate	Gifts From Thol
Spicy Chocolate	Love of Thol
Nutty Chocolate	King of Thol
Katz' Cat Series	Earth Calling Thol
Katz' Cat	**Sci-Fi Romance Adventure**
Bill Hill's Pills	Forced Dreams
The Detectives	**Dystopian**
The Pact	The Last Dog
	Texmexzona
Books by my Alter Ego ~ DG Ireland	
Bonded Shapeshifter Billionaire Series	
Bonded	
Tothars	
Titled	
Unforeseen	
Connected	
Need A Notebook?	
See my 54 themed notebooks on my website	
www.degreenfield.com/notebooks	
Screenplays formatted as books	
Plan B (Dark Comedy)	Where's Ralphie? (Family Comedy)
The God Child (Action Adventure)	Standing Dead (Drama/Tragedy)
The Far Corner (Sci-Fi/Psychological/Creatures)	
Screenplays as TV Episodes	
Hot Chocolate ~ Episode 1	Prophecy of Thol ~ Episode 1
Bonded ~ Episode 1	
See my screenplays and awards on my website: degreenfield.com	
Filmfreeway, ISA Network	

TO ALL MY READERS... if you discover bloopers in this book (or any of my books), PLEASE send me an email and tell me what the blooper is so I can fix it! dawn@degreenfield.com

ACKNOWLEDGMENTS

Many thanks to the Noun Project for their fabulous collection of icons, specifically Pedro Santos for the beautiful crown icon I have used between scenes.

A great cover says it all. Once again, Marcha Fox of Kalliope Rising Press delivered the goods.

Robert Beddow of robertbeddow.com is a graphics wizard. He placed the panther atop the crown, and it looks like it belongs there! Thanks, wizard!

Many thanks to Dr. Samantha Vanderslice (samantha-vanderslice.com) for her help with the herbal remedies Mr. Tran used in the book.

Nick at Bodleian Imaging helped me with information about scanning ancient manuscripts. I couldn't work that info into *Tothars*, but it will go into book 3, *Tilted*, in detail. https://www.bodleian.ox.ac.uk

ADULT CONTENT

CHAPTER ONE

GAGE STRYKER'S ENORMOUS BALD EAGLE LANDED IN THE middle of the lawn at the house in the woods. He transformed to his human form as gold, white and brown feathers pulled back through his pores and completely disappeared, leaving only tanned skin. He looked like a sandy-haired god as he stood naked in the twilight. His muscled structure was tense and glistened with sweat after the grueling search above the forest.

Shifters coming out of the woods joined Gage. Some in their human forms, some as their animals. Sherman Foo, the head of Panther Industries' Security Division met them. Sherm was one-hundred percent human; an Asian-American about to turn forty. A team of commandos followed him.

Someone had abducted Gage and Ari's life partner, Roman Davenport; shot with a tranquilizer gun while he was in his panther form and hauled onto a helicopter. Someone wanted him alive, but Gage didn't know why. Panther Industries Security waited for a ransom call to come through, but no call was forthcoming.

Roman, Gage and Ari were Tothars. Royalty. The kings

1

and queen of the entire shifter world—a secret world that most humans were unaware of. Ben Hatahle (Grandfather Silver Wolf), still sharp at one-hundred-two years old and confined to a wheelchair, had been thrilled when he met the Tothar kings. Eighty years had passed since he had last seen a Tothar in the United States.

At well over six-foot, Gage was stronger than the average man. His kind predated regular shifters. As a Tothar, his bald eagle was majestic—twice the size of a normal eagle with a wingspan of twenty-five feet.

"We can't leave here!" Ari yelled at Gage.

Ari Davis, a striking woman with waist-long, pure white wavy hair, looked like a wild woman as she stood on the grass outside the house in the woods. No one would ever guess her actual age. She was over seventy but barely looked fifty. While she was a Tothar, her bloodline was so weak there was no animal present, but Atsa, the Navajo shifter, insisted there was magic present.

Gage ran his hand through his hair in exasperation. "Ari, we need to go back to the city. Roman's not going to walk out of the woods. These bastards took him. They could come back for us."

"Ari, we retrieved the tranquilizer dart," Sherm said. He held up the baggie that held the dart. "We'll find a fingerprint and possibly someone will pick up a scent from it."

Leander, a king cobra shifter, and Gloria, a wolf shifter, hovered around Ari trying to calm her.

"Ari, my queen, you shouldn't stay here. Those people know where the house is. You're better protected in the city where our large family and your security detail are close by," Leander said.

"Come on, Ari, let's get everything gathered so we can get

out of here," Gloria said. They went into the house. They returned a few minutes later, Ari carrying her purse.

Gage grabbed his clothes off the chair by the sliding glass doors. He stepped into his briefs, then his jeans. He pulled his T-shirt over his head, covering the flying eagle tattoo that spanned his back, and the head of a bald eagle tattoo on each of his biceps. He sat and donned his socks and tennis shoes, then stood.

Sherm approached and huddled with Gage.

"I'll drive. You keep Ari close so she calms down," Sherm said. He turned to Grandfather Silver Wolf. "Want to ride in the helicopter?"

Silver Wolf's eyes bugged out. "Can I?"

"Do you think that's a great idea?" Gloria asked.

"All that can happen is I'd die," Silver Wolf said. "Going to eventually. Might as well have fun while I can!"

Sherm grabbed the back of the wheelchair. "Come on." He pushed the wheelchair through the trees to a clearing. He helped them into the helicopter and got them settled.

"Enjoy the ride." Sherm wiggled his eyebrows at Silver Wolf. "If you get motion sickness, there's a barf bag if you need one."

Sherm returned to where Gage was dealing with Ari. The shifters who came from the city to search the forest were clearing out in their vehicles. Leander was reluctant to leave while Ari was in a state of panic.

"Where are all the bags?" Sherm asked.

"Upstairs, first bedroom," Gage said. He had his arm firmly around Ari's waist, hugging her to his body.

Sherm and Leander headed upstairs and returned with the luggage. They placed them in the back of the SUV.

"You going to follow us?" Sherm asked Leander.

Gage eased Ari into the front seat, the middle position. He got in beside her.

"Yes. I'll stay close, just in case you need help," Leander said. No one stood a chance of getting to the royals while Leander was around. One quick shift and his king cobra could take down any man or beast with its venom.

Sherm got behind the wheel of the SUV and they headed out.

THEY ARRIVED BACK AT THE PENTHOUSE A LITTLE OVER two hours later. Ari bounced between rage and loss, her emotions all over the place. Roman and Gage were the loves of her life. The three of them were bonded Tothars, and the separation from Roman pulled on both Ari and Gage as if there were a physical hole in their hearts.

Gage settled Ari in bed with a sleeping pill left over from the anguished days of her own abduction.

It was late. He was worn out.

Gage grabbed the bourbon and a glass and poured himself a drink.

"What the fuck happened, Roman? Why didn't you call for help?"

He felt his best friend's loss. It hit him hard. For well over fifty years, the two men shared thoughts and conversations in their heads with their mind-talk. Snarky quips, warnings about danger, even menu items were a constant banter ongoing in their heads. It started when Roman rescued an injured Gage in the forest after being shot out of the sky by a hunter.

Gage knocked back the liquor, thought about having another glassful, but decided against it. He'd need his wits about him in the morning. He put the glass in the kitchen sink. Gage walked to the first hallway to Roman's room, where the three of them usually slept in Roman's gigantic custom bed.

He stripped his clothes off and joined Ari in bed. He dropped off into an exhausted, restless sleep, curled up against her.

GAGE CARRIED ARI'S BREAKFAST AND COFFEE TO THE bedroom. She was just stirring when he set the tray on the bedside table.

"Hi, honey. I've brought you something to eat."

Ari raised her head and focused on him. "Roman?"

Gage shook his head. "Nothing yet."

Ari turned her head into the pillow.

"It's going to be a very busy day. Come on, eat, shower and get dressed. We need to call the community together," Gage said.

He looked her over. She wasn't in the best possible mental place and appeared to have dropped back to sleep.

Gage dug his cellphone out and called Sherm.

"I want you to send two of the team up here to guard Ari. We need to have an emergency community meeting," he said. "I'm going down to the meeting room."

Gage kissed Ari's shoulder. He dug through the bags in the middle of the floor until he found Roman's clothes. He pulled out the shirt he had been wearing before he shifted. The elevator dinged and two of the security details arrived.

"She's sleeping right now. Make yourselves comfortable, but make sure she doesn't wander off," Gage said.

"Don't worry, we'll watch over her. No one's getting near her," one guard said.

The elevator dinged and Kevin and Jason, Ari's sons, rushed into the apartment.

"We just heard!" Jason said. He grabbed Gage in a hug. "I hope they don't hurt Roman!"

Kevin hugged Gage when Jason let go of him. "Is mom okay?"

Gage exhaled. He looked thoughtful. "We'll get through this. She's sleeping. Come on downstairs. I expect people to show up for a meeting."

He grabbed Roman's shirt, and they took the elevator downstairs to the lobby. He stopped at the reception desk. "I'm expecting a large number of people. You may need to issue a few badges."

"We'll take care of it," the security guard said.

Gage and the boys entered the event suite. Leander paced.

They all bumped fists.

Leander lifted his chin toward the shirt in Gage's grip. "That Roman's?"

Gage nodded. "I figured I'd bring it for anyone who didn't recognize his scent."

"Good idea," Leander said. "Any word from the satellites?"

Gage shook his head. The stress exhausted him. "How's Ari?" Leander asked.

"Not good," Gage said. "I hope this doesn't tip her over the edge. She's barely over her own ordeal."

Leander nodded.

Gage turned to Jason and Kevin. Ari's sons had recently discovered the shifter world their mother kept secret from them. "Sit tight. People will be curious about you since you're human, but no one should give you any problems."

People started arriving and in less than an hour the room filled.

Gage stepped onto the stage as everyone settled into chairs. The door opened again.

Atsa, Yiska and three shifters from the Navajo reservation in New Mexico entered.

Kevin and Jason stared as the Navajos marched into the room.

Gage raised his hand in welcome to Atsa and the men. He tapped the microphone. "Everyone, settle down. We've got serious business to discuss."

He waited a minute for the remaining shifters to take a seat and be quiet.

"I want to thank our Navajo shifter friends Atsa, Yiska and these men from the reservation in New Mexico for coming to our aid." Gage pointed out the Navajos.

"And most of you have not met your queen's sons, Kevin and Jason Davis." He pointed to them. A lot of curious faces took in Ari's boys.

"Roman was taken sometime between three and five yesterday afternoon. We don't know for what purpose, or who's behind it, or where they have taken him. He was in his panther form, and they tranquilized him and loaded him onto a helicopter."

Murmurs sounded throughout the room.

"We're running fingerprints from the dart to see if we get any hits that will give us a general idea of where to look. We don't have a motive. I thought perhaps someone wanted a panther for their collection, but I doubt that. Only a local shifter would know that a panther sometimes ran in the forest.

Who outside our community knew he was a shifter, or a Tothar?"

"Who would have known we would be at the house in the forest yesterday? There are so many unanswered questions. Our security team is watching satellites for the helicopter, and all airports within a three-hundred-mile radius. If someone is transporting him somewhere, they would require a private plane. So far, we have no information.

"I brought Roman's shirt. If you don't have his scent, please bend and inhale—don't touch the shirt—don't contaminate it with cross-odors. It will be difficult to filter them out. The only other scent on the shirt will be mine."

"He may be here in the city. We don't know where they might have taken him, so I want everyone in the community to be on high alert for his scent," Gage said.

The meeting wound down and people left.

Gage approached Atsa and his delegation. He flopped down in a chair. His body ached from the stress knotting his muscles.

Kevin, Jason and Leander joined them. Gage introduced them to the Navajos.

"This stinks of a pissing contest," Atsa said. Yiska nodded agreement.

"You told us if someone got their hackles up, they'd let us hear about it," Gage said. "So, you think there's another Tothar out there?"

"Either another Tothar, or someone with a large shifter community who feels threatened," Atsa said. "Have you had any problems with anyone lately?"

Gage explained about the two women. Celeste, the woman from five years earlier who had her eyes set on Roman, and Lisa, the cougar shifter who had attacked Ari more recently. He clarified that Celeste was a human who wasn't aware of the shifter community.

"I've got a call in to Lisa's alpha to find out if she's disappeared," Leander said.

"She's a total whack job," Gage said. He thought for a moment. "She would have known we would be at the house."

"I'll kill her," Jason said. His nerves were coiled tight.

"Calm down, young Tothar," Atsa said. "This is a time to keep your head on straight."

"Tothar?" Jason asked.

Jason and Kevin exchanged questioning looks.

Atsa nodded. "Like your mom, very weak, but the bloodline is there."

"You are princes," Yiska said.

Kevin, Jason and Gage were stunned.

"We never considered Kevin or Jason had any Tothar blood since Ari's was so weak," Gage said. "Why don't we go upstairs?"

Gage shut off the lights, and they rode the elevator to the penthouse. He nodded to the guards.

Gage settled everyone in the living room with coffee. He sat on the sofa and stared out the wall of glass to the mountains in the distance for a minute, then focused on his guests.

"I don't know what to do," Gage confessed.

"There's nothing you can do," Atsa said. "Whoever has Roman has an agenda. They will contact you in their own sweet time."

The elevator dinged, the doors opened, and Sherm stepped out.

Everyone focused on Sherm. He shook his head. "Nothing yet."

He flopped down in a chair. Gage went to the kitchen and

grabbed a cup and poured Sherm coffee. He handed it off to him and settled on the sofa.

Atsa and Yiska's phones constantly dinged incoming texts.

"I sent a picture of Roman in his human and cat form to my shifter network throughout the US," Atsa said. "So far, no one has seen him in any form."

Leander's phone rang. He looked at the name on the screen. "It's Trisha Anderson, Lisa's alpha." He clicked the speaker and answered the call. "Trisha, what's the word on Lisa?"

The woman sounded out of breath. She inhaled deeply. "I'm at Lisa's place right now. The place is ransacked as if a tornado went through here. I'm not sure if she was in a rush to get out of town, or if someone did this and took her."

"Do you pick up any scents?" Sherm asked. He slid to the edge of his chair, ready to spring.

"I've picked up unfamiliar scents," Trisha said. "I'm not sure what I detect."

"Stay there, we'll come over," Gage said.

A caravan of three SUVs screeched to a halt in front of a small house. Doors opened and slammed shut as everyone disembarked from the vehicles and headed up the walkway.

TRISHA ANDERSON OPENED THE DOOR. "MAYBE YOU'LL have a better chance at identifying these scents."

Another vehicle pulled up and parked. Sherm's forensics team unloaded their cases and joined the small crowd at the door.

"Better let the team crawl through there and see if there's

any evidence before we contaminate the place." Sherm had a moment. "On second thought, all shifters go inside. Keep your hands in your pockets. Don't touch anything. Walk carefully—don't shuffle. Get whatever scents are inside and come right back outside."

Kevin, Jason, and Trisha stood to the side with Sherm as the shifters, led by Gage, entered the house.

Gage stood in the center of the living room and inhaled deeply. He walked through the other small rooms, stood in the middle of each room, and pulled in deep breaths. He had the scents, but he didn't recognize them. He hoped someone in the community could identify the odor.

Leander nudged Gage. They left the house, followed by the other shifters.

Sherm nodded to his team to enter and start on the process.

"Whoever was in there emitted a strange odor," Atsa said. "I'm still trying to place it."

Leander nodded. "I think it's garlic and olive oil. But there's another scent mixed into those. Probably an animal scent that's doused in the stuff so I couldn't determine what type of shifter was in there."

The shifters nodded in agreement.

Gage stared at Leander for a moment. "Yeah, I think you're right. Garlic and olive oil. So, maybe someone who cooks?" He turned to Trisha. "Do you know if Lisa cooked? Has to be somebody who either cooks a lot with garlic and olive oil, or takes cooking seriously to leave that scent."

"Lisa didn't have much in the way of kitchen skills. She ate out most of the time," Trisha said.

"Did you notice anything in particular that looked suspicious?" Gage asked.

"The place is a wreck, so it's difficult to tell if there's something that stands out," Trisha said. "I will take her down if she was involved in Roman's abduction!"

"Stand in line," Atsa said.

THE FORENSICS TEAM DUSTED EVERY SURFACE FOR fingerprints. They sifted through every bit of trash and bagged all bits of paper regardless if it was covered in banana peels or grease from takeout food. They inspected every waste basket item. They examined all clothing for blood and collected all dust bunnies for testing. Boxes and bags stuffed in closets were dug through.

After every surface was thoroughly scrutinized, the forensics team vacated the house and returned to the lab with their finds.

"Okay, everyone. Let's head back to the penthouse," Sherm said.

"Why don't we grab something to eat on the way," Gage said.

They all piled into the vehicles and headed out with Trisha following in her own car.

CHAPTER TWO

GAGE CALLED POMODORO'S. IT WAS HIS, ARI, AND Roman's favorite restaurant. When they arrived, they were escorted to one of the side rooms used for small parties. The group settled at the tables, placed their food and beverage orders and limited their discussions to small talk until the restaurant wait staff was out of range.

Leander, Atsa, Yiska and Gage pulled in deep breaths. "You don't think it's someone from Pomodoro's, do you?"

Kevin was shocked at the thought. They'd been coming to the restaurant for years.

Gage shook his head. "Nope, I don't detect the specific scent here, but I had to check."

"That would make sense," Sherm said. "Let's face it, the perpetrators may very well be someone you know."

"This business with Lisa is awfully suspicious," Leander said. "It's too much of a coincidence her disappearing so close to Roman's kidnapping."

Atsa stood. "I'm going to walk around, just to be sure."

After lunch everyone headed back to the Panther Industries high-rise in downtown Reading. Gage left the Navajos at the front desk so security could assign them to a furnished apartment in the building, and give them access to a vehicle. Leander offered to be their guide.

Gage headed to the twenty-eighth floor to Sherm's domain. Everyone else resumed their duties. They agreed to gather again for dinner at the penthouse to discuss any findings and compare notes.

Sherm waved Gage over to one of the monitors on his wall. About forty fingerprints were lined up on the screen with accompanying data. "We're gathering shifters in the community we've identified from fingerprints in Lisa's apartment. We'll interview them to determine where they fit into the scheme of things."

Gage studied the screen. "None of ours should show up because we all kept our hands in our pockets."

"In the meantime, there's a team at your property installing cameras throughout the woods. Should have done this several years ago, but hindsight and all that," Sherm said.

Gage pulled his hands through his hair. "We should have done that after those dimwits stormed the house. I don't know what the fuck we were thinking!"

The door buzzed open and Ari and the two guards entered.

"Anything?" she asked.

Gage kissed her forehead and folded her in his arms. "Nothing."

Ari released a breath. She teared up and hid her face behind her hands. "No one's called?"

"No demands yet," Sherm said.

Ari sniffled. "I'm going to lie down." The guards followed her out the door.

"She's holding up better than I expected," Gage said. "How

could that helicopter vanish? Why haven't your guys been able to track it?"

"We've still got our eyes on the satellites. We don't know when they nabbed Roman," Sherm said. "We can only guesstimate. There're so many unknowns. Time and direction."

Sherm's desk phone buzzed. Caller ID showed Kevin was calling. He looked through his glassed wall and saw Lonnie looking over Kevin's shoulder at his cubicle.

Sherm put the call on speaker. "What'd you find?"

"I'm pretty sure I found that bird," Kevin said. "I backed up my search to just before three o'clock yesterday. I've captured satellite pictures beginning at two-fifty-six p.m. Lonnie's checking out the exact location of takeoff and it looks like your property."

Gage and Sherm were out the door to Kevin's cube. Lonnie's fingers clacked across a keyboard.

"Destination looks to be New Bedford Regional Airport in Massachusetts. Lots of private planes and jets. We're going to get on the phone and start calling," Lonnie said.

Gage let out a deep sigh. "At least we have something!"

"Maybe we'd better send a team with Roman's human and panther pictures," Sherm said. "And we may luck out with images of who took him via security footage."

"If he hasn't shifted, it would be hard to hide a gigantic panther in a cage," Lonnie said.

"Who do we have close by?" Sherm asked Lonnie.

"No teams in the area, but I'll gather someone from Bruce's team and we'll fly out within the hour," Lonnie said.

Gage's face lit up with a thought. "Take a shifter with you to see if he can scent him."

"Good idea. I'll let you make those arrangements," Lonnie said.

"I'll be back," Gage said. He took off from Sherm's office and went upstairs. He stepped off the elevator into the penthouse, nodded to the two guards, and went directly to Roman's bedroom. The bed was empty.

"Ari?" He retraced his steps and found Ari in the kitchen making tea.

He walked up behind her and wrapped her in his arms. "How are you doing?"

She turned in his arms and wrapped her arms around his waist. "Better. Any progress?"

Gage brought her up to date on what Kevin discovered. "Leander is with Atsa and his guys. Who would be the best type of shifter we can call upon to go with Lonnie?"

Ari abandoned her tea and rushed from the room, Gage on her heels. She headed to her suite and sat at her desk.

"Bears have the best sense of smell of all terrestrial mammals. I looked it up a while back," she said. "We have great bear shifters!"

She pulled up her shifter database sorted by animal groups. She tapped the screen. Bradley Parsons was the leader of the group. She pulled out a sticky note and wrote his name and number for Gage.

He whipped out his phone and placed the call. Then he called Sherm. "Bradley Parsons will have a bear shifter downstairs. Ari said bears have the best ability to scent, so when Lonnie goes searching, you'll have a bear to lend a hand."

Gage turned to Ari. "Now, all we have to do is wait for news."

LONNIE, TWO FROM BRUCE'S TEAM AND THE BEAR SHIFTER boarded the jet at Reading Regional Airport. The bear shifter was well over six feet tall and built like a lumberjack. Lonnie and his team were in Panther Industries Security Division uniforms. They looked as intimidating as the bear.

Lonnie's phone dinged a text from Kevin. He had arranged for a TSA security escort to be waiting for them when they landed in New Bedford. The TSA agent was a chipmunk shifter who would escort them throughout the airport.

He hoped they could make a quick trip of it and not have to stay overnight. They'd find out in a few hours.

After the jet came to a full stop, they deplaned and headed over to the terminal. They met Bucky, the TSA shifter who assigned them badges and explained the rules.

Bucky didn't have a great sniffer like the bear shifter, but it was decided Bucky and Big Bear Muchisky would be in the lead to scent each area they searched.

After two hours of asking questions, showing pictures, and the shifters sucking in air to pick up scents, Big Bear Muchisky suddenly grabbed Lonnie's arm. He pulled him to a stop.

The giant shifter, well over six-six, stuck his nose in the air and turned his head this way and that. He nodded to a hangar.

"Roman was there! I picked up his scent clear as day," Big Bear said.

Bucky stuck his nose in the air and picked up an animal scent. "Wasn't that long ago either?"

"Okay, let's go," Lonnie said. "I'll record this." He took his cellphone out of his pocket and set the voice recorder to roll.

Lonnie, Bucky, Big Bear and the two commandos walked over to the hangar. "I want one of my guys to walk the perimeter of this hangar building. Make it the two of you so you can cover from both sides."

As Bucky, Lonnie, and Big Bear stood at a section of the open hangar door, Big Bear sniffed.

"I just picked up the garlic and olive oil scent along with Roman's scent," Big Bear said.

A man in his forties, dressed in jeans and a short-sleeved shirt with a logo, approached them from inside the hangar. He eyed the group with a leery expression plastered on his face: TSA, a huge man, and some strangers.

"Can I help you?" The guy appeared nervous as his eyes wandered over the group.

Lonnie held out his hand, and they shook. "Have you seen either this man or this black panther?" Lonnie held out the photos.

The man took the photos and studied them. "Didn't see this man, but I did see the panther. What a beauty! And huge! They had him in a cage, and it looked like he was out cold. We fueled their jet, helped them load the crate, and they took off."

Lonnie let out a loud breath. "Would you be able to tell me who they were, where they were heading, and when they left?"

"What's this all about?" the man asked. "That's typically not done. There's FAA rules and regulations to keep these things private."

"We're just having a friendly conversation to identify where these people had their jet serviced," Bucky said. "No regulatory problems. We appreciate your time and willingness to talk to us."

"They stole the panther from a very wealthy businessman and he's not happy," Lonnie said.

The guy eyed Lonnie. "Have the cops been called? Animal control?"

"We work for that wealthy businessman I mentioned. He

prefers to handle his own problems with his own security detail," Lonnie said.

The men who had performed a perimeter search returned and joined their group.

They followed Bucky back to the terminal building, handed in their badges, and walked back to the Panther Industries jet. Bucky shook their hands.

"I'm sorry I couldn't help more," Bucky said. "Due to terrorism, flight information is highly guarded."

"Not to worry. We've got people who can figure things out. Your kings and queen appreciate your help. It's not our intention to jeopardize your position with the TSA," Lonnie said.

They boarded the jet. Lonnie sent information to Sherm, Travis, and Kevin. He told them to check the airport security cameras and to have Travis get into the computer system from the hangar where Roman's scent was evident.

TRAVIS HACKED INTO THE COMPUTER SYSTEMS AT THE airport. He cross-referenced the information from the private hangar to the flight tower, tail number of the jet, itinerary, destination, pilot's name and everything else.

Kevin hacked into the security systems and found a scratchy video showing Roman's panther in a cage being loaded onto the private jet.

"The manifest shows Stefano Bianchi as the pilot and contact person. They left at ten-forty-five last night," Travis told Lonnie and Sherm.

"The destination is Italy," Lonnie said. "How is it that they didn't give the exact destination? Did they pay someone off to be as vague as possible?"

They began a search for this Bianchi person.

Lonnie received a ding from one of the team. They identified the fingerprint on the dart as belonging to one Salvatore (Sal) De Luca.

TWO MORE DAYS PASSED. EVERYONE WAS TESTY, AND ARI seemed to be slipping. She slept more and talked less. On the evening of the fifth night, Gage, Leander, Atsa, and Yiska were drinking whiskey in the living room. The elevator dinged Jason and Kevin's arrival.

"Where's Sherm and Lonnie?" Jason asked.

"They're focused on that jet, trying to find the exact destination," Gage said.

Ari stumbled down the hall and into the living room in a tank top and panties. She swayed, grabbed the edge of the bar and steadied herself as she stared at the group.

"Atsa?" Her voice was groggy from the sleeping pill she had taken hours earlier.

Gage jumped to his feet. "Ari! Honey, we have company." He blocked her from the guests.

Kevin jumped up and ran down the hall. He returned with her bathrobe and helped her slip into it.

Gage and Kevin guided Ari to the sofa. Her hair stuck out like a rat's nest. She rubbed her face briskly and focused.

"I had a strange dream—or something—Gage. I sort of saw through Roman's panther eyes," Ari said. She rubbed her face to become more alert. "I'm positive it was real."

"Remote viewing?" Yiska asked Atsa.

Atsa nodded. "Sounds like it." He turned his focus to Ari. "What did you see?"

"He's in a cell, and he's all doped up. I don't know what they gave him, but he can't stand or anything."

"Focus on what's around him. What's in the cell? Do you see the room?" Atsa directed her.

Ari was quiet for a long moment. "It looked like an ancient building. Maybe a rounded room—like a tower? The walls were old stone, and I saw a small window way up high with bars. I think I saw a banner blowing in the wind."

Gage perked up. "Were there any words or symbols on the banner?"

Ari closed her eyes. She swayed on the sofa. "Something, something Palazzo."

"Those names were Italian," Gage said. "I assumed they might be with the Italian mob in Philly, Jersey, or New York. Perhaps I was wrong?"

"Rule nothing out," Atsa said.

"Ari, can you communicate with Roman?" Gage asked.

"I've tried and tried, but he's all groggy." Ari fretted.

"Whoever these fuckers are, they'll regret the day they thought of this plan," Gage said.

He pulled out his phone. "Sherm? He's definitely in Italy." Moments later the elevator dinged, and Sherm and Lonnie stepped into the penthouse. Gage explained Ari's vision and the banner.

"Italy's a big country," Sherm said. "He could be anywhere. Whoever has Roman must have paid off officials. If Roman were still in his panther form, he would have had to be smuggled into the country. So, we're looking for someone who has the money and ability to make people look the other way."

"Why don't you send the bears to Italy? There's fourteen," Leander suggested.

"We could quadrant off the country into a grid so they can track down this banner and tower," Lonnie said.

"Okay. We need to find out if they all have up-to-date passports. Maybe they could take their wives on a second honeymoon or something?" Gage shrugged.

"Remember, these guys are working stiffs. They're not going to have a budget for travel. Plus, they'll have to get time off from work, make arrangements for kids and schools—all those things," Ari said.

"As soon as I have a list of names, I can assign them each a temporary credit card," Jason said. "I'll need specific information for each one."

"Better get some Euros out of the vault," Gage said. "They'll need cash in a lot of the rural areas."

Jason made a list.

NOT ALL THE BEARS HAD PASSPORTS. THOSE WHO DID jumped at the chance not only to find their king but also to take a once in a lifetime trip. Panther Industries put money in their pockets, gave them an unlimited credit card, and paid all expenses. They would travel in the comfort of a private jet. They also set out with brand-new iPhones. They were loaded with telephone numbers and email addresses of their entire group, the top brass in Panther Industries, the Security Division, and a team that was currently in Europe.

As everyone settled into their seats on the jet, Sherm climbed the stairs and entered the large cabin.

"We really appreciate all of you taking this unscheduled trip away from your homes and obligations," Sherm said. "Do not take any chances. If you detect Roman's scent, you are to call me immediately. Then call everyone else in the group so you can all gather in one location and wait for further instructions."

"We'll find our king!" Big Bear Muchisky said. "Whoever these bastards are, we'll hunt them down!"

"Remember, call day or night. There's a European team that can be there to assist you within a short time," Sherm said. "It will take us longer to join you from the States, but Gage, Ari, and her sons will join you."

They ended their discussion, and Sherm left the jet.

TWO WEEKS PASSED WITH NO SCENTING OR SIGHTINGS OF Roman. Italy was a large country consisting of 116,347 miles with a population of over sixty-million people. The bears trekked through streets, alleys, rural villages, cities—there was still a lot of the country to get through. They all had the description of the stone tower from Ari's remote viewing, along with the banner.

Three days earlier there was excitement when one of the bear teams found a round stone tower. But time and environment partially destroyed it, and the tower contained no evidence of Roman's scent, and no banner was in the area.

Ari spiraled downward toward the middle of the second week. When she wasn't crying or sleeping, she stared off into space. Gage stayed by her side, not wanting to let her out of his sight for fear of her safety. She was unstable in her loss for Roman. He barely slept at night, afraid she would sneak out of the apartment to do God knows what.

Both Gage and Ari suffered from what they called separation anxiety from Roman. Their bond was iron clad. He had talked to Atsa at length about his fears. What if they never found Roman? What if Roman died? How would he and Ari survive? They were barely hanging on now.

"You will know, without a doubt, if Roman died," Atsa said

more than once. "You're going to find him and bring him home."

"My head is so quiet I can't stand it," Gage said.

GAGE, KEVIN, AND JASON STOOD AT THE FOOT OF THE BED. Ari clung to the bedding. Her hair was in a complete tangle.

"Come on, Ari," Gage begged. "We need to change the linens."

"Mom! For Christ's sake, you look like a woman in an asylum from the early nineteen-hundreds," Jason growled in anger.

"Please go take a shower and let us change the bed," Kevin said. "You stink and the sheets stink!"

Gage shook his head with looming regret. He turned to Ari's sons. "Ready?"

Kevin and Jason nodded, grim-faced.

Gage swooped in, flung the covers back and hauled Ari out of the bed. She screeched, clawed and bit him. He was glad she wasn't wearing shoes because her heels bashed his legs hard. He fought her to the floor, panting hard, and hovered over her.

"Mom! Quit it! You're hurting Gage!" Jason yelled. He couldn't believe his mother was acting like a maniac.

Kevin and Jason quickly stripped the sheets off the custom-sized bed and flung them on the floor.

Ari struggled under Gage. She tried to crawl to the pile of dirty sheets.

"Jeeze, Ari! Stop it!" Gage could barely contain her.

Kevin grabbed the dirty sheets and ran to the butler's pantry and threw them in the washer. Gage had already prepped the washing machine with a natural detergent and

Borax laundry booster, and vinegar in the bleach dispenser. Kevin pushed the button and started the cycle.

"Wash is started," he yelled.

Gage released Ari. She sprinted from the bedroom to the butler's pantry.

Kevin tried to block her from the washer.

"Move, Kevin!" Her face contorted in a crazy rage.

"Stop it, Mom! The sheets are filthy," Kevin yelled back. The water poured into the machine.

Kevin attempted to put his arms around his mother. She shoved him out of the way and pounded on the buttons to stop the cycle. She lifted the lid as it unlocked and discovered the sheets drenched.

Ari sank to the floor, wrapped her arms around her knees, and wailed. "You've taken away all I had left of Roman's scent!"

Gage entered the butler's pantry, gathered her in his arms and held her as Kevin and Jason stood nearby, uncomfortable about their mother's condition.

"Thanks, I couldn't have managed without you," Gage told them.

"You okay, man?" Kevin asked.

"Yeah. I'll take it from here," Gage said.

"We'll make the bed," Jason said. "Come on, Kev."

Gage gathered a sobbing Ari up in his arms and headed to the bathroom. "Let's get you cleaned up." He stood her on the floor, shut and locked the door, and started the shower. Gage stripped his clothes off, then removed her dirty long tank top and panties. He tugged her into the shower.

CHAPTER THREE

ROMAN WAS SPRAWLED ON THE COLD, STONE FLOOR IN THE tower room in his panther form. His cat had lost weight. Mouth open, drool dripping on the floor, his breath appeared shallow as he lost consciousness again. An hour later his eyes slowly opened. He shivered.

Mice scurried across the floor. Cobwebs hung from the ceiling at the cell door. The place smelled of urine and feces and reeked a dank, moldy old scent. A chill hung in the tower that settled in the bones. The stone floor sent an ache through Roman's body.

Giuseppe Genovesi stood over his prisoner. He leered down at Roman with cruel, cold eyes. Giuseppe's tawny hair was laced with white, but his face remained unlined. He grabbed the panther's scruff roughly, lifting Roman's head off the floor.

"You will die here by my hand and no one will know what happened to you," Giuseppe sneered.

Roman could barely focus his eyes. He couldn't shift to his human form. Didn't have enough energy to communicate with the Tothar king telepathically. He didn't know what the man wanted of him, other than to kill him—starve him to death.

The old Tothar king jammed a needle into the panther's shoulder.

Roman opened his mouth to growl, but no sound emerged. He fell back to the floor, out cold once again.

THE PANTHER BECAME CONSCIOUS AGAIN. HE SMELLED A human and detected footsteps echoing in the corridor as they approached his cell. A man in a long brown robe stood at the door to his cell and someone stood in back of him.

Roman tried to rise to his feet. His body did not possess the energy to stand. He flopped back to the floor and let out a low rumble of a growl.

He heard keys clang against the door and the snick of the lock turning. The hinges squeaked a bit when the door opened, and the two men entered his prison.

The first man approached him, fearless. The man got on his knees and performed a preliminary health check. He pulled a stethoscope out of his pocket and listened to Roman's heart. He first lifted one droopy eyelid, then the other. The man spoke in Italian to his companion, but Roman did not understand the language.

A large piece of raw meat slapped down on the floor inches from Roman's mouth. He heard water running, and the large metal bowl settled on the floor in the corner.

More words passed between the two men, then they retreated through the cell door. Moments later, they returned, hauling a bale of hay between them. They cut the cord and piled hay in a corner opposite the water bowl.

The man who examined him sank to his knees by Roman's

face. He pointed to the hay and said something in Italian. He uttered one word in English: bed.

Roman's eyes flicked in the hay's direction. Then his eyes closed once again.

DONATELLO, IN HIS BROWN WOOL ROBE, STOOD BEFORE Giuseppe Genovesi, humble. He clasped his hands together in front of himself to still their trembling, which had nothing to do with his sixty-year-old appearance or any medical condition. He waited for permission to speak.

"What news do you have to report, Donatello? Is the Tothar still alive?" Giuseppe asked. The old shifter sat at his desk and set his fountain pen aside. He carefully placed a blotter on the page and closed the journal. His tailored suit, of the finest wool, fit to perfection, as did his immaculate white shirt and diamond cufflinks.

The window by the desk overlooked a large brick courtyard with fountains, statues, and lush gardens. The room contained art in gilded frames and tapestries, along with statues and busts from centuries past.

Donatello bowed slightly. "He is not well, Master Giuseppe. He has lost weight and can't stand because he's too groggy from the drugs."

Giuseppe appeared satisfied with the report. "That is as it should be. There is only room for one Tothar king, and it isn't this American panther."

Donatello shifted. "What are your plans for the panther, master?"

"I have not decided yet," Giuseppe said. "What of my niece? What does she have to say?"

"She is enamored of this Roman Davenport and desires him as a mate," Donatello said. He cleared his throat.

"Yes? You have more to report?" Giuseppe skewed Donatello with an impatient mask.

"Lisa said he lives with a woman and a man."

"In what capacity?" Giuseppe appeared thoughtful.

"She did not give details," Donatello said. "Shall I get her on the phone for you?"

Giuseppe nodded.

Donatello approached the desk and turned the phone to face him. He picked up the receiver of the vintage porcelain phone and dialed the number. After the third ring, a man with a gruff voice answered the phone.

"Who's calling and what is your business?" the man asked.

Donatello got down to business, in Italian. "Giuseppe Genovesi wishes to speak to his niece. Put her on the phone immediately."

There was a grunt on the other end of the line, some muffled speech, then Lisa was on the phone.

"One moment, please," Donatello said. He turned the phone toward Giuseppe and handed him the receiver.

"Lisa," Giuseppe growled into the phone.

"Hello, uncle Giuseppe."

"Who is the woman and man that live with this panther?" Giuseppe asked.

"They're his business partners," Lisa lied.

"He lives with his business partners?" Giuseppe raised his eyebrows and shared a brief questioning look with Donatello.

Donatello shrugged and shook his head—it was a mystery to him.

"Yes. They live in a penthouse in the building where his company is," Lisa said. "He's a billionaire. If I marry him, I'll be rich."

"He is not the one for you," Giuseppe said. "There can only ever be one Tothar king, and I'm not stepping down anytime soon."

"But Uncle Giuseppe..." Lisa stammered.

"There is no *but*, Lisa. Those are the rules of our kind," Giuseppe's tone was icy. "Do not make me angry, little girl. You will not like the lesson I dish out."

He heard her swallow over the telephone line. "You're not going to hurt him, are you?"

Giuseppe huffed out an exasperated breath. "Have you not been listening, Lisa? There is only ever *one* Tothar king." He slammed the receiver down on the phone and cursed in Italian.

Donatello stood quiet, head slightly bowed. He waited for the storm to abate.

A young man entered the room carrying a stack of mail.

He bowed to Giuseppe. "Your mail, Master Giuseppe."

"You dare to enter my space without an invitation?" Giuseppe rose from the chair and was across the room in an almost untraceable blur. His hands transformed into claws and he slashed the young man from scalp to chin.

The mail carrier screeched in agony and the mail flew out of his hands as he clutched his bleeding face.

"Pick up the mail!" Giuseppe boomed.

The man wiped the blood from his face on his robe and dove to the floor. He retrieved the scattered mail from across the floor like a monkey scurrying about on all fours.

"Your mail, Master Giuseppe," the young man said, trying not to blubber. He held the mail out to Giuseppe with shaking hands.

Giuseppe snatched the envelopes and returned to his desk.

"May I be excused, master?" the young man asked.

Giuseppe nodded. The mail carrier hurried from the room, sniveling.

"I want to speak with this Roman Davenport," Giuseppe said. He noticed a tiny blood splatter on his shirt and growled loudly, his ancient cat furious.

"He can't shift, master. He's too drugged and too weak," Donatello said.

"Forego the drugs," Giuseppe said.

THREE DAYS PASSED WITHOUT BEING DRUGGED. ROMAN'S panther was weak. His ribs were visible beneath his pelt, which was no longer glossy. The key turned in the lock, and the cell door squeaked open. Donatello stood before the lackluster panther.

"My master, Giuseppe Genovesi, requests you to shift to your human form so he can speak with you," Donatello conveyed.

Roman's panther eyes shifted up to Donatello's face with eyes barely focused. He was starving. He had no energy. Roman couldn't shift if his life depended on it.

Donatello continued to stare down at him as if he expected Roman to respond to his statement. After a long, silent moment, he turned on his heels and retreated from the cell, locking the door behind him. He walked down the corridor to the stairwell and descended several floors. He arrived on the ground floor and passed several rooms with open doors.

"Donatello!"

He turned to the whispered voice, glanced around, then slunk into the dark room and closed the door behind him.

A middle-aged man in a brown robe stood in the shadows. "We can't stand by while this young Tothar dies!"

"Marco, what do you propose to do? Giuseppe will kill us—shred us to pieces!" Donatello whispered back. "I don't want this Tothar to die. He's so weak he can't shift. I worry as each day passes that Giuseppe will kill him."

"We need to contact his people to rescue him!" Marco wailed. His face was awash in pain, barely visible through the low light of the room.

"They'd better come with an army," Donatello said. "No one survives a confrontation with Giuseppe's beast."

"I'm going to contact this Panther Industries," Marco said.

"Be careful, my friend. He's not in a good mood—just ask Simon," Donatello said. He opened the door a crack and saw no one. He slipped out of the dark room and headed to his master's office.

CHAPTER FOUR

GAGE LAY BESIDE ARI IN THE BED AND LISTENED TO HER sleep. He wondered if he'd ever get another thorough night's sleep. Thoughts of Roman and where he could possibly be hidden in Italy clouded his mind. He and Ari hadn't made love since Roman's disappearance. He wondered what their future held. Would their bond hold if it were just he and Ari? He really didn't have the desire to make love, but the thought of the act was there in his mind.

He eased himself out of bed and slipped out the door, chest and feet bare, wearing pajama pants only. Gage quietly grabbed the bottle of bourbon and a rocks glass from the fully stocked bar. He didn't even bother with ice. Gage poured the whiskey into the glass and wandered over to the sofa. He eased onto the cushion and put his feet on the coffee table.

Gage stared out into the night sky and thought about flying. He rubbed his hands over his face. He couldn't recall a time when he was more despairing, other than when Ari had been abducted by that maniac serial killer.

Somewhere, his phone chirped. He stood, looked around,

and made his way to the kitchen. He backtracked to the bedroom and grabbed his phone off the nightstand, and slipped out of the room. Gage turned on a light in the living room and sat on the sofa. He saw a message from Sherm, opened and read it. He shot to his feet.

"Holy shit!" Gage bellowed.

The elevator dinged, and Sherm stepped into the foyer. "Thought I'd have to wake you." He saw the half-full glass of whiskey. "You got more of that?"

Gage waved Sherm toward the bar. "Help yourself, dude. Have you confirmed this?"

"What we've pieced together is that someone from Giuseppe Genovesi's organization is ratting him out," Sherm said. He guzzled a mouthful of bourbon and strode to the sofa. "What my team has discovered is Genovesi must be ancient; either that or there are generations of men with the same name and the exact same picture."

"If he's a shifter, he may very well be quite old," Gage said.

"Gage?" Ari called out. "Where are you?"

"Talking to Sherm. There's news from Italy," Gage hollered.

Ari ran into the room, tying her robe in place. "What do you know, Sherm? Is Roman alive? Do you know where he is?"

"Someone sent a message through the company contact form on the web," Sherm said. "We're trying to understand what's going on. He didn't leave a phone number, address, or even his name, but he gave us the name of the man who's holding Roman. Travis will have all the details within the next hour."

"When are we leaving?" Ari demanded. She was hyper-excited.

"I've contacted the team and the bears. I want them to send whoever is closest to this place and see whether they can detect

Roman. We're not going off on any wild goose chase," Sherm said firmly.

"I'll pack our bags so we'll be ready to leave whenever you have confirmation of the location," Ari said. She took off down the hallway.

"Go back to bed," Sherm suggested. "We have to wait for confirmation." He headed back to the elevator. "See you soon."

"Thanks, Sherm," Gage said. He chugged the rest of his bourbon, grabbed Sherm's glass and set them in the kitchen sink. He found Ari gathering clothes and filling three rolling suitcases.

Gage took inventory of what she was packing for them. She was almost finished. Ari settled a handful of folded shirts in his suitcase. Then she practically leaped into his arms and smothered him in a tight hug. She pulled back, looked deeply into his eyes and kissed him for all it was worth, her tongue tangling around his as she sucked him.

Gage wrapped his arms around her and lifted her. She wrapped her legs around his waist and pulled back from the kiss.

"I haven't felt so alive since Roman disappeared. I love you so much, Gage. I can't wait until the three of us are together again."

His teeth pulled gently on her lower lip. "I know, honey. This hole in my heart..."

"We'll be okay, we're going to bring him home," Ari said.

Her fingers grabbed his hair and pulled his mouth back to hers. His rock-hard shaft was against her stomach, and she pressed against him.

"Oh, Ari..." Gage whispered into her mouth as he walked them over to the big bed.

He untied her robe, slipped it down her arms and flung it to the floor. Her nighty flew through the air. He hooked his thumbs through her panties and slid them down her thighs.

She stepped out of them, then watched as Gage dropped his pajama pants. She scooted onto the bed, and he crawled after her. His shaft pulsed, waiting to join her. They were desperate in their mating.

Gage bit her shoulder at the base of her neck. Ari moaned with desire as he inched down her body. He latched onto her nipple and sucked, then scraped his teeth over the sensitive tip, causing her to moan loudly. He moved to the neglected nipple and lavished love on it.

His lips brushed kisses across her tight abdomen and his tongue seared her along the way. As he reached her sensitive nub, her hands grabbed his hair. He sucked on her clit and Ari's steeled fingers held his head in place. He eased two fingers inside her core. He felt her tighten around him, then she screeched in ecstasy as the first orgasm tore through her.

His mouth lowered to her slit, and his tongue took over for his fingers. He kept a thumb caressing all around her peaked bud to further enhance her orgasm.

Gage couldn't hold off any longer. He climbed her body and nudged her legs further apart with his knee, then plunged inside. There would be no tender lovemaking tonight. He needed to release pent-up carnal desires. He hadn't felt this good in a long time. Ari pounded back stroke for stroke as she let herself go. She screamed through another orgasm, but he kept stroking, pounding his frustration away. When he finally let loose, her name wrenched from his soul. He dropped on top of her, then flipped them so she was partially on top of him.

They panted, cooling down. Then Ari giggled. Her giggles turned into a full belly laugh, and Gage followed.

"Oh, honey. That was so good," Gage said.

"I didn't realize how bottled up we were," Ari said.

"Let's grab a shower. There's no telling when Sherm will call with news," Gage said.

Sherm and Lonnie watched as Travis's fingers flew over the keyboard. He rolled his chair over to the next station and drilled out more code. Their eyes lifted to dart from one huge wall monitor to the next as Travis followed the secret IP address.

The huge world map showed lines that crisscrossed and double-looped back across the globe.

"Christ, I can't keep up," Lonnie said.

Finally, a heart-shape pulsed over a region in Italy east and south of Rome.

"This dude skipped all over the place. Three-hundred and twenty false locations," Travis said with a bit of gloat.

His fingers clacked on the first keyboard. He zoomed in on the map so his bosses could see.

Fiuggi, Italy.

Sherm and Lonnie grabbed their phones.

"Get the jet ready. We'll be there in less than an hour," Lonnie said. He disconnected and called Bruce's team together.

"Gage, we're ready to go." Sherm disconnected the call and placed another. "Atsa, we're coming your way. Should be there before noon."

Then he called Bradley Parsons. "Gather everyone in a town called Fiuggi. It's in the Province of Frosinone, about an hour, maybe an hour and a half east and south of Rome. Get overnight lodging set up. We'll be there within 24 hours. Make sure you don't swarm the place. Look like a tourist group. There will be a large group of us joining you, but we won't require accommodations other than food and restrooms. Text me immediately when you catch Roman's scent."

Sherm made one more call. "Leander, we're getting ready to go. Is your suitcase packed? Okay, see you."

Sherm and Lonnie took off to their offices and grabbed their gear. Gage and Ari barged into the security office.

Ari spotted the convoluted map with the lines criss-crossing on the wall monitors. She walked through the door into Travis' area. She stared at the screen, then looked at the young man.

"You did this?" Ari asked.

"Yeah, a simple child's game," Travis said.

"I can't believe it," Ari said.

Gage joined her and stared at the map. "Travis, you earned your worth today. Good job."

Sherm stepped into the room, his commando clothing bag over his shoulder and a large weekender bag clutched in his hand. "Time's ticking, let's go."

Ari bent and kissed Travis on the cheek.

THE JET LANDED AT FOUR CORNERS REGIONAL AIRPORT IN Shiprock, New Mexico. Kevin slept, open-mouthed in his seat while Jason watched a movie. Ari and Gage were too keyed up to sleep, and Leander stared out the window.

Lonnie opened the door and lowered the stairs. Atsa, Yiska and three hefty young Navajos hurried to the jet. They boarded, stowed their bags, and greeted everyone. Once again, the jet was in the air.

"This is Ahiga, Hashkeh Naabah, and Tahoma," Atsa said as he introduced his young men.

Sherm, Lonnie, Gage and Ari recognized Ahiga from their

last trip to New Mexico. Ahiga was one of the guys posturing at their security detail.

"What are your animals?" Sherm asked.

Atsa pointed them out. "Large gray wolf, coyote, and bear."

Ari stared at the young men. "Tell me what your names mean."

"He fights," Ahiga said.

"Call me Hash. My name means angry warrior."

Tahoma was a little shy. "Water's edge."

"Oh, that's appropriate for a bear, isn't it?" Ari asked.

Tahoma nodded with an almost hidden smile.

Sherm stood. "The cabin is fully stocked. You'll find water and other beverages in the refrigerator. We'll be serving lunch and dinner. We have one stopover to refuel, but we won't be leaving the jet."

Lonnie poked Sherm in the ribs. "There're movies and games, and you should be able to pick up network news and shows. Bathrooms front and back. Blankets and pillows are in the front cabinet. Questions?"

"Damn, this is a hot setup!" Ahiga grinned as he looked around the luxurious cabin.

An Da Tran couldn't believe his good fortune. The job Panther Industries offered him was a dream come true. The thirty percent increase in salary and the loaded benefits had the sixty-four-year-old historian and translator practically cross-eyed. When Sandy, the human resources director, showed him some apartments in the building, he thought his heart would beat right out of his chest.

He couldn't get home quickly enough to turn in his notice at his boring job, arrange for packers and movers, and list his small house for sale. Within a week, he had a good offer from a cash buyer. Everything happened so fast his kids barely had enough time to lift their jaws shut.

He enlisted his two sons and two sons-in-law to help with loading and unloading the trunk of his car and the U-Haul of immediate needs. He liked being prepared while waiting for the movers to show up. After he and his family had all been badged, they marched from the garage in the high-rise through the lobby with arms loaded. One of the security guards stayed by the elevator to lend a helping hand.

His sons set up the blow-up queen mattress and showed him how to deflate it.

"Don't forget to lay that egg crate foam on top before you put the fitted sheet on. The mattress can be a little chilly," Number One said.

When Sandy had shown him the choices of living spaces, he had taken videos and pictures and sent them to his children. They helped him choose the right place and could not believe the luxurious space. His children were happy for him. They wouldn't have to worry about their father. The old neighborhood had declined over the years and they were glad he got out before the undesirables took over completely.

Once everything was unloaded in the apartment on the twenty-fourth floor, his first priority was to get his home office set up in the spare bedroom. They headed out to return the U-Haul and to grab a bite to eat. He brought his sons- and sons-in-law to Pomodoro's. He had enjoyed the lunch as part of his interview and wanted his family to experience the same great time.

"So, this is where they brought you?" his oldest asked.

"Yes. We sat right over there." An Da pointed.

They ordered food and sipped hot tea.

"This is very fortuitous," his first son-in-law said. "I hope the job lives up to its expectations."

"Oh, it will. The books are ancient, and it will take time to trace them to the correct dynasty. I've waited for a project like this my entire career," An Da said. "My employers are wonderful people. Hopefully, you will get a chance to meet them one day."

"Your apartment is huge, Dad. Are you going to be able to keep it up?" his younger son asked. "I'll bet the A/C is going to cost you. What's the square footage?"

An Da let out a huge breath. "Two-thousand square feet. Don't worry. I'll be able to afford a cleaning service. The apartment is one of the perks of the job, and there's a gym in the building."

The four men gawked at him.

"Damn, Dad. You hit the Motherlode!" his oldest son said. "I may have to move closer!"

"You should check out jobs at Panther Industries. They have a whole security department."

THE NEXT DAY, THE MOVING TRUCK ARRIVED. THEY SET UP the furniture, and the boys helped unpack books, kitchenware and linens. Then An Da sent them home so he could settle into his new space. He could barely wait to place his hands on the ancient books they hired him to translate.

Sandy showed him his new office on the twenty-sixth floor. She handed him a key to a locked cabinet where the books were secured and showed him around the floor so he could get his bearings. He met some office neighbors who worked in different departments, and they all seemed welcoming.

An Da unlocked the cabinet, discovered his requested newsprint paper on the bottom shelf, and a box of latex-free gloves. He unrolled a sheet of newsprint paper and taped it to the surface of his desk. He slipped on a pair of gloves, withdrew the books and placed them on top of the paper. His eyes carefully scanned the covers after he slipped his reading glasses on and studied the artwork and Chinese characters. Whoever had created them had numbered them, but he was sure his employers didn't know because they weren't in the correct order in the cabinet.

He shelved all but the first book and re-locked the cabinet. He sat before the book and studied the cover, then opened it.

CHAPTER FIVE

THE JET LANDED AT A PRIVATE AIRPORT OUTSIDE ROME. Three large white vans pulled up as Sherm and all the passengers waited onboard for the customs agent to approve their passports and paperwork. When that was finished and the customs agent left, the team deplaned.

Dewey, one of the bears and his wife, along with another bear couple had walked around the medieval palazzo, gawking like tourists. They pointed at every feature, took pictures of the architecture and each other standing in front of the place, and walked the path to the gardens. Around the back of the building they discovered the tower with the tiny window at the top with the banner flapping nearby. They took pictures from every angle imaginable. The bears sucked in a breath. Dewey pulled out his phone and sent a text to the entire group.

Roman is in the tower!

The bears could hardly contain their excitement. Dewey grabbed his wife in a bearhug and kissed her.

The door to the tower opened and a man in a long brown robe dashed to them. "Mi scusi, questa è proprietà privata.

Devo chiederti di andartene." (Excuse me, this is private property. I must ask you to leave.)

Dewey grabbed his wife's hand. They all hurried back to the front of the place and traipsed off into the village.

BACK AT THE HOTEL, SHERM HAD TAKEN OVER AN EVENT room and set it up as their war room. Dewey shared the pictures they took of the tower, the gardens, the sloped rear edge of the property, and an ancient cemetery with the team. He pointed out a door to the left of the tower.

Lonnie pulled his laptop out of its case and dug a printer out of a box. He set them up at one end of a long buffet table. The security man connected cords, turned on the equipment and grabbed the ream of paper he brought with them.

Lonnie uploaded all of Dewey's pictures. He and Sherm studied them and decided which to print. As pages spewed out of the printer, Sherm laid them out. Twenty minutes later, the last picture spewed out, and the printer went quiet.

"We have two choices," Sherm said. "We can either approach from the rear of the building and enter the tower, or we can storm the front."

Gage, Bruce, and Atsa scrutinized the photos.

"I'll bet those stairs are narrow," Atsa said. "There are most likely corridors and doors on each of these floors. We can't all go up the stairs. We'd be trapped if someone caught us."

"There's forty-six of us, and the European team will be here soon. Why don't we have five or six hit the tower, some flank the perimeter, and the rest of us take the front." Gage asked. He looked to Sherm and Lonnie for advice.

"The larger group would be a distraction from the tower," Sherm said. "We'll need a shifter to go up the tower with some of my commandos so they can easily find Roman. Plus, a shifter can send mind images."

"Shifters should bring a change of clothes," Ari suggested. "If they shift while dressed, they will shred their clothes, and we can't have naked people running through the town back to the hotel. And we definitely can't have a bunch of animals terrorizing the townsfolk."

"If there are shifters inside this place, we don't know what they are or what their capabilities are," Sherm said. "Since we don't know what we're walking into, we need a contingency plan. My people will be fully geared up with weapons. We don't want anyone getting hurt in a crossfire."

The door opened, and ten men and women entered. They looked like military personnel or guerrillas with the amount of unseen weapons packed into their uniforms.

Lonnie crossed the room. He and the team lead shook hands. "Good to see you, Tony. You're just in time."

"We've got the weapons you requested," Tony said. He indicated a crate that two of his team had set on the floor.

Gage joined Lonnie and Tony. "Is everyone on your team aware..."

Tony nodded. "I've briefed everyone."

Gage made eye contact with the group. "I don't want anyone getting trigger-happy when they see people shifting. There are a lot of bears in the room and one huge king cobra."

Tony and his team eyed the unfamiliar people. "Understood, Mr. Stryker."

"Call me Gage, please. Join us at the table. We're just making plans," Gage said.

Sherm made quick introductions to Tony's group: the

bears, the Navajos, Ari, and her sons. Everyone else knew each other.

"I think it would be a good idea if the bear families led the way through the front door. It would throw the occupants off by thinking a large tourist group is misinformed about touring the place. Once the confusion sets in and these people try to stop the bears, we can storm through the place," Sherm said. "Then we'll see what the tower team has to report when they get to Roman."

"I wonder if the person who contacted us will come forth," Ari said. "There's a possibility we may have help on the inside."

"Okay, first up, gather spare clothing. Meet outside at the white vans—we're only taking two since most of you can walk to the palazzo. Atsa, I'd like you and Tahoma to join Lonnie and one of my team at the tower. Commandos and the royals will ride in the vans. Can't let residents of the town get worried they're under attack. We don't want them to call the authorities."

Atsa and Tahoma nodded for their roles. Everyone murmured understanding.

"Then I want the bear families to get into groups of four to six so you look like groups of tourists. When you get to the palazzo, just barge into the place through the front door like you're supposed to be there," Sherm directed. "Leander, I want you in front of the bear group. You'll be the spokesperson to whoever greets you or tries to stop you."

"Sure thing," Leander said.

"My people will be on your heels, so get inside and don't crowd the door. When my teams are through the front, get in back of us. We'll see if this Giuseppe Genovesi wants to play ball," Sherm said.

"Gage, you, Ari, Kevin, and Jason follow behind us. You

too, Yiska, Ahiga and Hash. Protect Ari. Listen to any orders I give. Everyone understand their roles?"

Murmurs and nods were exchanged throughout the room. Bears headed to their rooms to gather clothes. They arrived outside in small groups. All the commandos geared up with weapons from the crate, then piled into the vans along with Gage, Ari, Jason and Kevin. Atsa and Tahoma sat with the commandos.

Leander looked the part of a tour guide as he led the groups of bears through the village to the palazzo. He pointed out the interesting architecture of the medieval town and other points of interest. They approached the front door. Leander didn't slow down for a moment. He grasped the door handle and stepped inside, followed by the group.

Leander and the bears had followed directions carefully. He blathered up a storm as he pointed out the artwork he recognized.

Two brown-robed men approached and spoke in Italian. Their panic was obvious as they tried to usher the group back out the door. Another brown-robed man quickly approached the group and stammered in broken English.

"No, no. You must leave. This is a private residence," he said. He attempted to grab Leander's arm and turn him around.

A loud, threatening hiss emitted from Leander. His cobra wasn't having any part of leaving.

The brown-robed man immediately unhanded Leander and stepped back.

The white vans pulled up on the intricately laid bricks and parked so their rear doors faced the doors of the palazzo. They thrust the back doors open, and the commandos piled out and swarmed inside and around the building. Gage, Ari, and the others pulled up the rear.

The bears parted like the sea while the commandos stormed inside, Sherm in the lead.

The brown-robed men raised their hands in fright.

LONNIE, ATSA, TAHOMA AND ONE COMMANDO RUSHED THE tower door. The commando tried the door handle. It was locked. Lonnie dug through his pockets and pulled out a pic and got the door unlocked. It opened with a tiny squeak, and he stepped inside. Satisfied that it was safe, he waved the group inside. Tahoma took the lead, allowing his bear to guide them to Roman. He pointed up and nodded to Lonnie and Atsa.

They climbed three flights of stairs. A door opened at the next landing. A brown-robed man stepped into the stairwell. He held his finger to his lips and motioned them to follow.

Tahoma glanced back at Lonnie. He nodded. They followed the man in the robe up another three flights and stepped into a corridor.

The man placed a hand on his chest. "Marco. Panther is not good. Very sick. Donatello contacted you. Rescue panther."

Lonnie dropped a hand on Marco's shoulder. "Show us." He waved Marco to lead them. "Atsa, contact Gage so he can let Sherm know what's going on."

Atsa nodded. He sent his silent message as they walked down the dimly lit corridor and stopped in front of a cell.

Roman was sprawled on the floor. His ribs protruded, his tongue hung out of his mouth, and his eyes were gummed up.

A piece of raw meat was nearby, flies buzzing around it. A water bowl was near the cell door, too far away for the emaciated panther to crawl to relieve his thirst.

Marco unlocked the cell. Lonnie rushed inside.

"Jesus Fucking Christ! Roman!" Lonnie burst out. "I'll kill this Genovesi with my bare hands!"

He kneeled on one side of Roman and Atsa kneeled on the other side.

GIUSEPPE SIPPED COFFEE FROM AN ANTIQUE CUP. His latest journal rested on the desk beside a Cross solid gold, limited-edition fountain pen, a blotter, and his ink pot. He heard a disturbing noise and sat straighter in his high-backed chair.

A knock sounded on the closed door. "Come!" Giuseppe called out.

Donatello entered, agitated.

"What is going on? I heard something..." Giuseppe asked.

"They're here!" Donatello twisted his hands.

"Who's here?" Giuseppe asked.

"The shifters and their army!" Donatello stood in fear before his master.

Giuseppe thrust his chair back and strode around the desk to the door. "Call our people! We will cut them down."

"But no one's shifted in decades!" Donatello exclaimed anxiously.

"Call them!" Giuseppe said. He swept out the door. A sea of brown robes fell into place behind him as they approached the wide, elegant staircase. They came face to face with the commandos and the shifters.

Donatello stood a little to Giuseppe's left and a step behind. His eyes searched the group and fell on Gage, then Ari.

We don't want to fight! Only my master wants this.

Gage's eyes went from the man in the brown robe to the

arrogant bastard standing out front, like the king he was. He nodded his understanding and saw the man in the robe let out a breath he had held in.

At that moment, Atsa's vision of Roman filled their heads. Ari plowed to the front of her people and shoved Sherm aside.

"What have you done to my mate?" She roared at Giuseppe.

Gage, Kevin and Jason surrounded Ari. Sherm attempted to get her behind him and the commandos, but stopped when he heard an unexpected growl. He quickly unhanded her and stepped away.

The American shifters recognized the threatening situation and shifted. The Kodiak stood on its hind legs and roared. Leander's cobra swayed and hissed.

Giuseppe's eyes widened in disbelief. "Four Tothars? Impossible!"

The Italian Tothar shifted into a saber-toothed tiger. He roared.

Ari's world tilted. Something happened deep inside her. In another instant she shifted into a gigantic white liger with black stripes. She stood over six feet tall and was at least twelve feet long. Her seven-hundred ninety-five pounds could easily topple the saber-tooth beast in front of her.

Kevin and Jason's Tothar heritage zoomed forth, brought on by their mother's shift. Jason emerged as a tiger and Kevin shifted into a lion. They flanked their mother, roaring their rage.

Ari leapt forward to challenge the Italian. She was beyond furious at the image Atsa sent of Roman, near death.

"Ari! We need him to tell us about our past," Gage yelled. Then he shifted, and his eagle took to the twenty-foot ceiling of the large entryway. He landed on the banister and overlooked both groups.

The Italians, led by Donatello, stepped back and crowded the walls. This was not their fight. It was their cruel master's fight.

Kevin and Jason attempted to join Ari in her fight with the Italian. She turned on them with a warning roar. They stayed behind their mother, giving her the right to dish out her wrath.

Ari attacked the saber-tooth tiger with a vengeance. They clawed and bit each other and rolled on the floor in a tangle of claws and snapping teeth. She towered over him and threw the saber-toothed tiger under her and grabbed him by the throat. Her enormous jaws ripped out his throat, and as she clenched down tighter, she heard bones crack. Lost in her fury, she shook the now dead Tothar like a dirty rag.

Gage flew down and landed on her back. He squawked loudly as his talons dug into her fur. He pecked her head until she released the dead tiger. They both shifted at the same time. Ari panted. She stumbled into Gage's arms and shook slightly as she released her emotions. When they parted, she noticed her sons in their animal forms.

Donatello removed his robe and approached Ari. He slipped the robe over her shoulders and nodded to Gage. "I'm Donatello. I'm so glad you received our message." He bowed deeply.

The Italians all bowed and curtsied to their new king and queen.

Donatello stared at his dead master, then his eyes roamed the room of shocked expressions on his brown-robed brothers.

Gage held out his hand. "I'm Gage Stryker and this is Ari Davis, my mate and queen. We're grateful that you contacted us. It looks like Roman is barely alive."

Anguish crossed Donatello's face. "When our master's men returned to the palazzo with the panther, our spirits rose. We thought perhaps we had a chance of this young Tothar defeating our king. But he kept him so drugged he couldn't even eat or drink. All he wanted to do was kill him!"

Marco rushed down the stairs to join Donatello. He bowed. "We tried to help him, but he's too weak to shift." A sob escaped. Marco looked devastated. "I hope he doesn't die!"

The American shifters shifted back to their human forms. Ari approached her sons. They were still in their animals. She laid a hand on each and ruffled their fur.

"Look at you! You're so beautiful. Looks like we found our animals. You need to shift back."

After a few moments of uncertainty, Kevin and Jason shifted.

Marco approached Ari and Gage. "We will need a stretcher or some way to get the panther down the stairs."

A man came forward and handed robes to Gage and the boys.

"Bring us to him," Gage said. He slipped into the robe and turned to Sherm. "Get everyone's clothing so they can get dressed. We can meet back at the hotel."

Gage, Ari, and the boys followed Marco and Donatello through a door to the tower stairs. They climbed up to the cell.

They gasped loudly when they saw Roman. Ari and Gage rushed forward, followed by Kevin and Jason.

Ari sank to the floor and grabbed Roman's panther head and placed it in her lap.

"Roman!" Gage bellowed in grief and pain.

"Roman!" Ari sobbed at seeing him in the flesh. "Roman, please hold on. We're here for you. We're going to bring you home."

"Even this thin, he's going to be very heavy. It's going to be awkward to get him down those narrow stairs," Gage said.

"I can get him down the stairs!" Ari said. "Stand back. Someone needs to lead me to the ground floor."

Gage pulled his phone out of his pocket. He called Sherm. "Bring one of the vans around to the tower door. Ari's going to carry Roman down the stairs. Grab her clothes, okay?"

Everyone scurried out of the cell and backed up against the corridor wall to give her enough room to exit the cell. Lonnie stood in the corridor and waited.

Ari dropped the robe and transformed. Her liger walked around Roman's panther. She licked his face several times, trying to clear his eyes. Then she reached down and gripped his scruff with her teeth and pulled him off the floor. His panther groaned as he dangled in the air, her form so large his feet barely reached the floor. She slipped out of the cell and followed Lonnie down the corridor.

They slowly descended the six flights of stairs to the open door. She brought Roman through the open door. There was no way she could fit through the doors of the van. Sherm, Leander and several of the big bears saw the dilemma. Ari stuck her head in the van's back, and two of the big bears entered through the side door. They grabbed the panther under his front legs and pulled as Ari let him go.

Sherm and Leander grabbed Roman around his middle while Atsa and Yiska grabbed his back legs. They all got Roman into the van onto the floor.

Tony, the European security lead, retrieved the emergency field medical kit. He and one of his team set up an IV to get fluids into the panther.

"This will help him a lot. Go take care of business. My

team will monitor him," Tony said. "I don't think we should leave here just yet. Let me get him stabilized."

Ari gave Roman's back leg a lick, then she ducked her head back out of the van and transformed. Gage brought her a change of clothes and shoes, and she dressed. She scurried into the van.

"Oh, Roman!" She took in his sunken stomach and matted, lackluster fur. "What have they done to you?"

Gage reached into the van and tapped her arm. "Come on, we have to go talk to these people." He led her by the elbow. Kevin and Jason fell into step behind them.

"Is he going to be okay?" Kevin asked.

"He'll pull through," Gage said.

They followed Donatello and Marco back inside and through a door that led them to the ground floor entry room.

"Are all your people here?" Gage asked Donatello.

Donatello searched the room with his eyes. "No, I don't think so." He turned to Marco. "Ring the bell. Make sure everyone is in attendance."

Marco rushed from the room and climbed the stairs. He reached the bell tower and pulled the long rope. The ancient bell rang out in glorious tones. No one had heard the bell peel in at least a decade. He rushed back down the stairs and joined Donatello.

More brown-robed men and women filled the room. They stared in shock at their dead king, then gazed upon their new royal family.

Gage stepped forward. "My name is Gage Stryker. Roman Davenport is the panther your king captured. This is our mate and queen, Ari Davis, and her sons Kevin and Jason. We are Tothars." His voice boomed when he announced what they were.

The entire room of brown robes bowed and curtsied. "Your

king is dead. Ari killed him. Does anyone have a problem with that?"

Heads shook around the room. Suddenly, and quite unexpectedly, clapping thundered among them.

"If you don't already know this, we are Americans, and we have our business and lives there. We will be your royalty from afar, but it will take time to establish a new connection with you. Don't worry, we will not abandon you. I will speak to Donatello and he will relay news to you."

Gage spoke quietly to Donatello and Marco. "Do you have a chain of command?"

"I was our king's assistant. Marco assists me. Everyone has their specific tasks," Donatello said.

"Okay," Gage said. He called Sherm and Lonnie over. "This is Sherman Foo, the head of Panther Industries Security Division, and Lonnie is his second in command. I want them to look at your computer system and set up communications between us. We will be leaving here within the hour to get Roman back home."

Marco turned and motioned for two people to join them. "These are our IT people."

They bowed to Gage and Ari. Then they led Sherm and Lonnie out of the room.

Gage threw his arm across Ari's shoulders. "Things happened pretty fast. I had hoped to talk sense into your fallen king—we wanted to find out more about our kind—Tothars."

"I'm sorry, Gage. It was like instinct taking over, and I was blind with rage." Ari looked crestfallen as she glanced at the dead Tothar cat.

Donatello held up his hand. "Not to worry! Come with me." He turned and walked to the stairs. They all walked down a hallway on the second floor to a locked door. Donatello retrieved a keyring and unlocked the door, and swung it open. He led them inside a room filled with over-flowing shelves.

Gage and Ari gasped in amazement. Thousands of journals filled the shelves. From the floor to the twenty foot high ceiling. The bookcases held journals of every type of material. Library ladders rested on all four walls.

"Our master was an actual saber-toothed tiger. He was ancient. Every day for as long as I have been in his service, he has written in his journals," Donatello said.

"When did you join him?" Ari asked.

"Eight-hundred years ago," Donatello said. A tiny smile crossed his face.

Ari's jaw dropped. "You're eight-hundred years old?"

"No, that's when I joined him. I was a hundred-fifty."

Donatello grinned. "He was much older than that—I think it would be safe to say he was thousands of years old. I had our IT people research saber-tooth tigers on the Internet. According to what we learned, smilodon, which is what they were called, were from the Pleistocene epoch, and around 12,000 years ago they died off in the Quaternary extinction."

Gage looked at Ari. "Roman and I are just kids!" He turned to Donatello. "We're one hundred. Ari is only seventy-five—just a baby, and her sons ARE babies!"

Ari hung her head. "I don't know what to say. This never should have happened. He should have been..."

Donatello placed his hand on her arm. "Stop. He was a cruel master—beyond cruel. I've dreamed of his demise so many times across the ages. All his people hated him. Now, perhaps, we can have peace." He looked askance at Gage.

"We do not rule by fear," Gage said. "Our people are like our family."

Kevin, Jason and Sherm found them in the library. Gage met Sherm's eyes.

"Lonnie is working with the IT people here and at home. We've established server connections. I think it would be prudent to have one or two of our people come here to get things squared away," Sherm said.

Donatello waited until they had finished talking. "Will you inform our late king's niece about his demise? She was instrumental in King Roman's abduction."

"Is that Lisa Hamilton?" Kevin asked.

"Yes, you know of her?" Donatello asked.

"Oh, yeah." Kevin and Jason could barely hold in their fury. Kevin's face sprouted long whiskers as his newly discovered cat wanted out. Jason laid a hand on his brother's arm to calm him.

"Do you have contact information for her? She's not at her house," Gage said.

Donatello summoned Marco. "Would you look up Lisa Hamilton's information?"

Marco read off her phone number and a different address than where the team had originally gone to search for her.

"Sherm, have Travis do his magic. Just locate her. Let no one take any action until we're back in the States," Gage said.

Sherm walked to the other end of the large room and placed his call.

"She's MINE!" Kevin roared.

Kevin and Jason were near to fighting for the right to tear the woman apart.

"Stop!" Ari thundered at her sons. "I understand how you

feel, and that you want to be the ones to deliver justice, but there are others who should be considered. Her alpha, for one, and Gage. Roman and Gage were together far longer than we have been in the picture. You two settle down until we decide."

Gage hugged her to him. "We'll work it out." He turned his attention to the boys. "Go check on Roman. Then see if you can help Leander with the shifters."

Jason and Kevin reluctantly left the room.

"They'll calm down," Sherm said. His phone dinged an incoming text. "Travis found her. I'll have someone watch her so she doesn't slip away." With that he messaged instructions.

Ari's eyes took in the room filled with journals. "Boy, Mr. Tran would have a field day in this room." She snapped pictures with her phone. "I can't wait to show him this room!" She turned to Donatello. "Would it be okay if I brought one of these journals back with me? Our historian, Mr. Tran, would be very interested to see what's documented."

"Do you think Mr. Tran would like something current, or something much older?" Donatello scanned the shelves then walked to the first bookshelf close to the left side of the door. "These are the earliest journals."

"You choose something," Ari said. "No matter what it is, he will be ecstatic!"

CHAPTER SIX

Gage and Donatello sat in the chairs in front of the desk in the old king's office.

"While I realize we are the new kings, queen and princes of the shifter world, we can't up and leave our world and people in America to rule you and your people. So, we will rule from afar. My IT and security departments will establish systems so we have a good rapport," Gage said. "We don't know you, Donatello. I can only surmise from your contacting us that you are a decent person. With that in mind, I will leave you in charge."

Donatello couldn't hide his surprise. "My king! It would honor me. These people here are good people. The late king kept us strangled for so long, and most of our people have not shifted in decades."

"Why would your king not allow you to shift? It's a natural process for our kind!" Gage's anger steamed at the thought of the Italians being trapped in a miserable existence. "And what's with all these brown robes? Are you part of a religious order?"

"The late king imposed these robes upon us," Donatello said.

"Burn them!" Gage said, "or donate them to a monastery. Your people can wear whatever they want from this moment forward."

Gage calmed himself. "We conduct scheduled meetings with our community. For the next one, the palazzo will join us by video conference. If you don't already have a large screen TV, some will be installed throughout the common areas so your people can attend and see how we do things."

Donatello's face lit. "We would love to see how our American shifter family conducts these meetings."

Gage stood. "I should get going. We need to get Roman to the jet and back home so he can receive medical attention."

Donatello stood and walked around the desk. He grabbed the journal and handed it to Gage. "Perhaps you would like to read what Giuseppe documented over the past few weeks? It could tell you why he did what he did."

"Thank you. I'm sure it will be interesting reading."

GAGE AND DONATELLO WENT DOWNSTAIRS AND FOUND Sherm and Lonnie.

"Tony and the team will stay here and continue to get things set up," Sherm said.

Gage asked about the large TV monitors and mentioned the Italians would join them online for the next meeting.

"Tony will have to order monitors," Sherm said. "They have little in the way of electronics here at the palazzo."

"Where's Jason?" Gage asked.

"He, Kevin and Ari are in the van with Roman," Lonnie said.

Gage got out his phone and texted Jason. *Set up an account for the Italians. They're going to require a lot of electronics. Tony will oversee the equipment. He can let you know what they require, but they'll order from Italy.*

Within moments, Jason texted back. *I'll set that up from the plane.*

"Jason will get it all set up from the jet. We need to discover where the money comes from that supports the palazzo," Gage said.

"The master was very secretive about his finances," Donatello said. "But Marco should be able to help with that. He has access to all the accounts and bank boxes. Let me get him for you."

Donatello rushed off.

"These people need cellphones! This place is huge. They can't be running all over the place when all they need to do is send a text," Sherm said.

"Jason can set up an account with an Apple store over here. Better have him arrange for on-site delivery and training sessions. I don't know if these people are electronically savvy or still in the Dark Ages," Gage said.

Donatello and Marco returned and joined them. They bowed slightly.

"Donatello mentioned you wanted to discuss the finances," Marco said. He produced a large ledger book that contained removable plastic tabs.

"Where can we sit down?" Gage asked.

Marco led them up the stairs to his office, which contained a small conference table. He moved several stacks of paperwork to his desk, and Gage, Donatello, and Sherm sat.

"This is my daily ledger I brought to meetings with the late king," Marco said. "It contains daily balances only. Other ledgers contain each account's activity."

"Wait. Are you saying you do all of this accounting manually?" Gage asked.

Marco nodded. "Our master wouldn't allow cellphones or computers."

"Only the IT people had those luxuries," Donatello said. Sherm and Gage groaned.

"That's all going to change immediately. You're all getting cellphones, and those who require laptops for their work are getting those," Gage said. "Now, tell me how this place supports itself. Do you produce a product or service to sell?"

"No, it's all here," Marco said as he patted the ledger.

"Give us the rundown. I don't read Italian," Gage said.

"There are dozens of bank accounts throughout Europe. Each account contains millions of dollars. There's cash in bank safe deposit boxes and investments and property worldwide," Marco explained.

Donatello tilted his head to the right, his eyes focused on Marco.

"Oh, and the vault room downstairs," Marco said.

"What do you mean by the 'vault room'?" Sherm asked.

"It would be best to show you," Donatello said. He led the way down corridors to a door. He pulled a keyring out of his pocket and fingered through the keys, then unlocked the door. Donatello grabbed a lantern off a shelf inside the door and lit it.

"There's no electricity down here. Please light a lantern and hold the handrail," Donatello said.

He descended the stone stairs, Gage, Sherm, and Marco following with lanterns. They finally came to the ground floor.

"I lost count at sixty-three stairs," Sherm said.

Donatello laughed. "My knees know every single stair, especially when I ascend!" He turned to the left, down a very wide corridor to another door. This one looked to be made of ancient wood.

"I will have to light the torches inside." He unlocked the door, set his lantern on a shelf, and took up an oiled torch and lit it with a grill lighter. He lit the torches in the sconces around the room.

"Come inside," Donatello said.

Gage and Sherm entered the cavernous room. Precious artwork, statues, and antique furniture took up most of the room. A wall of cubbyholes, small drawers, and shelves was on one side of the vault. The shelves held small busts and art objects from across eras.

Sherm recorded video of the vault. "What's in the drawers?" Gage asked.

Marco pulled open a drawer that was filled with rubies.

Sherm pulled open another drawer and found emeralds. He and Gage pulled open more drawers to discover diamonds, pearls, and other precious stones. In one drawer were chunks of gold. In another, silver.

"What's the bottom line?" Gage asked.

Marco opened the ledger to a specific page. "As of this morning, approximately just under a billion dollars."

"Billion? And you track this manually?" Sherm asked incredulously.

Marco and Donatello nodded.

"I'm going to assume that doesn't include what's in this vault," Gage said.

"No," Marco said. "I would not know how to go about determining the wealth in this room."

"I guess, being as old as he was, he accumulated this wealth a very long time ago," Gage said. "Jason and my people back home will determine how we want to structure this new company."

Sherm glanced at his cellphone. "We need to get going." Donatello took a large snuffer and snuffed out the torches. He locked the door, and they climbed the stairs and returned to the entryway at the front of the palazzo.

They stood and shook hands.

"Thank you for all your help," Gage said. "We'll discuss the changes in more detail once we are back home and Roman is settled."

THE VANS AND SUVs DELIVERED ALL THE AMERICANS back to the jet. They stowed the equipment and bags. Lonnie had secured a collapsible gurney, and they hauled Roman out of the van as gently as possible. Ari cringed as she watched the large bears maneuver the panther onto the gurney. They then lowered it and carried it up the stairs and inside the jet.

Gage followed Ari and the boys up the steps to the back of the plane where they settled Roman and found a place to hang the IV bag. One bear, who was an EMT, took over. He covered the unconscious king with a thin blanket so that the air conditioning would not chill him excessively.

Ari hovered over Roman. "I don't pick up anything from him."

Gage wrapped his arms around her. "He'll pull through."

"Who will treat him once we get home? I don't recall any vets or doctors from the list," Ari said.

"Ethan can take care of him," the bear EMT said.

"Who's Ethan?" Gage asked.

"Dr. Tanner," the man said.

"The doctor who took care of Ari?" Gage asked.

"Yeah, his wife is a shifter," the bear said.

Gage and Ari exchanged an incredulous look. He whipped his cellphone out of his pocket, went through his contacts and pulled up the doctor's information. He pressed the call button.

"Dr. Tanner please," he said. "Okay. Please tell him Gage Stryker called. It's an emergency." Gage rattled off his number and ended the call. "He's in surgery."

As the jet prepared for takeoff, everyone buckled up. Roman was out cold on the gurney on the floor. After they were in the air, Ari sat on the edge of the gurney and stroked Roman's face and ears.

Gage spent the next two hours with Jason sorting out what the Italians required to get them up to speed.

"Lonnie, is there a head count of how many people live or work in the palazzo?" Gage asked.

Lonnie worked his phone and communicated with one of the Italian IT guys. "Three-hundred-twenty-three."

"Ask him to get with Donatello and Marco to find out if there's an HR department so we can determine all the different positions. We need to find out who needs a laptop and who can get by with an iPad. When things settle down and Roman is over this crisis, we can return for an extended stay and get things more organized," Gage said.

He turned back to Jason. "Find out about extensive in-house training with Apple just to get these people up and running. Then we need to get people trained with office products so they can use Outlook, spreadsheets, and all the rest. They might need someone in-house for several months. There's plenty of room for classrooms."

"Do you know if the place is wired for Internet and cable?" Jason asked.

"No, they're not. That guy would only allow his office wired, and the room where the server and the two IT guys had offices," Lonnie said.

"Connect with Tony, Jason. You two will need to set up the purchase orders for all the equipment. He'll have to get with Donatello and the three of you—actually the five of you—counting the IT guys, can get everything started," Gage said.

Gage's phone rang. "It's Dr. Tanner." He answered the call. "Dr. Tanner, thanks for calling. We have an emergency. As you most likely heard through your wife, someone kidnapped Roman. We rescued him today, and he's in awful shape."

Gage listened to the doctor, then continued. "They practically starved him and kept him drugged to the point where he couldn't shift back to his human form. He couldn't even get to the bowl of water."

Ari fretted as she listened to the one-way conversation. "The EMT has him on an IV drip, but he hasn't opened his eyes. He's truly out of it." Gage listened. "Okay, we'll get one ordered. We won't land for another ten hours. I'll text you when we get home."

"How are we going to get him up to the penthouse?" Ari asked. "It's not like we can hide him."

"We'll use the freight elevator up to the thirtieth floor, then we can get him to the regular elevator," Sherm said.

"Jason, Dr. Tanner suggested we get one of those Purple™ king mattresses and put it on the floor for him. If we can get him hydrated and nourished, he may be able to shift back, but I think that will take several days," Gage said.

Jason searched for a Purple distributor and discovered he could get a California king at a local mattress store in Reading.

He placed an order and then alerted the lobby security to accept the delivery. Security could get the mattress and set it up in the spare room, which once held Ari's hospital bed while she recovered from her ordeal.

"When we touch down, I'll text him, and he'll meet us at the building," Gage said.

Sherm came over to join them. "We're going to be extremely busy for the next several months. What exactly are we going to do about Lisa Hamilton?"

"Leander, come join us," Gage called out.

The cobra shifter sauntered over and took a seat across the aisle from Jason and Gage. Sherm leaned over the seat back, preferring to stand.

Gage looked at Jason and Kevin. "You two can excuse yourselves and go up front. This will require constructive discussions and you two are still too hot to think rationally."

Ari's sons did not want to leave willingly. Since they were outnumbered and their mother glared daggers at them, they left their seats and settled into two seats near the front, grumbling all the way.

"So, what do we do?" Gage asked them.

"She's a traitor," Leander said. "She purposefully set out to harm king Roman."

"We can never trust her. She's a conniving witch who only has her own interests in mind," Sherm said.

"We should have taken her down that day at the house. I regret that with every inch of my soul," Gage said.

Ari stood and left Roman's side. "I am going to suggest something that may seem barbaric, but I think it's fitting for the crime."

Sherm, Gage and Leander stared at her, wondering what she would propose.

"I say we bring her out to the house in the woods and

contain her in a circle of shifters and we show her justice," Ari said.

The men nodded.

"That's a plan. Leander, you bring Trisha up to speed. Our security has Lisa under surveillance so she won't go far. No one is to take any action until we gather, bring her in and conduct a reckoning or trial," Gage said.

They all weighed the plan and nodded.

CHAPTER SEVEN

THE JET LANDED AT READING AIRPORT. JASON ARRANGED for a bus to meet them to take the shifters, Atsa and his team, and Bruce's team back to the Panther Industries building. He reminded Atsa that they would need their badges to get to the apartment he had allocated to them.

The bears helped bring the gurney and Roman down the stairs of the jet to a waiting van. They loaded him into the rear of the van, and Sherm took the wheel. Gage texted Dr. Tanner as they arrived at the back of the building where the freight elevator was.

"I'll block out the camera back here, and the one inside the elevator," Sherm said. "I sure don't want the guards to raise the alarm if they saw a panther. They'd assume you had an illegal exotic pet or something."

They wheeled Roman into the freight elevator and rode to the thirtieth floor. It was early—barely six thirty in the morning. Early birds didn't show until seven, so they felt it safe to transport the gurney through the main corridor to the elevators.

They startled when they heard the elevator ding. Sherm

quickly opened a door on the right side of the corridor, and they wheeled the gurney through the door and slipped in after him.

Ari heard someone whistling a tune as they walked past the room and disappeared around the corner. "Who do you think that was? It's awfully early."

"I'll look it up after we get settled," Sherm said. He eased the door open, looked both ways, and they darted out of the room.

They sprinted toward the elevator and slipped inside. Gage inserted his cardkey, and they rode up to the penthouse. Ari scooted around the gurney and rushed to the spare room. The Purple mattress was on the floor. She rushed to the linen closet and pulled out a matching set of sheets and a light blanket. She put on the fitted bottom sheet while they all waited.

Sherm lowered the gurney to its lowest setting. "Will we need help?" Gage asked.

"Want me to shift?" Ari asked.

"Not enough room," Gage said.

The elevator dinged. Kevin and Jason called out. "We're back here," Ari called.

"Help us get Roman on the mattress," Sherm said. "Kev, hold the gurney in place. The three of us should get on the bed and drag him from the gurney."

They got Roman in the middle of the mattress with relative ease.

Gage's phone chirped a text. Dr. Tanner was downstairs. He engaged the elevator app, and within a few minutes, the elevator dinged his arrival.

"Ari, go get Dr. Tanner," Gage said.

DR. TANNER SHOOK THEIR HANDS.

"I had no idea you were married to a shifter and knew about us," Gage said.

"At the time of Ari's abduction, I wasn't on board. It was after you called the first meeting, which my wife attended, that I found out you were also shifters," Dr. Tanner said.

He set his bag on the floor beside the mattress and examined Roman.

"I'm going to draw blood so I can find out what drug they used," he said. "His vital signs are within the normal range, so that's good. I need to be sure the drug is flushed out of his system. We need to get him to where he's conscious and can shift, so he can drink water."

"How long will that take?" Ari asked.

"How long has it been since they administered the drug?" Dr. Tanner asked.

"Let me find out," Gage said. He sent a text to Tony to ask Donatello.

A long five minutes later his phone chirped an incoming text.

Yesterday was four days.

Gage sent: *Does Donatello know what drug was used?*

Zoletil.

Okay. Thanks. The doctor is here. I'll contact you later, Gage sent.

Gage shared his screen with Dr. Tanner.

"Okay, that helps, but we don't know the dosage. They should have tranquilized him only once. It would have kept him out long enough to transport him. If they repeatedly drugged him, it may take a few more days to flush it out of his system," Dr. Tanner said. "I'll still draw blood to check the level of the drug, and I'll insert a catheter."

Gage pulled open a closet door that held supplies from

when it had been Ari's recovery room. He pulled out an IV stand and hung the bag.

Doctor Tanner went about inserting the catheter and the IV. "I'm going to use a TPN IV nutrition (Total Parenteral Nutrition). This solution contains complete daily nutrition, plus fluids. I think it's wise to begin a course of broad-spectrum antibiotics in case Roman picked up any bacterial infections."

The doctor placed the two vials of blood in a case and put them in his bag. "It might help if you brushed his pelt with a soft brush. It could bring him around. If that happens, try to keep him from yanking out the catheter or the IV. I don't want him to hurt himself while he's still groggy."

He pulled extra bags out of his case. "You'll need to replace the catheter bag frequently. Please save one so I can run a urinalysis."

Gage and Ari responded, "Okay."

Ari glanced at her boys. "Can you run to the store and find a nice soft brush?"

"Sure," Kevin said. "Is there anything else we should pick up?"

Ari had a thought come through. "Roman loves bacon. Pick up an organic package, or grass-fed with no antibiotics or anything you can't recognize—make it two. Maybe if he smells it cooking, he'll come around."

"I'm going to take off," Dr. Tanner said. "I'll check in with you this afternoon."

Dr. Tanner, Kevin, and Jason rode the elevator together.

Ari sat on the edge of the mattress and stroked Roman's face and ears.

Gage and Sherm watched her.

THERE WAS NO CHANGE THAT AFTERNOON, EVENING OR overnight. Ari had slept on the mattress against Roman's back, her arm across his shoulders. Gage had curled up with Ari. He couldn't sleep, his nerves stretched tight from horrible thoughts of his best friend not recovering.

Gage swapped out the IV bag while Ari slept and Roman was still out cold. Then he hit the bottle of bourbon and slugged back a rocks glass full of the stuff.

"Fuck it!" Gage said. He opened the sliding glass doors in the living room, stripped off his pajama pants, and transformed. His eagle hopped to the railing and leaped into the air. He soared over the city and headed for the forest and mountains in the distance. He recognized that he needed to loosen his mind from the trap he kept circling. His monkey mind wouldn't shut up for a minute.

The Italian Tothar king was dead. They needed to deal with the woman. Things were being put into place to get all the Italian people online and brought into the corporate side of Panther Industries for benefits and financials. Then there was the shifter organization that would merge once meetings resumed and they took part.

Another smaller eagle joined him and he recognized Atsa.

Couldn't sleep? Atsa sent.

Too worked up, Gage replied.

It's going to be okay. Let it ride. You have no control over this, Atsa sent.

Gage's eagle shrieked. He let the wind soothe him as he soared and let his mind calm. He returned to the patio an hour later and shifted. Gage watched as Atsa landed on a balcony several floors below him. He checked on Roman, slipped into his pajama pants and climbed onto the mattress in back of Ari. In less than ten minutes, he was out.

GAGE WOKE TO THE SMELL OF BACON FRYING. HE WALKED around the mattress and knelt beside Roman.

"Hey, buddy, Ari's cooking bacon for you."

He thought he saw Roman's nose twitch, but couldn't be sure. He rubbed his hand over the panther's head, down his neck, and patted him on the shoulder.

Gage went into the bathroom and brushed his teeth. He splashed water on his face and dried off, then left for the kitchen.

"What can I help you with, honey?"

They smooched.

"You take over the bacon and I'll make scrambled eggs and toast," Ari said.

They finished preparing breakfast and ate. Ari brought her coffee and a plate of bacon into the spare room. She placed the plate on the floor within inches of Roman's nose.

"Do you think he'll smell it?" she asked.

"I hope so. He's really been out of it and I'm worried about all the weight he's dropped," Gage said.

"I shouldn't have killed that man," Ari said. "That justice was way too swift. All because he discovered he wasn't the only king, like some spoiled brat throwing a tantrum because he wasn't King of the Mountain."

Gage draped his arm over her shoulders. "It's over and done with. Your animal took control when it recognized the injustice and the threat. I've got to tell you, that was something to see—you and the boys finding your animals!"

"I wonder how that happened. Both Atsa and Silver Wolf said we didn't have animals," Ari said.

"It could have been like a trigger response. Whatever brought it on, I'm so glad you have an animal. You'll never have to worry about being intimidated by anyone ever again," Gage said.

Ari's brows knit in thought. "Am I a lion or a tiger? Are the boys just cubs? I was much bigger than they were."

Gage snorted. "You're one of the biggest cats in existence—a liger. They're a cross between a tiger and a lion and can weigh seven hundred to twelve hundred pounds. The reason the boys looked so small was because you stood at least six feet tall and were ten or twelve feet long. I'll have to measure the next time you shift."

Ari's mouth hung open. "You're kidding!"

"Nope. Believe me, I thought Sherm was going to drop to the floor."

They sat in silence. Ari grabbed the plate of bacon and waved it in front of Roman's nose.

"Come on, Roman. Please wake up!" she pleaded.

Gage's phone chirped. "Dr. Tanner's coming up." He got up and headed to the elevator to meet him.

"Hi, Dr. Tanner," Gage said.

"How's Roman this morning?" Dr. Tanner asked.

"Ari's trying to entice him awake with bacon. So far, it's not working."

They walked back to the spare room. "Hi, Ari."

"Hello Dr. Tanner," she said.

Dr. Tanner didn't look happy. "The toxicology test came back. Roman had ten times the recommended amount of Zoletil in his system. We should bring them up on charges. No one should have administered that dosage.

"You'll hear it through the shifter grapevine, but the man who had Roman kidnapped and drugged is dead," Gage said.

"I don't know if Roman will have organ damage from this

overdose or not. He's not human. He's not an animal. Shifters are definitely in the gray area of a lot of health concerns," Dr. Tanner said. "Being a Tothar, and much stronger than a shifter, makes the equation even more questionable."

"What can we do to keep him as healthy as possible until he wakes up?" Ari asked. "He's lost so much weight."

Dr. Tanner checked the catheter bag. It was half-full. He pulled a new bag out of his case and disconnected the current bag secured to Roman's hind leg. He connected the fresh bag, then packed the full bag into a sealable bag and stored it in his case.

"He's urinating, so that's a good sign," Dr. Tanner said. "I'm reluctant to insert a feeding tube. That would also entail either wearing a diaper or having another bag. Let's see how he is tomorrow."

Ari picked up the brush Kevin bought, and she started at Roman's head and brushed his sides, back, and legs.

"Should we flip him to his other side so he doesn't get bed sores?" she asked.

"Let's wait until tomorrow," Dr. Tanner said.

GAGE RODE THE ELEVATOR DOWN WITH DR. TANNER.

"I sense you're holding something back," Gage said in the elevator.

"No, I'm just overly concerned," Dr. Tanner said. "They had him for over two weeks and tried, almost successfully, to kill him. I hoped he'd come around by now."

Gage pressed his hands into his eyes. "I'd feel a lot better if he'd opened his eyes. Licked his lips—anything to show us he's recovering slowly."

The elevator landed in the lobby, and they exited.

"Hang in there. You're doing everything you can to make him comfortable. I'll be back tomorrow," Dr. Tanner said.

They shook hands, and the doctor left. Gage rode the elevator up to the thirtieth floor and stopped in Jason's office.

"How's it going, Jason?" Gage asked.

"Good. I've got a spreadsheet of all the Italians for HR, and I've set up accounts for the purchase of all the equipment they'll need. Donatello and Marco are authorized on all bank accounts and safe deposit boxes. Should Panther Industries be added?"

Gage thought for a moment. "That's something we should discuss with Sandy and legal. I'm not sure how we'll explain the new Italian Panther Industries office, or how Roman accumulated these millions."

Jason rolled his chair closer to Gage. He whispered, then changed his mind. "Can we go see Sherm for a minute?"

Gage arched an eyebrow, stood, and they headed to the elevator. Sherm was in his office when they arrived at his doorway.

"You two look serious," Sherm said. "How's Roman this morning?"

Gage shared what Dr. Tanner related about the tox screen.

"If that bastard wasn't dead, I'd kill him," Sherm said. "Piece of shit."

"That brings up another discussion. All these millions and how Panther Industries will absorb the financials," Gage said.

"We could get around the question if, perhaps, Roman is declared next of kin," Jason said. He raised his eyebrows in question.

Sherm and Gage shared pensive looks.

"That might work. Documentation would have to satisfy the Italian and US governments," Sherm said. "I wonder if Donatello or Marco could produce something like that."

Gage looked at Jason. "When's everything going to be set up so we can make phone calls?"

Jason pulled his phone out and looked at his calendar. "The one basic line in Giuseppe's office still works. Tony has someone wiring the place for phone, cable, Internet—the works. That will take several days since it's such a big place."

"So, we can call the office phone?" Sherm asked. He clicked the keys on the laptop and brought up the World Clock. "Six-hour difference. They're ahead of us, so it's four in the afternoon there. Want to see if we can get Donatello on the line?"

"Yes. Maybe we can work this out," Gage said.

Sherm looked up the number on his cellphone and dialed it on the office phone. He hit the speaker button, and they listened to it ring—a strange ringtone not common in the US.

Donatello answered the phone on the fifth ring. "Panther Industries, Donatello speaking."

"Donatello, this is Gage. I'm here in Sherm's office with Sherm and Jason," Gage said.

The man sounded joyful. "Oh, Master Gage! I'm so glad you called! Marco and I have devised a plan that may be helpful," Donatello said. He put his hand over the mouthpiece and yelled out, "Marco!"

"There's no need to call me, or anyone else, *master*, Donatello. I want you to inform everyone there that they can call us by our first names. Or, if they prefer a more formal title, they can call us by our surnames," Gage said. "Have you all ditched the robes?"

Both Donatello and Marco laughed.

"We donated them!" Marco said. "I'm wearing jeans and a T-shirt!"

"So, what did you two come up with—you said something helpful, Donatello?"

"Several things, actually, but I'm sure you will approve," Donatello said. "First, we buried our former king in the little cemetery on our property. Then we placed an obituary in the Fiuggi newspaper, which should run today or tomorrow—we will have our IT people email you a copy. Then we contacted a notary who is a very good friend and who created a testament. That's what you call a will, along with supporting documentation that states Roman is Giuseppe's only known relative."

Marco interrupted him. "No, he disinherited his niece, remember?"

"Oh! That's correct, Marco. He left Lisa Hamilton ten thousand dollars. I'm sure she didn't know what his net worth was. The last time she was here, she thought this was a monastery, so the brown robes came in handy."

Gage, Sherm and Jason smiled widely at what the two Italians had accomplished.

"You two have been busy!" Gage said.

"No one will question the signatures on all the documentation?" Sherm hitched an eyebrow in concern.

Donatello laughed. "The joke's on Giuseppe! I've been signing all of his paperwork for the past two-hundred-fifty years! But we need to get signatures from you, Roman, and Ari on all the accounts. This modern age requires more due diligence, and it will make me nervous until everything is set up properly."

"How is Roman?" Marco asked. Gage related what Dr. Tanner said. Donatello cursed in Italian.

"As soon as Roman has recovered, we will make a trip over there. In the meantime, it looks like things are. You should have new equipment showing up with on-site training. Call Jason direct for questions about accounts or billing," Gage said.

CHAPTER EIGHT

GAGE, JASON, AND SHERM COULDN'T HELP THE WIDE smiles plastered on their faces. The Italians solved a huge problem for the late Tothar king's estate by transferring ownership to Panther Industries.

"You know good and well that Donatello and Marco could have made themselves heirs to the fortune, don't you?" Sherm said.

"I honestly don't think they have it in them to do that," Gage said. "That man was so vile and hated by everyone in the palazzo to the point I'm surprised they didn't do him in."

"Mom was awesome, wasn't she?" Jason asked. "I can't believe Kevin and I shifted. I can't believe our animals materialized after what Atsa said."

"Wait until Roman sees her—plus you and your brother when you shift," Gage said.

His phone rang. Ari was calling. "Hey, is everything okay?" He heard coughing in the background.

"Gage! Roman's coughing! He was panting, so I tried

squeezing a little water into his mouth. I hope I didn't hurt him!" Ari panicked.

"Be right there!" Gage was up and out of his chair in a second. "Roman's coughing."

All three rushed to the elevator. They bolted as soon as the doors opened in the penthouse. They heard the panther coughing, and they ran into the room.

Roman was still in his panther form. He raised his head, and leaned to the side, almost as if he were going to stand. He coughed several times.

Gage rushed up to his friend. He slapped his back with enough force to dislodge whatever had caused his coughing spell.

Roman's eyes were open, and he looked at each of them. He saw Ari's stricken face. Read the worry and the fear there. Relief flooded Gage's face while Sherm showed deep concern. Jason comforted his mother.

Roman tried to stand, but his body wouldn't allow it. He collapsed back on his side.

"You're too weak to stand, Roman. Don't try for at least several hours until you can eat. If you aren't aware of them, Dr. Tanner has you on an IV drip and a catheter, so be careful." Gage said.

When did I get home?

"Yesterday. You were at the palazzo for over two weeks," Gage told Roman.

How did you find me?

"There's so much to tell you," Jason said. "You wouldn't believe half of it!"

Roman glanced at Ari and Jason. His eyes drooped. He yawned.

"Get some sleep. When you wake up, I'll heat up the bacon I cooked for you this morning," Ari said.

Roman's eyes closed.

Gage worked his phone. "I texted Dr. Tanner. He said not to worry about the coughing for now. He'll come by later when he's finished with his rounds at the hospital."

Three hours later, a thought popped into Ari's head.

Hungry.

She bolted off the sofa in the living room and rushed to the spare bedroom.

Roman was awake, blinking. She flopped on the floor beside the mattress and ran her fingers over his face, stroked his neck and shoulders, then kissed his forehead.

"Want to try some bacon?"

Yes, please. Water...

Roman maneuvered his body to raise his head. Ari picked up the squeeze bottle and twisted open the top. She lightly squeezed to trickle water into his mouth. He lapped at the spout of the water bottle.

"I'll be right back," she said. She rushed to the kitchen, removed the plate of bacon from the refrigerator and heated it in the microwave just enough to remove the chill. She grabbed a few paper towels and returned to the bedroom and kneeled on the floor.

She held out a piece of bacon to Roman's cat. He gently snatched it from her fingers and chewed. Ari continued to feed him until the plate was empty. Her phone alerted her to the elevator app. Then she received a text from Dr. Tanner.

"Dr. Tanner's here. I'll be right back," Ari said. Ari and Dr. Tanner entered the room.

"Hi, Roman, it's good to see you awake and alert," Dr. Tanner said. "Tell Ari how you're doing—she'll be the interpreter."

I feel weak, still a little groggy.

Ari passed on the information.

"You had ten times the amount of the tranquilizer in your system. It's going to take a few more days before you're fully recovered," Dr. Tanner said. "Do you want to try to shift?"

Roman blinked, thinking. *I don't want to get stuck.*

"Then wait until tonight or tomorrow before you attempt to shift," Dr. Tanner said. "I'll remove the IV and the catheter. If you can't shift, or are too wobbly to stand on your own, someone will have to assist you to go to the bathroom."

Dr. Tanner turned to Ari. "I know this sounds gross, but if he's eating and can't shift, he'll have to defecate and urinate in the bathtub. Unless, of course, he can figure out how to use the toilet in his cat form."

"That's what they make bleach for," Ari said. "We'll work something out."

Dr. Tanner disconnected him from the tubes, then checked Roman's vitals. "You're in decent shape now. Don't rush anything. Even after you shift, I highly suggest that you stay in bed for two or three days, or longer. Your body has taken a beating and you've lost twenty or thirty pounds."

My pelt is loose and my stomach feels hollow.

"What should I feed him?" Ari asked.

"Roman, do you like venison?" Dr. Tanner asked.

Yes.

"My brother-in-law just dressed a deer. I'll have him send over some large slabs of meat. You should eat as much protein as you can to build up your strength," Dr. Tanner said. He turned to Ari. "Cut it into bite-sized pieces for him, whether he likes that idea or not. He's too weak to stand, so he's going to need help with the food."

Dr. Tanner patted Roman on the shoulder. "Take it slow. I'll be back in a few days to check on your progress."

I will. I promise.

Ari walked Dr. Tanner to the elevator. "Thanks so much. I don't think I could have gotten through this without your taking care of Roman."

"I'm glad to help. Be on the lookout for the box of venison," he said.

Dr. Tanner left, and Ari returned to the spare room. She sat on the edge of the mattress and stroked Roman.

I have to go to the bathroom.

Ari examined the room for space. "I'll be right back. Boy, are you going to be in for a big surprise."

Ari, I need to go right now. I can't wait for your surprise!

Ari ran out of the room to the living room. She stripped off her clothes and willed herself to shift. Her gigantic liger stepped forward. She trotted to the spare room.

Roman's panther stared at the giant cat that approached the bed.

Ari? Is that you? What...

There's so much to tell you. It happened instinctively in Italy at the palazzo. The boys also shifted. Gage said Sherm almost passed out.

Ari's liger grabbed Roman by the scruff and she carried him to the bathroom.

Number one or number two? Do you want to try the toilet or should I put you in the bathtub?

Both, I'm afraid. This is so embar...

Stop it, Roman. We almost lost you. That bastard almost killed you.

She held him in the tub, keeping a grip on his scruff as he did his business.

Hurts to urinate.

That might be from the catheter. I'll text Dr. Tanner to be sure. I hope you don't get an infection.

Finished.

She lifted him out of the tub and brought him back to the mattress. Ari's cat settled Roman gently on the bed, licked his face, then she shifted.

"I'll be right back," she said. She slipped out of the room and returned, dressed once again.

Ari climbed on the bed and spooned Roman's back. She threw an arm and a leg around him. The panther purred, and they drifted off to sleep.

Gage returned to the quiet apartment. He entered the spare room where both Roman and Ari slept. He noticed the IV stand missing and the catheter bag was no longer strapped to the cat's leg. The eagle shifter removed his shoes and climbed onto the mattress in back of Ari. She stirred slightly, sighed contentedly as she sensed him, and slumbered. Gage dropped off to sleep immediately, worn down from the stress of the past few weeks.

Two hours later, Ari's phone rang. They all woke. Ari crawled over Gage to reach her phone.

"Hello? Oh! Is it heavy? I'll send Gage down. Thanks. Dr. Tanner's brother-in-law sent a box of fresh venison meat for Roman. Can you go downstairs and bring it up?" she asked.

"Sure. What's the plan for the bathroom?" Gage asked.

Ari's now acting as my mom. She shifted and brought me to the tub.

"Damn, wish I could have seen that. Were you as shocked as everyone else when you met her liger?" Gage asked.

We're lucky these rooms are large. She's got to be at least ten feet long, if not more.

"Yeah, I want to measure her the next time she shifts," Gage said.

"I'm so happy I have an animal! Roman, Jason is a tiger and Kevin is a lion," Ari said.

Gage went downstairs and returned with a hefty box. He set it on the kitchen island and opened it. There were plastic bags of venison steaks and stew meat. He grabbed a bag of stew meat and set it aside, then opened the refrigerator and moved things around to gain shelf space, then emptied the box onto the refrigerator shelf. He opened a cabinet and took out a plate and dumped the stew meat on the plate.

Roman's cat sniffed the air. He licked his lips as Gage entered with the plate of cubed meat.

"Should we heat it if it's cold?" Ari asked.

No.

"Here you go, buddy. There's plenty more." Gage set the plate on the mattress.

Roman shifted his weight to raise his upper half and dove into the raw food.

More.

"You'd better wait a while," Ari said. "Your stomach hasn't digested food for over two weeks, so you don't want to push it. You might vomit and make things worse."

Roman yawned. *Okay. But I'm hungry.*

The elevator dinged. Kevin, Jason, Sherm, and Lonnie joined them in the spare room.

"Well, you're looking better," Sherm said. "Doesn't look like you're knocking at death's door."

"You can't shift?" Kevin asked.

Not yet. Too weak.

Gage translated for Sherm and Lonnie.

Ari, I have to use the bathroom.

"Okay, I need to shift so I can take Roman to the bathroom, and the largest space is the living room. So, if you don't want to see me naked, stay here."

She left the room to undress and returned in her mighty liger animal form.

The newness of her animal stunned everyone. Sherm and Lonnie couldn't help themselves. They stroked her sides. Gage stood in front of her and grasped her face in his hands. He made her lower her head, and he stayed forehead to forehead with her for a minute.

"You're spectacular, Ari. Just spectacular." Gage kissed her head.

Ari gently grabbed Roman by the scruff and lifted him off the mattress. She walked to the bathroom and lowered him into the tub while she kept a firm grip on his scruff. He did his business, and she returned him to the mattress.

"I'll clean it up," Gage said. He noticed a dustpan and a bottle of bleach beside the tub. He scooped up the poop and dumped it in the toilet. Then he ran water in the tub so the urine would drain. He set the stopper and poured bleach and water in the tub.

"Let the bleach stand in the tub for a little while before you drain it out," Ari called out.

DURING THE NIGHT, ROMAN SHIFTED TO HIS HUMAN form. He stood on wobbly legs beside the mattress and gazed down at Ari and Gage sound asleep. He stumbled to the bathroom and used the toilet, thankful that he didn't require help. He made it back to the bed, settled in and engulfed Ari in his arms. His hand settled on Gage's arm wrapped around Ari. It felt so good to touch his life partners. Within minutes he drifted to sleep.

They woke within moments of each other. Gage and Ari sensed something different and were happy Roman was in his human form. They had a moment. All three of them lay in an embrace, the way they had spent the past several years sleeping.

"The separation almost killed me," Roman said. "I couldn't shift because I was so drugged up, couldn't eat or drink. I thought I would die on that floor and never see either of you again."

"My gut and my heart ached," Ari said. "It was torture for us; I can't imagine how you felt."

"How did you find me?"

"Ari had this odd experience where she remote-viewed through your eyes. She saw a banner through the barred high window and a couple of bear shifters identified the tower," Gage explained. "We sent twelve bears and their wives to Italy and had each couple assigned to an area to find you. But what found you was a message from Donatello, who was Giuseppe's assistant, through our online contact web form."

"I don't remember anything or anyone," Roman said.

"Well, buddy, you're millions of dollars richer," Gage said.

He and Ari took turns explaining everything that Donatello and Marco had done.

"Sounds like there was no love lost there," Roman said.

"That bastard made them wear those robes, wouldn't even let them shift, and no one had any electronics except for him," Ari said.

"What you'll find interesting is that Marco tracked all the accounts manually in ledgers," Gage said.

"Oh, and we found the Motherlode of history for our kind, which reminds me, where are the two journals we brought back with us?" Ari asked. "I'd like to give that ancient one to Mr. Tran."

"I'm going to try to read the journal that was on Giuseppe's desk. There should be answers about how this kidnapping all fell into place." Gage looked at Roman. "Lisa Hamilton is the dead Tothar's niece. She's responsible for everything on our end."

Roman's face transformed from his relaxed form to show he seethed in anger. "That bitch is going down!"

CHAPTER NINE

ARI BROUGHT HER WALKER AND CANE FROM HER RECOVERY to the spare room. "Here, you need to stabilize yourself until you're back to your full strength."

Roman didn't hesitate. He grabbed the walker and pulled himself to his feet. His arms shook slightly as he rolled the walker out of the room. "I want to take a shower."

"Let's go to your room. Your shower is the biggest," Gage said.

Gage reached into the shower stall and turned the water to full blast. He and Ari undressed, and all three entered the large shower stall. Gage and Ari each held one of Roman's arms. He tilted his head back and let the water rush over his face and hair.

Roman groaned with pleasure. It had been a long time since he had a clean body, and the water felt like pure luxury.

Ari grabbed one of the bath scrubbers on a stick, poured a dollop of Dr. Bronner's body wash on it and scrubbed Roman's back. Gage poured shampoo into his hand and rubbed it through Roman's hair. They scrubbed every inch of him while he held the bar on the shower wall and turned when they directed him.

When all three of them rinsed off, Gage shut off the water and grabbed a towel. He rubbed Roman's head, wiped the man's face, and threw the towel across his shoulders. He and Ari led Roman out of the shower stall. Ari placed a towel on her vanity chair.

"Sit," she instructed. They dried their partner.

Ari wet Roman's toothbrush and lined it with toothpaste. "Here, brush your teeth."

He stood on shaky legs before the sink and brushed, turned the water faucet on and rinsed his mouth, then the toothbrush.

"I feel like a million dollars," he said.

Gage laughed. "You mean millions and millions."

Ari left and returned with sweatpants, a T-shirt, and a sweatshirt. "How's your body temperature? Do you want to wear a T-shirt or sweatshirt?"

"T-shirt should be okay," Roman said. "Am I going commando?"

"I figured it would be easier for you," Ari said.

She handed him the T-shirt, and he slipped it over his head.

Gage grabbed the sweatpants and crouched before the chair and helped Roman get them on.

Ari grabbed her robe and slipped into it. She and Gage helped Roman over to the walker and hovered as he made his way to the living room sofa.

"I'll get dressed," Gage said. He hurried out of the room.

Roman let out an exhausted sigh. "I've never felt so tired in my entire life."

"Rest up while I get breakfast. Do you want more venison, or would you prefer a steak with your eggs?" Ari headed to the kitchen and opened the refrigerator.

"The venison was good. Just sear it so my human form can tolerate meat as raw as possible," Roman said.

Gage strode into the room barefoot, dressed in jeans and a T-shirt. He kissed Ari. "Go get dressed. I'll take over."

The elevator dinged Jason and Kevin's arrival.

"You're here early," Ari said as she stopped to kiss their cheeks.

"We figured we'd stop before going to work," Jason said. He glanced into the living room and saw Roman on the sofa.

"Roman! You shifted!" Jason said as he loped over to the gaunt man and threw his arms around him.

"Man, you're bone thin," Kevin said.

"You boys want steak and eggs?" Gage called out.

"Sure," they both responded. They never turned down home-cooked meals.

Ari returned, dressed, and joined Gage in the kitchen.

They broiled steaks, made toast, and Ari scrambled eggs.

"Help Roman over to the table," Gage said.

"I'm good," Roman said. He grabbed the walker and stood up. His arms and legs shook. He rolled the walker a pace. His legs wouldn't cooperate. Standing in the shower had zapped his energy.

"Come on, man," Jason said. "You're too weak right now. Eat first and see if your energy returns."

He grabbed one arm and Kevin grabbed the other, and they helped Roman over to the table. Sweat shone on his forehead as they settled him into a chair.

Gage placed a plate in front of him, along with a steak knife and fork. "Start with this; the rest is coming."

Roman lit into the food like a starved man. His hands shook, but he managed to cut the steak.

Ari and Gage brought plates to the table and handed them out. Everyone sat and dug into the food.

"Now that Roman's shifted back, are we going to have an international meeting?" Jason asked. "I'll check with Tony and see if the IT people have everything they need."

"Let's wait a day or two," Gage said. He nodded to Roman. "He wouldn't want to look weak to the masses."

Ari studied Roman from across the table.

"I think I need another twenty-four hours," Roman said. "I'm not worried about how I look with the weight loss, but I don't want to appear physically weak, as Gage mentioned."

"For our local community, make this a mandatory meeting," Ari said. "While Lisa is under surveillance, we need to make sure she's at the meeting. Sherm should hold her under house arrest in the cell downstairs until we make a final determination about what to do with her."

Kevin looked pensive. "That Italian guy is dead, which means you're the kings and queen of the shifters worldwide. Every shifter community should be part of this meeting."

"Call Atsa and find out how to connect with all the groups in the US. Donatello and Marco should be able to inform us of groups that were under their old king," Gage said.

Roman pushed his empty plate aside and pulled the plate that held his scrambled eggs and toast toward himself. He dug in.

"Want more?" Ari asked him.

"I'd better slow down and let this digest, but I think my body will require several smaller meals for the next couple of days," Roman said.

Over the next four days Roman fed his ravenous body, while

Gage and Ari contacted the Italians and the Navajos. Leander helped establish a network throughout the United States, while Donatello and Marco did the same for the overseas groups. They set a time for the online meeting that was agreeable to everyone. Eight o'clock in the morning for California, eleven in Reading and reasonable hours for overseas.

ARI DRAFTED A MESSAGE FOR EMAILS, PHONE CALLS, AND mind-blasting out to each group. They discussed how to present the meeting. Should they remain in their human forms? Should they shift? Shifting presented a problem—they'd be naked on the stage if they shifted before the meeting. Neither Roman nor Gage had a problem with that, but they wouldn't allow Ari to be naked before the shifter world. Even if that part of the shift was natural to their kind. She was their queen and needed more protection than they did.

Last-minute details were sorted, and IT held a test run with the online meeting venue. Parts of Russia and Albania experienced glitches, but their IT people corrected the problems.

Leander came up with a solution to the shifting. He suggested the royals shift to their animal forms so a photographer from the community could take a picture for display on a screen as a backdrop.

That happened on day five.

They made emails, phone calls, and mind-calls to gather their kind. Their local community gathered downstairs in the meeting room. Trisha Anderson's eyes swept the room, looking for Lisa. The young woman finally showed and Trisha grabbed her arm and led her to a chair. Two commandos joined them. Lisa tried to stand, but they forced her to stay in the chair.

Roman had a timer set on his phone. It counted down to the exact time when the worldwide shifter community came online. There were additional large monitors mounted on the wall with screens within screens to show the dozens of communities. The Tothars sat in chairs on the stage.

Roman's phone vibrated. He silenced it. "Greetings! My name is Roman Davenport. This is Ari Davis and Gage Stryker. We are your kings and queen. This is Jason and Kevin, your princes. We are the last living Tothars."

The photo of the royals in their animal forms was directly above them, all labeled so the world would understand who was who.

Sherm, Lonnie, and a team of commandos were onstage fully geared up. Roman and Gage wanted the world to see they were not helpless.

"We recently experienced a power-play with Giuseppe Genovesi, an Italian Tothar. He kidnapped me in my animal form and kept me drugged and starved for two weeks. Unfortunately, Mr. Genovesi is no longer among us," Roman said. His eyes sought Lisa in the room. "We discovered a traitor among us. A young woman here in our Reading community who plotted with her uncle and arranged for my abduction. Her actions led to her uncle's death."

Roman's cold eyes fell upon Lisa. The room was deathly silent.

Lisa was not aware of her Tothar uncle's demise until that moment. Her face displayed shock. She shot out of her chair, but the guards grabbed her. Trisha growled at her.

"You killed my uncle?" Lisa screeched.

"You are a disgrace to our kind," Trisha spat out.

Roman nodded to the guards. They hauled Lisa out of the room. "She will be dealt with."

Gage shifted slightly in his chair. "We wanted to take this time to introduce ourselves to you and to assure you that we are fair and just leaders. We recently learned that the Italian Tothar ruled with an iron fist. He stifled his own people to the point where he forbade them to shift. We deplore that action. We will never deny our people their natural abilities. They were not allowed any electronics to communicate with the world."

"While we live and work among humans, we should always be true to our nature. That does not mean we will condone any shifter who goes wild and attacks a human. I want to be clear on this point. You shall cause no harm! If you are having a problem with a human, if you are being treated cruelly, or witness an act of cruelty, you are to report it to your immediate leader," Gage said.

"They will go up the chain of command and we will decide the course of action. Don't take matters into your own hands. Shifters have a precarious place in the world, and we don't want to bring our kind into the spotlight." He looked to Ari.

"Hello everyone," Ari started. "We have a daunting job to organize our worldwide community. Our headquarters is located at Panther Industries here in Reading, Pennsylvania, in the United States. We will send contact information for shifter-related issues, which will include our new overseas offices in Fiuggi, Italy."

THE MEETING LASTED FOR CLOSE TO FIVE HOURS. Each region introduced itself and discussed how it ran its organization. So many revelations of hardship disturbed Ari. She noticed that Jason took careful notes of those things.

After the meeting closed, the Reading leadership team, consisting of the royal family, Leander and Sherm, met in the penthouse and discussed a plan of action.

"We need to understand these hardships," Ari said. "Is it

because most shifters don't have an education? What seems to be the problem?"

"That's what I was wondering," Jason said. "I noticed only a small percentage of people in business attire. I realize that's a strange observation. It seems to me, if you were meeting your new royal family for the first time, you'd put more effort into your appearance."

Sherm huffed out a sigh. "Remember when we met the Reading community for the first time? Most people were in work clothes—more like laborers or low-paying jobs. There were a few exceptions," he nodded at Leander. "But mostly, I'm willing to bet most shifters live in abject poverty, or close to it."

"Perhaps they were held back from the time they were children?" Leander asked. "I wonder how this all came about. It seems like a social problem."

Roman shook his head. "This makes little sense. Gage and I surely can't be the exception. I mean, Leander, you're a successful businessman. Trisha Anderson is a successful businesswoman. So, what happened to all the other shifters?"

"Possibly, it's just missed opportunities," Kevin said. "If you recall, both Jason and I were in low-end jobs when we first met you two. If it hadn't been for your hiring us, we'd still be floundering around and eating at mom's most of the time. Most likely sleeping on her sofa."

Roman looked pensive. "You're right, Kev. I think it would be a good idea to investigate the situation on various levels. This will take a lot of work, but we have to bring our people up in the world."

Gage nodded. "We could put a stop to this social problem, which will enrich future generations. We need to discover the cause. Could it be low self-esteem because they think themselves beneath humans? Did their leaders have something to do with this? How can we identify the problems?"

Their discussions continued for another hour. Then Roman, Gage, the boys, and Leander left with Sherm. Ari decided she needed a nap.

The guys rode the elevator down to the basement where only the Security Division, Roman and Gage, had access. Sherm stuck his cardkey into the security panel and tapped in a long code on the keypad. The door snicked open, and they entered the room.

Lisa sprang to her feet in the six-by-eight-foot cell, which contained a cot with a pillow and blanket, a toilet, and a sink with a plastic sixteen-ounce cup. The cell was designed with no extended ceiling fixtures or breaks in the bars, and the bed was bolted to the floor. There was no opportunity to hang oneself for an easy way out of a situation that landed someone in the cell.

Her face was tight with angst as she finally understood the mess she got herself into. Her uncle was dead, and it was all her fault. She thought she could claim the panther king for herself. The eagle king would have the queen, so she didn't know why she would have been rejected. Why did the queen have two kings? Why was she, a beautiful cougar, spurned?

The six men who stood on the other side of the bars glared at her with malicious intent.

"Do you understand what your traitorous actions led to? What harm you did to your king?" Gage asked.

He sent her images of Roman close to death in the Italian cell.

She flinched. "I had no idea! I never thought my uncle would do anything like that! He told me he wanted to see who the other Tothar king was."

Roman still needed to gain weight to fill out. His cheeks were still sunken, and his clothes hung on him. He wobbled slightly, worn out from the meeting.

Leander grabbed a chair from the vacant desk and set it in back of the king.

Roman nodded his thanks and sat. "What you did was vicious and selfish. You are a danger to our community—our entire kind."

Lisa swiped at a steady stream of tears. "I'm sorry. I swear I won't ever cause harm again."

Roman stood. The men turned to walk out the door. "Please, can I have something to eat?" Lisa begged.

"I didn't eat for over two weeks while I was a *guest* of your uncle's," Roman said. "But we aren't that cruel."

Kevin opened the door, and they filed out.

CHAPTER TEN

THEY STOOD OUT BY THE ELEVATOR.

"We need to set a precedent," Gage said.

Leander was thoughtful. "Remember that movie about the woman who had to wear the letter A because she committed adultery? That would be a just punishment if we branded Lisa with the word traitor—just a suggestion."

"We should have torn her apart at the house!" Kevin railed.

"Well, we didn't, and there were dire consequences. We can't go around murdering people who cause us harm, but we can take justified actions," Sherm said. "Leander's suggestion has merit."

Roman nodded. "Would that ironworker be able to create a brand?"

"You mean Wendel Smith?" Leander asked.

"Yeah, I remember him mentioning that he creates things in metal in his off-hours," Gage said.

"I'll find out," Leander said.

WENDEL SMITH WORE A LEATHER APRON AS HE WORKED at the anvil at his forge. He held a hot piece of iron with tongs and a fireproof glove, picked up the large hammer and beat the edges of the iron on the anvil.

Leander and Gage arrived in the BMW sedan. They got out and approached the large barn. The double doors were open to let the heat from the forge escape.

Wendel stopped what he was doing as he saw them approach. "What can I do for you, gentlemen?"

They shook hands and got down to business. "Can you make a cattle brand?" Gage asked.

"Sure, those are pretty simple. What do you have in mind?" Wendel asked.

"Two things," Gage said. He caught Leander's questioning look. "I want the letter T, then another brand with the word Traitor."

"You sure you want brands and not tattoos?" Wendel asked.

"Tattoos won't show through a shifter's animal fur or skin," Gage said.

Wendel nodded. "You're right. The brand will."

The three discussed the brands. Gage explained that the T was for the forehead and the full word was for between the shoulders.

"Yeah, I can do that. Should only take a day or two," Wendel said.

"What will you charge?" Gage asked.

Wendel waved a hand. "Don't worry about it."

"You're in business, Wendel. The company has funds. Do me up an invoice and we will pay you immediately," Gage said.

"Okay," Wendel said.

Gage and Leander left. As they buckled up and Gage

backed the car out of the parking space, Gage asked Leander his opinion.

"In order for the brand to be effective, Lisa should be in her cat form. That way, it will burn her fur, not just the skin underneath. Same with her forehead," Gage said. "Or does it matter?"

"No, that sounds right," Leander said. "It seems to me if she were branded in her human form, the brand would be beneath her fur. This would be a good question for Atsa."

"Good idea." Gage engaged the phone app in the car and called the Navajo. He and Leander took turns explaining what they were doing and which way would be the best for the brand to be visible at all times.

"For the branding to be visible at all times, she should be in her cat form," Atsa said. "So, you're going to brand her, then kick her out?"

"Yeah. Sherm wants to chip her," Gage said.

"How's Roman?" Atsa asked.

"He's put on a little weight, but he's still exhausted," Gage said. "It will be a few more weeks before he's fully back to himself."

"That's to be expected. I gathered from what everyone said, he had quite an overdose of that drug in his system. Everything else okay?" Atsa asked.

"We're getting things organized," Gage said.

GAGE DROPPED LEANDER OFF AT HIS SHOP AND HEADED back to the penthouse. He stepped off the elevator into the foyer and went in search of Roman and Ari. He found them in Roman's bed, sleeping.

He slipped off his shoes and climbed onto the bed and wound himself around Ari.

Roman lifted his head. "Hey. Get everything taken care of?"

Gage reiterated the conversations between himself, Leander, Wendel and Atsa.

"Good. The sooner we put this behind us, the sooner we can focus on other things," Roman said.

"How are you doing today?" Gage asked.

"I still feel off," Roman said.

Gage studied Roman's face. He had shadows under his eyes, and his face wasn't as filled out as when he had been in perfect health. "It will be a challenge until you can gain the weight back. Would it help to shift and hunt fresh game?"

Roman shook his head. "I don't have the energy to hunt. I don't even have the energy to make love." He looked embarrassed.

Gage grabbed Roman's shoulder across Ari. "Listen, man, getting your dick wet should be the least of your concerns. You almost died. We almost lost you. Ari and I only made love once while you were gone, and that was the night we discovered where you were."

"You don't have to wait for me," Roman said. "You two shouldn't have to suffer."

"You don't understand, Roman. It's not the same," Gage said. "Our bond does something. It makes me wonder what would happen to us if one of us were to die. You remember how we suffered when Ari was down. She and I experienced something similar when you were gone."

Ari turned over onto her back. "No one's going to die! Stop getting all dark and dreary. Roman, you will gain the weight back, and that will make your strength return. We're not teenagers. We can survive without sex for a few weeks."

"I don't even think I can get it up," he said.

"Want to try?" Ari asked.

Roman and Gage exchanged a glance.

"Let's wait until tonight. After I've had more sleep and a lot more food, maybe I'll have the energy. But I can barely keep my eyes open," Roman said.

They sandwiched together. Ari kissed Roman and laid an arm across his shoulder. Gage spooned Ari, his hand around her waist. They drifted off to sleep.

ARI PREPARED GINSENG TEA FOR ROMAN WHILE GAGE seared a venison steak in a frying pan.

"Want any salt and pepper or Worcestershire sauce on this?" Gage asked.

Roman shook his head. "Plain is best."

Gage dropped the blood-rare steak on a plate and handed it to Roman. He fished out a fork from the drawer, then opened the knife drawer and carefully pulled out one of the razor-sharp steak knives.

Roman cut a hunk and shoved it into his mouth and chewed. Ari set the steaming cup of tea in front of him. By the time he finished with the steak and tea, his coloring seemed less pasty.

"I feel better," Roman said. "Thanks."

"Let's go see Mr. Tran," Ari suggested. She scooted off to her room and returned with the ancient journal.

They rode the elevator down to the twenty-sixth floor and found his office. Ari tapped on the open doorframe.

"Hi, Mr. Tran," Ari said. "Do you have a minute?"

An Da looked up from his project, grabbed a sticky note and placed it on the edge of the ancient paper. "Come in!

Come in! It is so good to see you." He peeled off the gloves and threw them in his recycling bin.

He looked at Roman and studied his gaunt face and thinner frame. He jumped up and hurried around the desk, and guided Roman to a chair.

"You do not look well! What happened?" Mr. Tran asked.

Gage dipped out of the office and returned with another chair. He and Ari sat.

"Someone kidnapped me and nearly starved me to death," Roman said.

"They kept him drugged," Ari said.

"What was this drug? Do you know?" Mr. Tran asked.

"Zoletil," Gage said.

Mr. Tran stared at the three who sat in front of his desk. He got up, walked to the door, closed it, and returned to his desk. He folded his hands on the desk—more to keep them steady because he knew a big secret was right in front of him.

"Why did they use an animal tranquilizer on a human, or does this have something to do with the context of these ancient books?"

There. He asked the big question. All they could do was fire him, but he didn't think they would. They needed these books translated, and in addition to being a translator, he was an expert historian, and he had signed a non-disclosure agreement so secrets would be safe.

Roman studied the older man. He glanced across at Gage and Ari. "Show him."

One by one, they showed their animal faces.

Mr. Tran's hands flew to his heart. "I remember when you interviewed me. You told me I might consider the content strange. Now I understand."

Ari explained about the kidnapping. Gage explained the difference between Tothars and regular shifters.

"So, this Italian Tothar king is dead. Are you the only Tothars?" Mr. Tran asked.

"Ari's sons are Tothars," Roman said. "There won't be any more attempts at a takeover."

"Mr. Tran, there's a room full of Giuseppe's journals," Ari said. She handed him one of the earliest texts. "I haven't even looked at this, so I don't know what language he used, or if you will understand what's in the journals. Donatello told us that the king could have been twelve-thousand years old."

Mr. Tran took the journal and studied the outside. The cover was made from tree bark and was tied with a brown vine. He carefully slid the vine off the journal and opened it. His eyes went wide. He lightly ran a finger across the page, which was a large leaf of some type. He worried that the natural oils in his fingers would damage both the leaf and the substance that made the symbols.

An Da yanked open one of his desk drawers and pulled out two sterile gloves and slipped them on. He lifted the first leaf out of the book and studied the images.

"This is extraordinary! You said there's a room filled with these journals?" His eyes lit up as if he'd won the lottery. "I suggest you hire more translators and historians."

The royals conferred silently.

"We'll start by sending a worldwide request to the shifter world," Gage said. "Do you know anyone from the societies you belong to?"

An Da silently considered the people he knew. "There is only one I respect and trust. I'm sure he would jump at the chance to work with these ancient documents."

"He will have to understand that he can't go public with any information in the books or journals," Ari said. "No one can publish a paper or speak publicly about these journals."

"And we will have to trust him with the knowledge of the shifter world," Roman said. He swayed slightly in his chair. "I need to go back to bed."

An Da looked over Roman. "I may be able to help you." He turned to Ari. "May I keep this journal?"

"Yes. I was afraid to open it," she said.

Mr. Tran stood, closed the bigger book he was translating, and brought both to the cabinet, locking them inside. He tore off the gloves.

"Please come to my apartment. I will prepare an elixir for you," he said. He led them out of the office to the elevator. They rode to the twenty-fourth floor, then walked down a hall and around a corner, where he unlocked the door and escorted them inside.

He walked to the spare bedroom with his employers following him. His desk chair was against a solid wall, and his desk faced the door to protect him from psychic or any other attacks. Tall white cabinets and bookcases stuffed with books, texts, and binders lined part of the wall. A large, oblong table was in the center of the room. He grabbed a chair and motioned for Roman to sit.

Mr. Tran opened three of the cabinets packed with labeled jars of different sizes, shapes, and colors. A fourth cabinet held bags and larger containers of dried herbs.

His eyes scanned the shelves. He grabbed bottles and jars and set them on the table in the center of the room.

Gage and Ari walked around the room and studied the contents of the various shelves and cabinets. Ari stood at the table.

"I only recognize two or three things," she said. "Ginseng and Vitamin C, and that looks like honey." She pointed to a jar of liquid.

"Raw honey in twenty percent agave alcohol," he said.

Mr. Tran pulled his pestle and mortar from a cabinet and ground the herbs. When he was satisfied with the consistency, he pulled an empty jar from a cabinet and grabbed a sheet of printer paper. The herbalist rolled the paper into a funnel shape and propped it inside the empty jar. He dumped the herbs into the funnel and filled the jar.

Next, he opened a box and retrieved two silk tea bag pouches.

He tapped each jar in front of him with an explanation.

"Take one tablespoon of the dried herbs and put it in the silk tea bag. This is reusable, so don't accidentally throw it out." He made sure he had their attention. "Boil water to make the tea. Add one or two tablespoons of honey to a cup—you can adjust the taste later. Add your boiling water and stir the honey to mix in completely. Then steep the bag in the water for twelve minutes—use your phone or a timer. Start with one cup today. Tomorrow, drink one cup in the morning before breakfast and one at bedtime. The next day and for the rest of the week, drink three cups a day. One before breakfast, another four or five hours later, and the last at bedtime."

"This will make me feel better?" Roman asked.

"Your energy will return, and you'll gain your weight back. Your body won't spend all its energy fighting your exhaustion. If you don't seem better in two days, I'll adjust the formula."

Gage spread his arms wide. "Is this a hobby of yours?"

He thought for a moment. "My maternal grandfather was, ah, known for his elixirs. Many people called him a wizard."

He slipped the silk pouches into an envelope and handed it to Roman. He handed the honey to Ari and the herb jar to Gage.

"I will call my colleague," An Da said.

They all shook hands, and Mr. Tran bowed slightly as his employers left his apartment.

CHAPTER ELEVEN

THE NEXT MORNING, WHILE ROMAN DRANK MR. TRAN'S herbal tea at breakfast, Jason arrived with his laptop.

"Good morning, son, have you had breakfast?" Ari asked.

"I'll never turn down a home-cooked meal, Mom!" Jason sat at the table beside Gage and opened the laptop.

"What do you have?" Gage asked.

"The Fiuggi facility is now wired and online. They've installed all the wide screens," Jason said.

"How many were installed, and where?" Gage asked.

"We may have gone overboard, but I took into consideration that this facility will be the main meeting place for all of Europe. I'm not sure if Russia or the Far East will have a center, or if it all falls to Italy," Jason said. "So, there's a large screen in that huge foyer room, three more in the first-floor meeting rooms, and smaller screens in some key offices upstairs. Tony installed ten throughout the place."

Ari joined them at the table. She handed a plate of bacon and eggs to Jason, and he dug in.

"Have all the laptops and equipment been delivered? And

what about the training?" Ari looked over his shoulder at the spreadsheet on the screen.

"I'd like to take a trip so I can sit with both Donatello and Marco. We need to go over the purchase order protocols, and I want to provide them with templates for their location. Plus, I want to make sure everyone is getting the training they need," Jason said between bites. "I can't imagine being as old as some of them are and having never used a cellphone or a laptop. It seems wrong."

Roman chuckled from across the table. "Jason, look up the year 1918—that's our birth year. Think about all Gage and I saw and experienced in the past one hundred years."

Jason stared at Roman. "That never crossed my mind. Mostly because I always think of you as my age."

"For some reason, and we don't know why, we stopped aging," Gage said.

"Maybe Mr. Tran will come across something in the big books," Ari said.

"Anyway, would it be okay if I booked a flight to Italy?" Jason asked.

"Get with Sherm and see if there's anything that requires attention—anyone who should accompany you on the trip," Gage said. "You might also want to check with Sandy. Find out if there's any HR-related information you need to collect, or any other paperwork we may have overlooked."

"Take the jet," Roman said. "Otherwise you'll be miserable, even in first class. Remember, there's a bed in the back."

"Make sure you put in your food order so they can stock the galley for your flight," Ari said.

Roman sipped his bedtime tea while propped against pillows against the headboard. Ari and Gage came into the room and climbed onto the bed, Ari between them, as usual.

"This tea tastes terrible, but it seems to work. I feel stronger," Roman said.

"Looks like you're filling out, so you're finally gaining more weight," Gage said.

Roman tipped the cup and finished. He set it on the night-stand, then lowered himself into a sleeping position, turned toward Ari. She turned toward him, and Gage spooned her. Roman ran his arm down her side. Then he cupped her breast. He pressed himself to her body and kissed her along her neck.

Gage looked on and waited for the final sign that the game was on with them.

Ari reached out and ran her hands through Roman's hair. "I feel you against me... you've got it up."

Roman raised up a little and made eye contact with both of them. "I think I'm ready... and capable. Let's try." He grasped her face between his hands and laid a kiss on her lips. His tongue slid into her mouth and entwined with hers. He dropped his mouth to her neck and slowly licked and kissed all the way down to her chest.

Ari turned to Gage, and they kissed. His mouth was all over hers.

Demanding.

Impatient.

Wanting an entry.

She turned onto her back and they both sensually engaged with her.

Roman's tongue circled one of her nipples while Gage's teeth scraped the other one. They sucked and licked and nipped at her soft, smooth, satiny skin.

Roman placed one of his knees between her legs, making Ari spread for access. He slid between her legs and his mouth latched onto her clit.

Ari's hips shot off the bed as she yelled out his name.

Gage's mouth ravished her nipples and her flesh. He stretched up and his teeth taunted her lips. He ran his tongue across her lips and slid inside.

Ari was one hot, writhing mess as Roman's slipped a finger inside her slick, wet core. She couldn't control her hips. They continuously rose to meet the actions of his mouth and fingers.

Roman's tongue circled her sensitive bud, then his mouth sucked until Ari was nearly comatose with ecstasy. She screamed through her first orgasm. Roman brushed Gage out of the way as he slid up her body. He slowly launched into her and groaned with pleasure.

He rested his forehead on hers and stared into her eyes. "Being inside you is like coming home."

He moved slowly at first, then picked up the pace. Ari wrapped her legs around his hips, her heels firmly against his butt, holding him in place. She moved with him, keeping pace with his deep thrusts. She came undone as her second orgasm roared through her. Her pussy clenched down on his cock, and Roman slammed into her as his own orgasm ran through him.

When every last pulse of ecstasy had been released, he rolled off her and kissed her tenderly. Exhausted, he dropped off into a deep sleep.

Gage went into the bathroom and returned with a warm washcloth. He wiped Roman's juices from between Ari's legs. He pulled her away from Roman's side.

"He needs to sleep," he said.

Gage wrapped his arms around Ari and drew her to him. They kissed passionately as their hands explored each other. Ari wrapped her hand around his thick, long cock and stroked. His eyes closed, and he moaned. He nipped her earlobe and licked the rim of her ear.

He made his way down to her breasts and sucked and lapped at her nipples. He kissed his way down across her abdomen to her mound. When his tongue circled her heightened pebble, her hips rose and smashed into him. His mouth latched onto her and didn't let go.

"Gage!" She whispered his name over and over while her head turned from side to side wildly. She sobbed through an orgasm and pulled his hair, forcing him to let go of her clit. He climbed her body to settle his throbbing manhood between her legs.

He rammed into her, and she wrapped her legs around him, riding out the storm of passion. They came together—Gage roaring his pent-up lust and Ari gasping through a powerful orgasm. He collapsed upon her, then rolled to the side.

They giggled at their reactions to their lovemaking. It hadn't been that long since they had made love—but that one time had been a quick release, knowing they would bring Roman back home. This was more typical of the threesome sessions they were used to. Raw passion between the three of them was always fulfilled.

"I'm so glad Roman is better. We all needed this tonight," Ari said.

"This bond is scary," Gage said. "It entwines our lives in such a way that it makes us more powerful. On the other hand, it makes us more vulnerable."

He looked thoughtful. "I wonder about Jason and Kevin. Do they have a bond, or are they individual Tothars?"

"That's to be seen. I don't think Kevin has dated anyone since he and Amanda broke up. We never even got to meet her," Ari said. "Do you think they'll both fall for the same woman?"

"There's no telling. Roman and I aren't brothers. We're not related through DNA, just our Tothar connection," Gage said. "It's mysterious. I wish we knew more."

"Mr. Tran..." Ari said.

"Do you realize how long it will take to gain anything from those books and journals?" Gage let his frustration out.

Ari pondered. "We could help ourselves, you know. All of us need to study languages immediately. I don't know how long our lifespans will be, but we can enrich ourselves with language skills. I'll talk to Sandy tomorrow and put into motion another employee benefit: a Rosetta Stone subscription for all the languages they support."

"That's an excellent idea," Gage said. He hunkered down, yawned loudly and snuggled up to Ari.

Ari nudged Roman. "Time to wake up, Roman. Drink your tea."

His eyes slowly opened. "What time is it?"

"Nine. I wanted you to have your tea before breakfast," she said. "You need to keep to Mr. Tran's schedule."

He grasped the cup by the handle and took a sip. His face screwed up. "God, this stuff tastes horrible. I'm starving."

"I have your plate in the warmer." She leaned in and kissed him on the forehead. "I'm so glad you're on the mend."

"I'll be glad when everything's back to normal, and we can go to our new Italian headquarters," he said.

He tipped the cup and swallowed the remaining bitter tea, then slid out of bed. "Lead the way."

His stomach growled loudly as he followed Ari into the kitchen. She grabbed a potholder and retrieved his plate from the oven and set it on a placemat in front of Roman.

"Careful, the plate is hot," she warned. She pulled another smaller plate out of the refrigerator and set it beside the hot plate.

"What's on your schedule today?" Roman asked. He dug into the food with gusto. In no time, the four eggs, two slices of toast, rib-eye steak, stuffed tomato with cottage cheese, and sliced avocado disappeared.

Ari set a cup of café mocha in front of Roman, and he slurped some down.

"Last night Gage and I were talking about the translations. I'm going down to Sandy's office and set up another employee benefit." Ari explained about the language courses through Rosetta Stone and their need to learn as many languages as possible.

"Have it set up so that the shifter communities can take advantage of this as well—maybe with a special word or code," Roman said. "Let's bug Kevin and Jason to use the programs. We should all try to learn the most common languages: Spanish, French, German, and Italian. Where's Gage?"

"He's helping Jason pull things together for his trip to Italy," Ari said.

"We still need to deal with Lisa Hamilton," Roman said.

"She can rot in that cell for all I care," Ari said.

"I want her out of here," Roman said. "The branding irons should be finished, and we can get on with it."

ROMAN STOPPED IN MR. TRAN'S DOORWAY. THE OLDER man sat at his desk, absorbed in his translation. Roman tapped on the doorframe.

"Hi, Mr. Tran," Roman said.

The older man looked up and acknowledged Roman. "Mr. Roman! You look much better today."

Roman stepped into the office and slid into a chair in front of the desk. "I wanted to thank you for your tea. Tastes awful, but does the job."

"You are gaining weight and filling out," Mr. Tran said. "My friend I mentioned was at a symposium, and we spoke this morning. He is very interested in working on the translations."

"Wonderful! You sure could use the help. Ari is blasting a message out to the community to find other translators. In the meantime, is your friend sending his resume?" Roman asked.

"Let me check my email," Mr. Tran said. He nudged the mouse to wake his computer and checked his Outlook inbox. "Here it is. Do you want me to print it for you? I will forward it to you."

"A print copy would be great. Forward it to Sandy and she'll get the ball rolling," Roman said.

The printer clicked to life and several sheets of paper spat out into the tray. Mr. Tran stapled them together and handed them over to Roman.

"After tomorrow you can stop drinking the tea. I feel sure your body is fully on the mend and it has expelled all the poison from your system," Mr. Tran said.

"Okay. I won't miss it," Roman said. "I can't thank you enough."

Roman stood, followed by the older man. They shook hands, and Mr. Tran bowed slightly.

As Roman rode the elevator to the twenty-eighth floor, his cellphone dinged a message from Gage.

Wendel Smith has finished the branding irons. Do you want to come with me?

The elevator doors opened and Roman headed to Sherm's office.

"Dang, you look a lot better!" Sherm said as he came around the desk.

"Hang on a sec. I have to answer Gage," Roman said.

I'm with Sherm. Yes, I want to come along.

The elevator dinged Gage's arrival. "Hey, Sherm. Want to come with us?"

"Where are you going? Do I need to bring a team?"

"We're going over to Wendel Smith's forge," Gage said.

"I've never been to a forge. Yeah, count me in," Sherm said.

They all piled into the elevator and rode down to the ground floor, then exited into the garage. They piled into an SUV and headed out. Wendel's property was on the outskirts of Reading. Gage pulled into the long driveway and drove up to the barn. Smoke plumed out of the smokestack.

They entered the barn and approached the forge. Wendel hammered a piece of iron on the anvil. He set the work aside, removed his big gloves and came around to greet the men.

"Wendel, this is Roman and Sherm," Gage said.

"Good to meet you in person," Wendel said. "I've got your brands ready." He walked over to a large bench and retrieved the branding irons.

They examined the letter T, then the full word, Traitor. "These will do," Roman said. "Really fine work, Wendel."

Sherm glanced around the barn. "This is an impressive space."

"Been in my family for a few hundred years," Wendel said.

"Did you turn in an invoice?" Gage asked.

"Not yet," Wendel said, looking embarrassed.

"We'll send you five hundred dollars. Does that cover the cost?" Gage asked.

Roman opened his wallet and drew out five bills. "Here. Paid in full." He nudged Gage. "Might not want to track this expense."

"Oh! Hadn't thought about that," Gage said.

"That's way too much...," Wendel said.

"Take your wife out to dinner," Roman said.

They piled back into the SUV and headed back to the city.

"So, when are we going to do this, and where, specifically?" Sherm asked.

"I've been tossing that around," Gage said. "She needs to be in her cat form. We can either do it downstairs, or go out to the house in the woods."

"Need a fire source," Roman said.

THE BRANDING IRONS RESTED ON THE ROCKS SURROUNDING the fire pit, their ends in the roaring fire.

The royals, Leander, Sherm, Lonnie, Trisha, and Bruce's team surrounded Lisa. She was in her cougar form on the ground, warily looking around.

Roman stood in front of her. "Your traitorous actions have caused a lot of harm. Your uncle is dead. I'm recovering from being starved and drugged. It would have been very beneficial if we could have met your uncle and learned more about our kind. But you had your own agenda, Lisa."

"When you discovered your uncle's plans, you could have gone to Trisha and told her. Instead, you ran away to hide the knowledge of your participation. Our kind will never forgive you. When we are done here, you will leave Reading and never return. You will find your car and clothes on the private road," Roman said.

Trisha turned her back and stripped. She shifted to her cat and grabbed Lisa by the scruff of her neck as Roman walked over to the fire, picked up the heavy glove and grabbed the brand with the letter T.

Lisa hissed and growled when she saw her fate. She tried to back away, but Trisha had a firm grip on her scruff while Sherm and Lonnie's fingers dug into her sides and rump, holding her down.

Roman pressed the branding iron into the fur on Lisa's forehead. The smell of burning hair filled the air.

Lisa's cat howled in pain.

Trisha's cat scooted around, still firmly gripping Lisa's cougar by the scruff.

Sherm hovered over the cougar with a hypodermic needle and inserted a microchip into Lisa's scruff. He made sure she didn't see the needle. They wanted to keep the tracking device knowledge to themselves.

Roman retrieved the other branding iron from the fire and stepped around limbs. He planted the brand between her shoulder blades.

The cougar shrieked in agony.

"Never, ever return to Reading," Gage said. "Cause no harm to either the human or shifter worlds. Do you understand?"

She snarled.

"Let her go," Roman said.

The cougar took off into the woods.

"Someone needs to make sure she leaves this property," Ari said.

"I'll stay," Trisha said after she shifted and dressed. "She's my responsibility."

"Not anymore, but I appreciate it," Roman said.

"I'll douse the fire," Leander said.

CHAPTER TWELVE

They shipped Jason off to Italy for two weeks to organize the Italian office. Kevin was in the Middle East with one of Sherm's teams, and Ari didn't even want to know what he was doing. She figured it was best to stay out of that part of the security division.

Trisha Anderson reported that Lisa Hamilton had returned to her car, shifted, dressed, and drove away. They all sighed in relief.

Gage, Roman, and Ari spent a leisurely week at the house in the woods. Ari let her liger loose in the forest. Roman showed her the boundaries of their property. The original two thousand acres and the newly purchased acreage where the community came together and constructed a dozen cabins were on the other side of the private road.

Ari's animal was so large, and the forest was so dense, she didn't have room to run at top speed. Roman ran by her side, and sometimes Gage's eagle rode on her back. Her magnificent white coat with the black stripes was striking, and Roman's cat rubbed against her often.

The panther detected a deer—a true animal, not a shifter, and he taught Ari how to hunt. Her liger instincts hadn't kicked in, so he schooled her in being wild. He wanted her to fend for herself, to be self-sufficient so she would not be at the mercy of an unknown situation.

They ate their fill. Gage's eagle joined in, but stayed out of their way. They returned to the house, but lounged on the back patio. Ari licked Roman from head to tail. She tried licking Gage's eagle, but he was having none of that.

Gage shifted. "I'm going to shower. Interested?" Ari's liger stood. She blinked. *I can't shift!*

Roman shifted. "What do you mean? It should come naturally to you."

I'm thinking of my human form, but I can't shift!

"Stay calm," Gage said. "Walk around for a minute. Rest your mind."

The liger strode around the lawn. She stopped occasionally, trying to shift with no luck. She roared with anger.

"You're not helping matters," Roman said. He shifted back to his panther and nudged her.

Her temper was at its peak. She snarled at him, her huge teeth gleaming as her face contorted in a deadly threat.

"Ari!" Gage yelled. "Get your act together. Don't you even think about hurting Roman's panther! It's not his fault you can't shift, so don't take it out on him."

The liger looked contrite. She shook herself, then lay down on the grass. Roman licked her face.

Try, Ari.

I'm trying. I'm sorry I got mad, but I don't know what to do.

"I'm going to get dressed and call Atsa," Gage said. "He may be able to talk you through this."

He slipped into the house, quickly clothed himself and

grabbed his cellphone. He returned outside while the phone was ringing on the other end in speaker mode.

"Hey, Atsa," Gage said. "We've got a little emergency and hope you can lend some advice."

"You need to move closer," Atsa joked. "What's the problem?"

"Ari can't shift back. She's in her liger form and can't seem to shift," Gage said.

"That happens sometimes, but it's not permanent," Atsa said. "Ari, clear your mind. Shut down your mind talk as best you can. Try to get quiet."

Roman shifted. He kneeled behind her back and ran his hands over her pelt. "Just relax." He massaged her shoulders.

She yawned.

Roman stumbled forward when Ari suddenly shifted to her human form.

"She did it," Gage said. "Thanks so much, Atsa!"

"Ari, for the first year, don't shift when you're alone. You have to get used to your animal, and remember, you're massive. It's not like the guys can load you in the back seat of the SUV and bring you back home," Atsa said.

"I was so scared, Atsa!" Ari said. Her lips quivered. "Do others experience this?"

"Yes, it's a common occurrence, so don't think it's just your newness."

"Thanks so much, man," Gage said. "We'll talk later."

"Let's go take that shower," Roman said.

The three of them went into the house as twilight approached.

THEY ARRIVED BACK IN THE CITY AND SETTLED INTO THE penthouse. After a home-cooked meal of lasagna, salad, and crusty bread, they lounged in the living room with glasses of wine.

"I don't think I want to shift again," Ari said.

Roman and Gage stared at her as if she were daft.

"Oh, come on, Ari," Gage said.

"We haven't talked about this. You need to understand that if you suppress your animal and don't let it out enough, you'll discover an internal war between the two of you," Roman said. "I'm telling you this from firsthand experience."

"What are you talking about?" Ari asked.

"This was before Gage and I found each other. I was building my company and working ridiculous hours," Roman said. "I neglected myself and my panther. Had a handful of women I was juggling, drinking a lot, not getting enough sleep —I was a mess."

"Sounds like a bachelor's existence," Ari said.

"Yeah, well, when you have an animal inside clawing to get out, it can take over at the worst possible time. I had a young lady over that my cat didn't like at all. In the middle of the night, I shifted and could not shift back. I ended up sneaking into the bathroom and staying there for hours, pleading with my cat to just let me shift. I promised to go to the house in the woods and let him free for the entire week."

"Oh my God! I don't know what I'd do!" Ari said in a panic.

"You will respect your liger. You will let her have some free time and she'll work with you," Roman said.

"So, what happened?" Gage asked.

"I could finally shift back. I packed up that woman and sent her on her way. That was a wakeup call," Roman said.

Roman, Ari, and Gage sat in the conference center having an online meeting with Jason, Donatello, and Marco.

"Well, look at you two," Gage said. "No brown robes!"

Donatello wore a charcoal gray suit, a bold red, black, and gray striped tie, and a crisp white shirt. Cufflinks were visible at the cuffs that extended just below the suit jacket sleeves.

"We found two monasteries that needed them," he said.

Marco was dressed less formally in a white button-down shirt and black slacks. "Two of our brothers won't give them up."

"You both look nice," Ari said. "You realize that a suit and tie are not required, right?"

"I enjoy dressing for my role," Donatello said. "I doubt if I'll ever wear brown again. The old king forced us to wear those robes for centuries! In the early years, we could wear nothing remotely like traditional clothing under the robes. At least that changed in the twentieth century."

"Imagine living in this drafty place with only a robe for cover," Marco said. "We were fortunate he allowed us to wear socks."

Roman stared at the two Italian shifters. "Why didn't you revolt? There's enough of you—seems like you could have gotten out from under that oppression long ago."

Donatello shook his head. "Mostly, it was a peasant complex. We were so browbeaten, no one could organize an uprising. It will take our people a long time to understand that they can make their own decisions. Even to understand the chain of command. There was only one way, and that was Giuseppe's way."

"So where are you with transitioning everything to electronic files?" Ari asked.

"There's a lot of progress. Before we get into that, there's now a HR department that will oversee everyone on this side of the world," Jason said. "Sandy and I are divvying up the benefits. She's handling all the insurance contracts, which will include veterinary care, in addition to traditional health benefits."

Roman and Gage exchanged a look. That was a line they hadn't wanted anyone else in the company to cross. Even though Sandy had been with the company for years, the only employees aware of shifters were Sherm, Lonnie, and Bruce's team. And Mr. Tran.

"Sandy knows about our animals?" Gage kept his agitation in check, but Jason heard the hard edge of Gage's question loud and clear.

"Look, I know you trust Sandy. What you don't realize is that to make this work, there is a great need for veterinary services and the insurance to cover it. Those needs have to go above and beyond dog and cat pet care," Jason said. "Don't worry. She understands what's at stake. Sherm helped by explaining a few things."

"Jason, never make a decision like that again without talking to us first," Roman said.

Ari placed a hand on Gage's and Roman's arms. "What's done is done. We can set up protocols later. Let's move on."

Jason let out a breath of relief. "I think Marco is in love with Excel."

"My abacus now sits on a shelf collecting dust. Jason taught me how to set up spreadsheets. I'm studying YouTube videos to learn different ways to format cells. I love my laptop!" Marco grinned as if Santa turned his coal to diamonds. "We've decided to only take the current year and enter those into the various spreadsheets. There are too many ledgers, and it would take too long."

"Have you hired staff? There're payables and receivables, not to mention taxes and the various laws and rules across borders," Gage said.

They talked for another hour, then concluded their business.

"Let's get lunch," Roman said.

"Upstairs, or do you want to go out?" Ari asked.

"Let's go to that Indian food buffet," Gage suggested.

They piled out of the room and headed to the garage. Roman and Gage flipped a coin to see who would drive.

"You two and your games!" Ari grabbed their coin and climbed into the driver's seat. She stuck out her tongue as she started the BMW.

"We've been bested—I know when to quit," Roman said.

Gage grumbled from the back seat. "Stop dilly-dallying. I'm starving."

Ari backed out of the parking space and eyed Gage in the rear-view mirror. "You're always starving. I swear, sometimes I wonder if you have worms. I should be a lot hungrier than either of you. Look at the size of my animal."

Ari maneuvered out of the parking garage and eased into traffic. She drove around the block and two streets over, pulled into the parking lot of the Brasserie restaurant. They piled out and headed for the door. Tantalizing aromas wafted out when Gage opened the door.

One of the staff rushed over and greeted them. "Would you like a menu, or are you going to try the buffet?"

A man in a suit approached them. He nudged the other guy out of the way.

"Hello Mr. Davenport. Ms. Davis. Mr. Stryker. Come right this way. I have a table in your favorite area."

"Thanks, my mouth is watering!" Roman said.

The man escorted them to a table, and he pulled out a chair

for Ari. He snapped his fingers at two of his staff, and within moments a fresh basket of naan bread and glasses of iced tea were on the table.

Ari led the way to the buffet line. She grabbed a plate and skipped the salad offerings. She piled chicken tikka masala on her plate along with basmati rice, saag paneer, one tiny piece of lamb vindaloo, yellow daal and tandoori chicken.

She grabbed the last piece of salmon and headed back to their table.

Roman and Gage plowed through everything with two plates each.

They settled at their table with their linen napkins across their laps and dug into the food.

"I can't believe you only took one piece of lamb vindaloo," Gage teased.

"It's too spicy," Ari said.

A man stopped at their table. "Hello, Ms. Davis."

All three looked up into the smiling face of Detective Valk.

Roman grabbed his napkin and stood. He shook the detective's hand.

"How are you, Detective Valk?"

"Doing fine," he said.

Gage stood. "Join us?"

Valk looked across the room to his small table then back to their table for four. "Sure. Thanks."

Roman got the attention of a server and made sure they didn't hold Valk's table.

"How are things at the jail?" Ari asked.

Gage tapped her foot under the table.

Why are you asking that?

The rats, remember?

"Any more problems with those rats?" Roman asked.

Detective Valk draped his napkin across his lap. "Man, we

had every known agency crawling through the jail, along with exterminators. It was a nightmare." He looked across the table to Ari. "I'm happy to see you fully recovered, Ms. Davis."

"Ari, please. It was rough going at first, but I made it. Were all those other women identified?"

The detective shook his head. "All but one of the older skeletons. What a nightmare. It was tragic contacting all those families."

"What are they going to do about that unidentified woman?" Gage asked.

"They sent the skeleton to the FBI lab," Valk said.

They ate in silence for a few minutes.

"I realize you don't have to worry, being in the penthouse and all, but when you go to your house, be on the lookout for a bear. We've had complaints about this bear around town. I don't understand how a bear can wander around downtown in the middle of the night, getting into dumpsters and just disappear," Valk said.

Roman, Gage, and Ari controlled their faces. Gage coughed into his napkin, then stood. "Excuse me for a minute."

He left the restaurant and pulled his phone out of his pocket far away from the front door and foot traffic. He scrolled through his contact list and connected to Bradley Parsons. "Brad, this is Gage. Is one of your bears in trouble?" He listened for a minute, then explained the situation. "Find out what's going on and get back with me."

He entered the restaurant and joined the others at the table. "Sorry, I had to get one of my allergy pills."

Ari raised her eyebrows.

Brad Parsons will find out what's going on with his bears.

Roman nodded discretely.

"So, how's things going with Panther Industries?" Valk asked.

"We opened an office in Italy," Ari said.

"Business must be good," Valk said.

They finished their meal, and the detective rushed off as his phone pinged with multiple messages.

Gage's phone rang. "It's Brad... What'd you find out?" He stared at Roman with wide eyes. "Okay. Keep everyone calm. Let me get with Sherm and see what he can do. I'll get back with you."

Roman stood. "Let's go."

They piled into the car and Ari drove them back to the building. They went to Sherm's office.

They caught him with a napkin tucked into his shirt while twirling spaghetti on his fork. "Hey, what's up?"

"Slight problem. A bear by the name of Greg McMahonas got picked up by animal control. Brad Parsons said that evidently he's been off his medication for depression, and he's been wandering through dumpsters downtown," Gage explained.

"Where are they holding him?" Sherm asked.

"Some place called Claws' N' Paws in the Poconos. It's a wild animal park," Gage said.

"That's a good two hours away. I'll find out if they have cameras. God, I hope he doesn't shift!"

They all looked nervous. Roman pulled out his phone. "Brad, have you been able to communicate with this guy? Does he realize he can't shift? We aren't sure if they have cameras all over the place. Let me know."

"This could be a disaster," Roman said.

"I wish Kevin were here. He's a whiz with camera systems," Sherm said.

Ari raised an eyebrow. "Really?"

Sherm coughed into his napkin. "He has many new skills, Ari. Let's leave it at that, shall we?" He clacked on the keyboard. He picked up his phone and made a call. "Dyson, listen, man. I need you to work with Travis and determine whether there're cameras at this place in the Poconos called..." he looked at Gage.

"Claws N Paws," Gage said. He pulled up the information he had saved on his cellphone and showed the screen to Sherm.

"Claws N Paws," Sherm told Dyson. "Search specifically where they keep bears, and any pathway leading up to that, including parking. I need the best intel you can provide."

Sherm listened to Dyson. "No. Someone's bear got picked up by accident. It's tame. They want him back without a lot of fuss from multiple authorities that would entail fines and confiscation."

The call ended. "The lies I have to tell just to get through the day."

"You know damn good and well you'd die of boredom at any other job," Roman said.

Sherm smirked. "Yeah. The only way I'd leave this job is retirement, or in a box. I'm sort of hoping for retirement with benefits."

Roman's phone dinged a message from someone he didn't recognize. He looked at the message. "This is from a shifter in Montana. They spotted Lisa Hamilton. He sent this picture."

He opened the picture showing Lisa with a scarf covering her head and draped over her forehead to hide the T brand.

"Tell him to spread the word. They need to keep an eye on her," Gage said.

"After her punishment, do you really think she'll cause more trouble?" Ari asked.

"There's no telling," Sherm said. "Some people don't like justice. She could go rogue."

"Rogue? What do you mean?" Ari asked.

"She could find other shifters that aren't in an organization

—people who don't want to conform to any rules or regulations
—outcasts, so to speak," Roman said. "Atsa mentioned rogues at
one time."

"It's a good thing you chipped her, Sherm," Gage said.
"Yeah, looks like a project for Travis. He can set up tracking
and keep us informed where she is at all times," Sherm said.

Sherm's phone rang. "What do you have, Dyson?" He
listened for a minute. "Okay, that sounds doable. I'll get back
with you."

He faced Roman, Gage and Ari. "The bear quarters are on
the Northeast side of the facility. Dyson looked at the place
from the satellite and said there's security, but he can override it
and block all cameras on that side. They have two guys who
walk the place during the night. They take forty-five minutes to
an hour and a half to get to the bear quarters."

Roman and Gage nodded as they thought through what
Sherm said.

"Take two shifters with you on this run, Sherm. When do
you want to send a team? I'll see who Brad can rustle up."

"I'd say the team should leave here at ten tonight. They'll
get there after midnight. Travis or Dyson can track the ground
people and let us know the timing while they block all the
cameras and security on the Northeast."

Gage pulled up Bradley Parsons' contact info on his phone
and made the call. "Brad, we've got a plan. We want to have
two shifters go with the team. Can you have two people downstairs at ten tonight?" He nodded to Sherm. "Okay. We'll be
waiting for you."

"Never a dull moment." Sherm smiled like a schoolboy as
he twirled another forkful of spaghetti and slurped it into his
mouth.

Big Bear Muchisky and one other bear shifter arrived at the building at nine-fifty. The guard looked over the giant man and called Sherm's cell.

"Sherm, someone by the name of Big Bear Muchisky is here to see you."

The door to the garage opened and Sherm entered, phone in hand. He and the bears shook hands. "Let's get going." Big Bear Muchisky held up a bag. "Clothes."

"Good idea. Hadn't thought of that," Sherm said.

They all walked to the garage and met two from Bruce's team.

"Everyone ready?" Sherm asked. "Let's roll."

They piled into the big SUV that held eight comfortably. Two hours later, they wove through the area and came to the place where Travis determined it would be safe to park.

Sherm texted Travis. He shut down the security cameras. The guards were due to walk the bear enclosure within the next ten minutes. Sherm opened the rear of the SUV and pulled out his night-vision gear. He handed goggles to Bruce's people, then offered the gear to the bears.

Big Bear Muchisky pointed to his eyes, then to Sherm's goggles.

Sherm got it. The bear's vision was just as good as the technology. He pulled out his cell phone and opened his EarthNow app. After a few moments, he zoomed down and watched the progression of the guards. They walked from facility to facility, checking secured doors and the well-being of the animals. They approached the bear facility, made their checks, and continued on. When they were far enough away, Sherm motioned for the group to go. It amazed him how quiet the big men were. Bears weren't known to be quiet on their feet.

They approached the bear facility. Sherm pointed to Big Bear Muchisky and motioned for him to mind-call Greg

McMahonas. Muchisky nodded. After a moment, Big Bear Muchisky gave Sherm a thumbs up.

One of Bruce's team picked the lock and got the door open. They entered the facility with Muchisky in the lead. He waved them on, following silent instructions from the locked-up shifter. He stopped in front of a locked door and pointed. They saw the bear on the other side of the door, eyes wide, pleading.

Bruce's guy picked the lock, and the bear rushed out. He locked the door behind him. The bear shifted. He opened his mouth to say something, but Sherm clamped his hand over the shifter's mouth and shook his head.

Muchisky handed the clothes to Greg, and he dressed. Big Bear shoved the empty bag inside his shirt.

One of the team wiped down the door lock and handle to obscure any fingerprints, then the group backtracked out of the building, locking it and repeating the wipe-down. They jogged back to the vehicle. Sherm had one of the team members drive while he manned his phone.

Once they were on the road, the talking started.

"You ever pull that shit again and you'll stay a bear that wears one of those clown hats for the rest of your life," Big Bear Muchisky growled.

"I'm not sure what happened," Greg said.

"Get your ass in to see Dr. Tanner," Big Bear Muchisky said.

For the next thirty minutes the ride was quiet.

Sherm coordinated with Travis to reset all the cameras and security systems.

CHAPTER THIRTEEN

THE NEXT MORNING AFTER BREAKFAST, GAGE, ROMAN AND Ari sat watching the news. Police, animal control and the Claws N Paws people were scouring the area looking for the missing bear. It was a mystery how the bear escaped with everything locked up. A newscaster joked that there must have been a magical *poof,* and the bear was gone.

"There you go, *poof* sums it up," Roman said.

Gage lounged in a corner of the sofa with Ari's head on his shoulder. Roman's head was on her shoulder, his arm draped across her waist.

Roman scooted down and breathed hot air onto Ari's mound. Since his abduction and slow recovery, he had not initiated sex, so Ari was surprised, if not delighted, in his display of desire.

Gage clicked the TV off and turned slightly. He grasped Ari and pulled her body slightly so her head rested on the sofa arm. His lips claimed hers while Roman slid her leggings and panties down her legs. He tossed them over his shoulder, and they landed on the coffee table. He pulled off his T-shirt and settled his face between her legs, licking her slit then latching his mouth to her clit.

Ari moaned through Gage's kiss. One of his hands caressed her breasts and pinched her nipples. She grabbed Roman's hair. She arched her hips, not wanting to break the contact with his mouth on her hot sex.

Roman slid his hands under her butt and held her in place while he sucked and licked her engorged nub. He slipped a finger into her slick core. She broke lip contact with Gage when she flung her head back and scooted an inch or two.

"Bed!" Gage said.

Roman was on his feet within a split second and grabbed Ari up in his arms. He and Gage walked fast to Roman's bedroom, and he crawled onto the bed with Ari. Gage stripped his clothes off and climbed onto the bed. His lips latched onto one of Ari's nipples while Roman shed his jeans and boxers.

Ari ran her fingers through Gage's sandy blond hair as she moaned his name.

Roman settled between Ari's legs and continued his assault on her nether regions. Two fingers slipped into her dripping wet core. His tongue circled her most sensitive spot, alternating with his lips slightly tugging at her clit. She writhed between the men, her back arching. She screamed out an orgasm.

"Move," Roman growled to Gage.

Gage was shocked when Roman growled.

Roman positioned himself, ready to enter Ari as his partner pulled away from her nipples. Roman lunged into her—a total surprise to Ari and Gage because he was typically the gentler lover of the two men. His mouth captured hers, his tongue twining with hers. He kissed down her jaw and neck and made love like a man starved. Roman thrust hard, then fast, changing his pace, but not his thrusts.

Ari sank her heels into his butt. She muttered his name over and over while her hands roamed his back and arms.

Roman changed positions, getting on his knees and pulling her legs over his shoulders. He plunged into her again.

Gage watched, fascinated with his partner's change of love-making style. The abduction and near-death experience had changed something in Roman. He seemed almost desperate.

Roman continued his thrusts for several more minutes, then arched into his orgasm, letting loose a loud roar.

Ari's eyes startled open as she watched Roman's face. An almost tortured expression crossed his face.

He collapsed on top of her, breathing heavy. He kissed her gently, eyes closed, then extricated himself from her and left the bed and the room.

Gage and Ari watched his back as he left, then their eyes met in silent question. Neither was interested in making love now.

"What just happened?" Ari whispered.

"I'm not sure. Are you okay?" Gage said. He got up, pulled on his jeans, and left the room.

"Yeah. He didn't hurt me." Ari grabbed her robe and followed.

Roman was spread out on the sofa, naked, an arm covering his eyes.

Gage sat on the coffee table in front of Roman, and Ari sat beside him.

"Roman?" Gage asked.

"Leave me alone," Roman said.

"No!" Gage said, not quite a shout.

Roman sprang to a sitting position and let his panther show. He released a warning growl, his face twisted into a snarl. His claws came forward.

"Roman!" Ari yelped. "What's wrong? Talk to us!"

He sprang off the sofa and hurried to his bedroom, dressed and headed to the elevator.

Gage and Ari stood in the living room in a deafening silence. Gage rushed animal-fast and blocked Roman's escape.

"What the fuck is wrong with you?" Gage bellowed.

Roman grabbed Gage and tried to thrust him aside. Ari watched, a panic across her face as the two men hammered on each other. Furniture shattered, artwork fell to the floor.

"Roman! What are you doing? Gage! Stop it!" she screamed. Suddenly, her robe shredded as she shifted, and her liger roared. She lunged at the two men and swiped a paw that knocked them both on the head and caused them to fall to the floor.

Ari positioned herself in front of the elevator, making it clear that no one was leaving the apartment. She roared again, her teeth bared at her lovers.

Roman panted on the floor. Gage untangled himself from his partner, his chest heaving.

Roman looked warily at Gage, then his eyes swung to Ari's liger. "I'm sorry. I honestly don't know what came over me."

Ari's cat hissed. She didn't believe him.

The elevator dinged, and the doors opened. Sherm, focused on his phone, plowed into Ari's cat.

"What the fuck?" He walked around Ari's cat and stood taking in the event he missed. He looked at the two men on the floor, bruising already starting to show on their faces, and broken furniture and shards of glass across the floor.

"What the fuck's going on? What happened? You were fighting?" Sherm's words ended in a higher, tighter pitch than he ever used.

"Just a misunderstanding," Roman said.

"Like hell," Gage yelled to his partner. He was furious. "That was not you in our bed. What the fuck, Roman?"

Sherm held up a hand. "I don't want to hear anything about what goes on in your bedroom!"

"Nothing unusual goes on, Sherm. We're not into bondage or S&M," Gage said. "Something happened, but Ari and I don't know what's going on and Roman won't talk."

Sherm focused on Roman. "Is it possible you're having a PTSD episode?"

Ari's liger walked out of the room. She shifted and dressed quickly, then joined the men in the living room.

Roman sat on the sofa with his head in his hands.

Gage swept broken glass from a destroyed framed picture into a dustpan and dumped it in the trash receptacle.

"I think you need to talk to Lorraine," Ari suggested. Roman shook his head. "Won't do any good. Can't discuss shifter..."

"Check the list. There's got to be a professional in the community. If not, get with Dr. Tanner," Gage said. "Something's bottled up inside, Roman. This can't happen again. I can't have Ari at risk."

Roman lifted his head and choked out a laugh. "How could Ari be at risk? She could take either, or both of us out in a split second."

"You know what I mean," Gage said. His anger simmered.

"Go to the gym and work off some of your aggression," Ari commanded. It was not a suggestion.

Roman stared at her for a long moment. He nodded, went to his room, changed and went downstairs.

Ari plunked into a chair at the kitchen table, lost in thought.

Gage kneeled before her. "You okay?"

"Yes, but I'm really worried about him. I'm not even sure what happened," she said.

Sherm joined them. "What exactly happened?"

"Roman is typically a gentle lover with Ari. I'm more aggressive," Gage said. "But today, it was like he was—not brutal, but overly aggressive for him, almost desperate. I don't know what the fuck happened."

"He refused to talk about it," Ari said. "That's when the fight started. They've never even been mad at each other for as long as we've been together. My head's spinning. I don't know what happened."

"Can Mr. Tran help?" Sherm asked.

Gage shook his head. "I don't think so. He doesn't have the experience within our shifter world. Maybe Dr. Tanner can help, or recommend someone."

PEOPLE IN THE GYM KEPT THEIR DISTANCE FROM ROMAN. His posture and expression warned them off. He set up his weights to bench press, placed his towel on the bench and laid on his back.

A bulky guy strolled over. "Hey, man, want me to spot for you?"

"No thanks," Roman barked out.

"You sure? You've got three hundred pounds there," the guy said.

"I'm good, thanks," Roman said. "Leave me alone."

"What an ass," the guy said as he walked away.

Roman roared out an ARRRRRHHHH, set the bar and weights on the rack and jumped off the bench just as Gage entered the gym.

Gage made a mad dash to get between Roman and the guy. The guy spun and turned as Roman's fingers gripped his shirt.

"What the fuck do you think you're doing?" Gage

bellowed. They struggled for a moment, then Roman seemed to come around. "Go home, right now." He turned to the guy. "Sorry. He's having a PTSD flashback."

"Fuck that," the guy said and stormed off.

Gage turned and caught up with Roman. "Come on, we're going to Dr. Tanner's."

Ari, get Dr. Tanner on the horn. I'm driving Roman over there right now.

I'll get the car, Ari sent.

Roman pulled away from him.

"Don't make me call in the bears, Roman. Come peacefully, or come knocked out, your choice, but this shit has to stop."

Gage pushed the elevator button. The bell dinged, and the doors opened. Ari stood there, her face a mask of worry. Ari handed Roman a T-shirt and jeans. They rode the elevator down to the parking garage in silence as Roman tore off his gym clothes and dressed. Ari grabbed the tank and shorts he had discarded on the floor. She was seething.

Ari pressed the remote for the BMW and slid into the driver's seat.

"Get in!" she roared.

Roman got into the passenger side and Gage slid into the back seat.

The BMW screeched out of the parking space, through the garage and pulled out into traffic.

"Take it easy," Roman said.

Ari quickly glanced at him. "Don't tell me to take it easy, buster! You sit there and shut the hell up."

She drove several blocks, took a right, and zigged and zagged through different streets. Ari pulled up in front of a house converted into a doctor's office. She pulled the BMW into the long driveway to the rear, where there was a small parking lot. Only one other vehicle was present. They all piled out and approached the door with a sign that said Enter Here.

An old-fashioned bell rang as the door opened. They stepped into a hallway with an arrow that pointed toward the front of the house and entered a small reception waiting room.

An attractive woman sat at the desk. She looked up, spotted Ari, and said, "You must be Ari. I'm Vanessa, Dr. Tanner's wife." Vanessa stood and came around the desk, and shook hands.

"Why don't you all come with me?" She led the way through a door to Dr. Tanner's office.

The doctor stood and shook their hands. "What's going on?" He looked from Roman to Gage, assessing their facial bruising.

Ari and Gage dove right in. Dr. Tanner listened and nodded. "Okay, why don't you two go back up front while I spend some time with Roman?"

Ari and Gage left the doctor's office and returned to the front.

"There's an ice-cream shop right up the street," Vanessa suggested.

"That sounds like a good idea," Gage said.

Vanessa pointed to the front door. "Turn to your right and it's half a block down on this side of the street."

Gage and Ari stepped outside.

Roman was tense. He bent over and placed his arms along his legs.

"So, what's going on?" Dr. Tanner asked. "Tell me what's going through your head, no matter how frivolous you think it is. Something is triggering these outbursts. It's not uncommon for someone to experience PTSD after such a harrowing experience."

Roman sat up. "I'm not sure. It's been weeks. I don't know where all this shit came from. I've never been aggressive to Ari or Gage. Never!"

"I'm wondering if the drug is still messing with you," Dr. Tanner said.

"Mr. Tran, our historian and translator, is an expert herbalist. He gave me this tea to drink to help my body expel the drug and get my energy levels back up, and to help gain my weight back. You can call him and see what he has to say," Roman said.

"What's his number?" Dr. Tanner wrote it down and placed the call. They talked for several minutes, and Mr. Tran discussed the properties of the herbs and the effects they would have. "Hold on a minute, Mr. Tran."

"Roman, do you want me to tell Mr. Tran what you're experiencing and see what he has to say? There may be a correlation between the drug, your body, the herbs—beyond what I have experience with."

"Sure, Mr. Tran might be able to help. We can even go see him if you'd like to meet him. He has an apartment in our building," Roman said.

Dr. Tanner clicked the hold button and got Mr. Tran back. They talked for several more minutes, and Mr. Tran invited them over.

Dr. Tanner and I are heading over to see Mr. Tran.

Want us to meet you there, or leave you alone? Gage sent.

Meet us there.

Dr. Tanner escorted Roman back to the front. Vanessa was the only one there. "We're going over to the Panther building. Do I have any appointments this afternoon?"

Vanessa looked at the calendar. "Nope, you're all clear."

Dr. Tanner led Roman down the long hallway to the rear of the building.

Gage and Ari met with Roman and Dr. Tanner as they stopped by Mr. Tran's office. Roman introduced Dr. Tanner, and they all headed to the elevator. Dr. Tanner's eyes bulged when he saw Mr. Tran's home business.

"I have quite a few online orders," Mr. Tran explained.

"This will be fantastic for the shifter community," Dr. Tanner said. "Many times, the prescriptions I have to write aren't the best choices for my patients."

"I would be happy to help the community. If I get too busy with my herbal business, I'll hire someone to help," Mr. Tran said. He shifted his gaze to Roman and Gage, studying their bruises. "Would you bring in more chairs from the dining area?"

Roman and Gage brought three chairs from the next room. They all sat.

"When did you first experience this aggression?" Mr. Tran asked.

Roman thought about it. "This morning."

"Have you had night sweats?" Mr. Tran asked.

"Not that I'm aware of." He turned to his partners. "Have you noticed anything?"

Ari shook her head.

"I don't think so," Gage said.

Mr. Tran focused on Ari. "Has he hurt or frightened you?"

"Only this morning. He didn't hurt me, but his lovemaking differed completely from what I've experienced all these years." Ari was thoughtful. "The fight with Gage was brutal. I had to shift to get them to stop."

Mr. Tran focused back on Roman. "Do you dream? Tell me if you've had dreams of what you experienced in Italy."

Roman moved around in his chair. It was obvious that

something bothered him. He glanced at Ari, then at Gage. "I've had nightmares." He rubbed his eyes with one hand. "Everything's all fuzzy because of the drugs. I keep seeing these brown robes and sandals, the stone floor and walls, the bars on the cell. These two monks brought in straw to build me a bed so I could get off the cold floor, but I couldn't move—this part is real. I couldn't even crawl to the straw. I could barely understand what they were saying."

He stopped talking and looked at the floor. "I was so hungry and thirsty. So dizzy. Could barely lift my head off the floor. Pissed and shit all over myself."

Dr. Tanner, Ari, and Gage didn't make a sound. They now understood what Roman experienced and knew it was healthier to let Mr. Tran lead him. Ari had tears in her eyes. She kept her emotions under control, so she didn't distract Roman.

"Does it bother you to talk about this?" Mr. Tran asked.

Roman blinked as he looked at the man. "I don't like talking about it. Makes me feel weak, exposed."

"Do you feel guilty?" Mr. Tran asked.

Roman thought about that. "No... Sometimes... I'm not sure."

"You need not carry guilt. You were the victim, Roman. The guilt is on your abductor," Mr. Tran said. "Do you practice yoga or meditation?"

"No."

"I would like you to join me every morning so I can teach you how to meditate," Mr. Tran said. "Once you get the hang of it, you can meditate at your own place, or in the park—wherever you're comfortable."

"Okay. What time should I come down?" Roman asked.

"How about seven o'clock in the morning?" Mr. Tran asked.

Roman glanced at Ari. She nodded encouragement.

"Wear sweatpants and a T-shirt," Mr. Tran said. "Now, let me mix up two potions for you."

Mr. Tran perused his cabinets and shelves and pulled out six jars of herbs. He lined them up on the table, then opened a cabinet and pulled out his mortar and pestle.

He went to another cabinet and pulled out eight dark amber bottles that contained liquids, along with a small, empty dark amber bottle, and set them on the table.

Dr. Tanner joined him at the table and looked over the jars and bottles. He recognized none of the herbs, and the labels were in Chinese. "What are these, Mr. Tran?"

Mr. Tran recited, tapping each jar. "Chamomile, lemon balm, valerian, skullcap, hops, and passionflower. All excellent for a calming tea."

"What about these Bach Flower Remedies," Dr. Tanner read off the bottles.

"Holly for anger; cherry plum for fear of losing control; rock rose for terror and panic attacks; willow for feeling like a victim and resentment; mimulus for fears that can be named; aspen for anxiety and fears without a specific cause; star of Bethlehem for shock, sorrow and grief; and walnut to help him adjust to changes and to fulfill his ambitions free from the influence of others."

"One of my patient's needs help," Dr. Tanner said. He turned to Roman, Gage, and Ari. "Greg McMahonas might benefit from Mr. Tran's formulas."

.   They told Mr. Tran about the bear shifter's exploits. "I will mix something up for him," Mr. Tran said.

When Mr. Tran finished, he presented Roman with the dark amber bottle and a package of tea. "Do you still have the tea bag?"

"Yes, and the spare," Roman said.

Mr. Tran pointed to the label on the bottle of liquid. "Tap the bottom of the bottle five to ten times. Take four drops four times a day. Stand in front of a mirror and use the dropper. Count four drops under your tongue. When you run out, we will meet and you can tell me how you're feeling. I may have to adjust the formula, or if you determine you are more settled and calmer, you can continue with the original remedy."

"How long will I have to take the drops?" Roman asked.

"Three weeks," Mr. Tran said. "After that, you will stop for one week, and we'll all get together and assess your progress."

He led Roman to the sink and a mirror. "Take four drops right now."

Roman tapped the bottle, unscrewed the dropper cap and counted four drops under his tongue.

"That wasn't too bad, was it?" Mr. Tran asked.

"No, there's hardly any taste," Roman said.

"You have my phone number in your cell?" Mr. Tran asked.

Roman pulled out his phone and checked it. "No, I don't."

Mr. Tran rattled off his phone number, and Roman created a contact form. The herbalist returned to the table and handed the other bottle to Dr. Tanner. "This is for your bear shifter. Have him monitored to make sure he takes this formula. Four drops before breakfast, lunch, dinner, and at bedtime. He is not to take this with food. He should take the drops, then wait fifteen minutes before his meals."

"Thanks, Mr. Tran. I hope we can get him under control. We can't have a bear walking around getting into trouble. I was worried he would shift at the wrong time with witnesses around," Dr. Tanner said.

Mr. Tran returned his supplies to their cabinets. "Now, let's all get back to work! I have books to translate!"

"You should take the rest of the day off, Mr. Tran," Gage said.

"Ah, I would if it wasn't for such interesting and exciting work," Mr. Tran said with a huge smile.

They all piled into two different elevators, Dr. Tanner and Mr. Tran going down while Roman, Gage and Ari rode up to the penthouse.

CHAPTER FOURTEEN

THEY STEPPED OFF THE ELEVATOR, AND ARI LET A SOB escape. She ran down the hall to her bedroom. The door slammed shut behind her. Roman and Gage stood stock-still in the foyer, then glanced at each other before taking off at a run down the hall.

Roman was through the door with Gage on his heels. Ari was head into the pillow, sobbing.

"Ari! What's wrong?" Roman's voice escalated in fear. "Honey, talk to us," Gage begged.

They climbed onto her bed, one on each side of her in their typical bedtime positions.

Roman pried her face out of the pillow. "Don't suffocate yourself. Come on. Calm down and talk to us."

Gage reached into her nightstand drawer and pulled tissues out of a box. He folded her hand over them. "Dry your eyes and blow your nose."

Ari continued to cry, her chest heaving with angst. Once she gained control, she pulled her pillow against the headboard.

"What's going on?" Gage asked.

Ari crossed her legs and sat. She looked at Roman. "Why didn't you talk to us? Tell us about your nightmares, what you were feeling?" Tears started up again.

Roman looked crestfallen, his face filled with guilt. "I thought I was long past all that while I recuperated. Until today, I did not understand I harbored such anger about my abduction. No clue until Mr. Tran questioned me."

Ari sniffled. "But you never would even talk about anything. It was as if it hadn't happened. You nearly died, Roman. We nearly lost you."

Roman stared at the bedspread. "Honestly, there's not a whole hell of a lot to talk about. I was so drugged I wasn't able to call out to either of you. I had no muscle weight. Couldn't crawl to the water or the straw. Couldn't lift my head to see anything other than the hem of brown robes and sandals."

Gage was quietly thoughtful. "Maybe the online meeting with the Italians triggered your aggression."

"I don't know, but that makes sense," Roman said.

"Is there a chance you recognized either Donatello's or Marco's voices?" Ari asked. "Maybe that's what did it."

"I don't feel mad, or like anything's bottled up inside," Roman said. "And to be honest, I'm not sure I was mad when we fought. It seems surreal now."

"Let's hold off going to Italy until we know you don't have any issues with them," Gage said. "There's no hurry. Jason is more than capable of getting them completely situated."

Roman yawned. He slid down on the bed and grabbed one of Ari's pillows. "I really need a nap."

The next several days were smooth sailing. Roman met with Mr. Tran each morning until he got the hang of meditation and could continue on his own. He drank the tea and took the drops. He engaged with the Italians during online meetings with no disruptions, and even enjoyed getting to know Donatello and Marco.

They all met with Mr. Tran at the end of the week, except for Dr. Tanner, who was tied up with patients.

"There have been no incidents?" Mr. Tran asked. He glanced from Ari to Roman and Gage.

"No problems," Roman said.

"Nightmares?" Mr. Tran asked.

Roman shook his head.

"We're considering a trip to Italy to our offices," Gage said.

Mr. Tran shook his head emphatically. "Too soon. Please wait until the end of the three weeks. If anything crops up, I expect it will be within the next two weeks. The potions help to resolve issues. Sometimes issues you aren't aware of consciously."

"Okay, we'll continue on this course for the next two weeks then," Ari said. "There's no sense in pushing the envelope."

"Exactly," Mr. Tran agreed.

After the session was over, Ari, Roman, and Gage went to Pomodoro's for dinner. They ate their dinner amid comfortable conversations.

"Seems strange without the boys here," Gage said.

"I'm glad they like their jobs," Ari said. "They floundered for so long before you two hired them."

"They just needed to be grounded to something that resonated with them," Roman said. "It isn't fun working a job without the joy of personal accomplishments."

"Ari, I was a mess until I hit fifty," Gage said. "After Roman and I met up and merged our businesses, things came together. I grew up. There's no other way to say it. So, theoretically, Jason and Kevin may have a way to go yet."

"They *came out* rather late for our kind," Roman said. "I'm wondering how that will affect them—if it even has any bearings on anything."

Ari scrutinized the men. "What exactly does Kevin do now?"

Gage stared at her. "He no longer installs cable TV."

"We should leave it at that, Ari," Roman said. His lips lifted in a little smirk.

She sighed in exasperation but knew when to quit.

THEY MADE LOVE LIKE THEY USED TO BEFORE THE abduction. A long session with the three of them entwined together in erotic ecstasy. Satisfied with each other. Falling into a languid sleep afterwards.

Toward three in the morning, Roman woke up shouting a roar. Gage and Ari were immediately alert. Roman shifted to his panther, bedclothes flying. His panther clawed out of the sheets and leaped off the bed.

"Roman? What happened?" Gage asked, fully awake.

"Roman, settle down. Shift back so we can talk about what caused you to shift," Ari said. She was kneeling on the bed, Gage beside her.

The panther walked in a circle, growling, then jumped on the bed, snarling ferociously as he closed the distance between them.

Gage shoved Ari behind him as Roman sprang. He threw his arms around Roman's chest, missing the brunt of his claws and teeth.

Ari shifted. The bed frame collapsed under her enormous animal weight. Gage and the panther tumbled together and bashed into the collapsed headboard as Ari's liger stepped off the bed. She turned around and snatched Roman up by his scruff and hauled him off the bed. She growled and shook him.

Gage scooted off on the other side of the bed, keeping his distance from the cats. There wasn't much he could do as a shifter; his eagle was big, but defenseless against the two predators.

Roman's paws fought the air, claws extended. He growled in rage.

Ari shook him by the scruff again until he calmed. When it appeared he submitted to her, she settled him on the floor. He shifted, but stayed on his back, his belly exposed to her as he stared up at her somewhat dazed.

She hissed, showing her teeth. There was no mistaking that she was all business. After several long moments staring Roman down, she shifted. Her chest heaved with anger, then she settled into worry about what just happened.

"What woke you?" Ari didn't take her eyes off Roman.

Gage finally came around the bed and reached a hand down to his partner. He pulled Roman to his feet. He grabbed their robes off the hooks on the door, tossed Roman his, and handed Ari her robe. They went to the living room and sat separately, facing each other.

"I don't understand why I shifted, unless my dream—nightmare, triggered it," Roman said. He rubbed his face with his hands. "I remember getting shot with the dart. Those men grabbing me and hauling me through the forest."

Roman sucked in a ragged breath.

"We have the fingerprint from the dart. Some guy named Salvatore (Sal) De Luca," Gage said. "I don't know whether he's from Italy or lives here in the States. I'll check with Sherm."

"There's no information about this Sal character?" Roman

thought about it. "We need to pay him a visit. Make sure he knows his boss is dead."

"Was that all?" Ari studied Roman. "Can you recall any other bits from the dream?"

Roman stared at Ari but looked through her, remembering. "I seem to recall waking up on a plane. I was sick to my stomach from whatever they drugged me with. They didn't offer me anything to drink or eat. Some guy shoved a needle in my back leg and I was out so fast."

Gage tried to control his fury, but it covered his face like makeup. "I'd like to kick Sal's ass. Come on, Roman. Let's go see Sherm."

"It's four in the morning. We need to get back to sleep," Ari said. "We'll have to find someone to repair the bed. I'm sorry, Roman. I didn't mean to destroy your bed frame."

They headed down the hall to Gage's room, where they rarely slept.

"If you feel a tendency to shift, Ari, please get off the bed first," Gage joked. "I'm really going to miss Roman's bed. We could stretch out unrestricted on that huge thing."

"I'll find a carpenter in the morning. Should be fixable," Roman said.

AFTER BREAKFAST, THEY HEADED DOWN TO THE SECURITY department. Ari went in search of Lonnie. She was helping catch someone who had stolen from a client. As a forensic accountant with the nickname "The Sifter," it was difficult to hide things from Ari.

Gage and Roman cornered Sherm about Sal. Sherm's fingers clacked on the keyboard.

"Okay, here's what we know about DeLuca. He's one of

the late Italian Tothar king's thugs. He has a rap sheet two miles long. Everything from breaking and entering to breaking legs. No murders, as far as I can tell. He's a Fiuggi citizen, so let's assume he lives there and not here," Sherm said.

Gage nodded. "I'll have Donatello get more information on him."

"We getting ready to go back to Italy?" Sherm asked. "We weren't there long enough to sample the food."

"Is that all you think of? We won't be going anywhere for at least two more weeks," Roman said. "Mr. Tran has me on two different potions and suggested I wait until I'm finished with them. Which reminds me, I have to look at our list and find a carpenter."

"What do you need a carpenter for?" Sherm quirked an eyebrow, wanting details.

"Ari shifted and broke the big bed," Gage said.

Sherm barked out a laugh. "You guys never have a dull moment."

"We think this stuff up so you won't get bored," Gage said. He fiddled with his phone and pulled up the world clock meeting planner. "It's after nine here, so it's a little after three in the afternoon there. Let me call Donatello."

Gage put the call through and switched to speaker. An Italian answered the phone.

"Buon pomeriggio, industrie della pantera. Come posso aiutarti?" (Good afternoon, Panther Industries. How may I help you?)

"Donatello, please," Gage said.

"Un momento per favore," (One moment, please.)

"Donatello parlando," Donatello said. (Donatello speaking.)

"Donatello, it's Gage Stryker," Gage said.

"Gage! How are you? What could I do for you today?" Donatello asked. You could hear the smile in his voice.

"We identified the man who tranquilized Roman on our property here in the States," Gage said. "Someone by the name of Sal De Luca. Is he there in Fiuggi?"

"Hold on, I'll find out," Donatello said. He yelled across the hall to another office. "Dov'è Sal DeLuca?" (Where is Sal DeLuca?)

Gage listened to the yelling between offices. "Donatello, you should text instead of yelling. That's what makes cell phones so great."

"Oh, it's no problem. It will take us a while to get used to the technology. We're used to yelling all over the place for information," Donatello said. He laughed at their own lack of tech knowledge.

More yelling through the offices.

"Ah. Okay, Gage. Sal's here in Fiuggi. He doesn't stay at the palazzo—Panther Industries' new home. He has a house in town."

"Keep an eye on him. We can't be there for a couple of weeks, but we want to talk to him when we get there," Gage said. "See if someone will snap a picture of him and where he lives without him knowing."

"We can do that. How is Mr. Roman?" Donatello asked.

"I'm doing fine," Roman said.

"We love your boy, Jason," Donatello said. "We may not want to give him back."

"I would hate to lose him, even to another Panther location," Roman said. "He's a valuable asset."

"Donatello, even though he's a grown man, his mother might have something to say about that. She likes her boys close by," Gage said.

Donatello laughed. "Roman, are you sure you only want us to watch Sal? We could haul him into the cell for you."

Roman, Gage and Sherm shared a silent moment. "Jason may be impulsive if you had this thug locked up. I would not mention our interest in De Luca to him," Roman said. "I'm sure he'd contact his brother, and they'd take matters into their own hands."

"We want him alive to question him," Sherm said.

"Okay. I'll set up surveillance and will keep you informed of his actions," Donatello said.

"Make sure Jason uses the new Rosetta Stone language program so he gets proficient in Italian," Gage said. "All of you should take advantage of your benefits."

"We have a team from Apple teaching us how to use our devices. We're getting everyone through that program. What it boils down to is getting used to technology," Donatello said.

Sherm, Gage, and Roman heard something in the background.

"Hello everyone, Marco here." Marco was Donatello's second in command. "After decades of being restricted from all this modern communication equipment, we are now practically in technology overload. But we're getting used to cell phones and laptops. I think everyone is happy with the transition."

"That's good. Technology isn't going away," Gage said. "We need to get going. Thanks for taking care of that for us, Donatello," Roman said.

They ended the call.

"So, what are your plans for Sal?" Sherm asked. "The only redeeming quality I can gather is that he follows orders."

"We need to get a better idea of what he did for Giuseppe. I wonder if the journals have any information about Sal," Gage said.

"Did we give the most current journal to Mr. Tran?" Roman asked.

Gage shook his head. "I've been remiss. I'll bring it to him—I've tried to read it but my Italian is not quite up to par."

"That was the journal on his desk, so I'd think there would be something in it about Sal and his services," Sherm said.

"Okay, that's the first line of business. We'll ask Mr. Tran to translate this and look for anything related to Sal," Roman said.

ROMAN MET WITH DICKIE STONEBRIDGE, A SHIFTER carpenter who worked at Nana's Hovel, which was anything but. Rita Richards, the master carpenter, owned the beautiful place. They discovered the three beavers in the community, and Rita was the head of the group. Dickie built and repaired furniture.

Dickie, Roman, and Gage removed the custom mattress and stood it against the wall, followed by the box springs. The carpenter climbed among the slats and determined the damage to the large custom bed.

"No major damage," Dickie said. "The headboard is okay, but I should replace this brace along the back and these eight slats, along with the middle supports. Could have been worse."

Roman looked relieved. "I'm so happy it's repairable. This bed and the mattress and the box springs cost a small fortune. I waited over a year for delivery, thirty years ago."

"It's a beautiful bed. Looks hand-carved," Dickie said.

"It is. I found the furniture maker in Taiwan. He has exquisite designs, and while today they're mass produced, back then, he carved them himself. Took a while to get the custom mattress and box springs created here in the States," Roman said.

"I'll take measurements and go get what I need," Dickie said.

"Appreciate it," Roman said. He shook Dickie's hand.

CHAPTER FIFTEEN

Mr. Tran stepped out of the elevator into the penthouse apartment. Gage and Roman met him. They noticed the journal in his hands with several sticky flags attached to pages.

"Come in, Mr. Tran," Gage said. "Would you like something to drink?"

Mr. Tran shook his head. "No, thanks. I'm good. As you can see, I found several places where this Salvatore DeLuca is mentioned."

"Let's get Sherm up here," Gage said. He texted Sherm. A few minutes later, Sherm joined them.

They sat in the living room. Mr. Tran opened the journal to the first flagged location. "It appears if anyone was out of favor with this old Tothar king, he'd tell Sal to make them disappear." He read the first passage out loud.

I instructed Sal to extract information from Rosario Rossi, the Bank of Fiuggi employee assigned to the palazzo accounts, to determine where the missing money went.

Mr. Tran flipped pages to the next flag.

Rossi used the money to buy his mother new appliances. I've instructed Sal that Mr. Rossi should sign over his property to the palazzo for his embezzlement. Then Rossi will take a little trip and drown.

He flipped to the next flag.

My niece has informed me there is a Tothar king in America. As soon as she provides details of his activities, Sal will go pay our new king a visit and bring him back to the palazzo. There can only ever be one Tothar king, and no one will usurp me from my throne.

Lisa Hamilton's scheming came to light at the next flag.

Lisa called with details of the American king's schedule. Sal will go to this Reading, Pennsylvania and wait with his team for the Tothar to show up. Hopefully, by the end of the week, he will be in custody. Lisa fancies this Roman Davenport for herself, but she is too ignorant to understand the concept of <u>ONE</u> king, or she wrongly assumes I will hand him over to her.

Mr. Tran turned to the next flag.

I have incarcerated the panther in the cell. I will keep the panther drugged so he can't attempt to escape. I have yet to determine what to do with him, but perhaps starving him is a just end.

Finally, Mr. Tran opened the page of the last flag.

I plan for Sal to remind Donatello and Marco that they answer to me and no one else. I suspect they are too soft and will help the panther.

The room was quiet as the last entry sunk in.

"He was going to kill Donatello and Marco?" Gage thundered, his anger erupting.

"At the very least that sounds like they would have an accident—perhaps break an arm or leg. It's a good thing he had not moved forward with that plan," Roman said. "You must have shown up by that time, because there are no more entries."

"The rest of the journal is just as bad. This man evidently thought he could do as he pleased, outside of the law," Mr. Tran said. "When I translate the entire journal, I will keep the English version with the original Italian."

"So, Sal was the go-to guy for all the dirty work. Giuseppe must have had the authorities on his payroll for them not to investigate people disappearing," Gage said.

Roman stared at the journal. "Change of plan. Sherm, get Tony on the phone. Tell his team to apprehend this guy and dump him into that cell. We don't really know whether Giuseppe mentioned anything to Sal about Donatello and Marco. I'd rather not take any chances. I'll call Donatello and warn him."

"Mr. Tran, where are we with your friend, the other translator?" Roman asked.

"Abbot Benston," Mr. Tran said. "And, no, he isn't a priest. He told me they picked on him as a kid. When I met him, most of the people in our professional society assumed he was a priest, and he never corrected them. I believe he has an interview."

Mr. Tran stood. "I will provide you with the English translation before your trip."

"Thanks, Mr. Tran," Gage said. "I can't tell you how much we value your service."

Mr. Tran nodded, pleased. Then he entered the elevator. Sherm contacted Tony about the situation with Sal.

Roman walked into the kitchen to call Donatello, then changed his mind. He called Jason instead.

"Jase, a little problem cropped up," Roman explained, referring to the journal entries. "Sherm is on the phone with Tony. I want you to tell Donatello and Marco to cancel their plan to have Sal monitored. We don't want anyone bumping into the wrong person."

"I'll make sure they recall anyone they sent to take pictures and watch the guy," Jason said. "What a sick fuck this Tothar bastard was. If he weren't dead, I'd kill him all over again."

"Jason, one day you may rule. Make sure you are a just and kind ruler, but not a pushover," Roman said.

"What this guy did was uncalled for on so many levels. The more I'm around the people here at the palazzo and the town, the more I realize what a celebration it is that Giuseppe is dead," Jason said.

"We'll see you in a couple of weeks," Roman said. He ended the call and walked back to the living room to find out how Sherm made out with Tony.

Sherm ended his call and faced Roman. "Tony and his team are going to surveil the house for forty-eight hours. Once they determine the schedule Sal and anyone else who lives there keeps, they'll gather forces and take Sal into custody. The first order of business is to determine who lives in the house, who visits, and their activities."

Four days passed with no word from Tony. Roman and Gage expressed their concerns with Sherm.

"Look, Tony will stay silent until he has everything he needs. If we don't hear from him by the end of the week, I'll contact him. There may be more to this Sal guy than we are aware of," Sherm said.

"You don't believe there's a chance they caught Tony?" Gage asked.

"His team would have been in contact immediately," Sherm said. "Did you talk to Jason or anyone at the palazzo today?"

"No," Roman said. "Let me call Jason so we can get a feel for the atmosphere there. He's transparent, so I wouldn't worry if he says everything is okay."

Roman pulled up Jason's phone number and placed the call. "Hey, Jase. How are things going?"

He felt the smile in Jason's voice while he reported on all the progress he had made at the palazzo. Roman gave the thumbs up to Gage and Sherm.

"We're waiting on a few things to sync before we fly over there. Make sure you tell us if you need us to bring something," Roman said. He ended the call.

"Okay, so everything's under control there. We'll wait for Tony to report in. Evidently, there's something going on and he's monitoring it," Sherm said.

ROMAN AND GAGE RETURNED TO THE PENTHOUSE. ARI was making sandwiches.

"Hungry?" she asked. "Always!" Gage said.

"You finished working with Lonnie?" Roman asked.

"Uh huh. As the song suggests, *Another One Bites The Dust*," Ari said. "People don't realize just how stupid they are when it comes to embezzlement."

"Especially when a terrier is nipping at their heels," Gage said. He smooched her on the lips.

"So, what did I miss?" Ari asked.

They sat at the table, and the guys brought her up to date while they noshed on sandwiches, pickles, and iced tea.

"I can't imagine that bastard would hurt his two most valuable people. Who did he think could step into their positions?" Ari ranted furiously. "God! I hope we hear from Tony soon. What will we do with this Sal?"

"I'm not sure." Gage raised his eyebrows at Roman.

"I want to take him out back and shoot him between the eyes, but I'm not sure. It depends on what intel Tony delivers and what he can extract from this guy." Roman silently ate while thinking things over.

"We should take Mr. Tran with us. He could meet Donatello and Marco and explore the library," Ari said.

"We don't really know what those journals contain. Could be our history, or maybe that sick fuck's notes on who he had killed or maimed," Gage said. "Either way, we need to protect that library."

All their phones dinged an incoming message from Sandy.

Attached are six resumes for translators. I have Mr. Tran's friend scheduled for an interview on Tuesday. Let me know whether you want to interview these other people.

"Want me to print these resumes?" Gage asked.

"Yes. I need to hold a piece of paper instead of reading off a tiny screen," Roman said.

They heard Gage's printer kick in. He got up and went down the hall to retrieve them. He returned with six resumes and three pens. They sat and read through the pages.

"This woman looks good on paper," Roman said. "I'm not sure this man has enough language background to be a good translator. Mr. Tran needs to look these over."

"Good idea. Now that he's seen two of these journals, and he knows the content of the big books, he might have a better idea of who he needs for help," Ari said. "I'll forward the resumes to him."

Ari worked on her phone and sent Mr. Tran the resumes.

"This Arthur Doyle has a good background," Gage said. "He speaks Italian, Latin, Mandarin, Portuguese, Spanish and French."

Roman stuck his hand out and Gage handed him the resume.

"Anyone from the shifter community?" Ari asked.

"Doesn't look like it," Gage said.

"I don't understand how there could be no one in our community that has the background we need for these positions," Ari said.

"Why don't we schedule a world-wide meeting," Roman said. "There has to be people... shifters who qualify for these jobs."

Gage and Ari nodded.

"Let me work on setting this up," Ari said. "We should do this before we leave for Italy."

"Good idea. What it boils down to, is job security for several people," Gage said.

"How does tomorrow before lunch sound? It will be eight in the morning in California and a decent time overseas," Ari said.

Gage and Roman nodded. "Perfect," Gage said.

"I'll send out an email alert," Ari said. "Gage, send out a text message to the world group leads. Roman, blast out the message."

They all got busy on their messaging.

THE MEETING ROOM DOWNSTAIRS FILLED WITH PEOPLE from the shifter community. Ari had three of their favorite restaurants cater finger foods. At eleven on the dot, the shifter world came online and little windows opened on the big screens showing each area.

Ari, Gage and Roman sat on chairs on the stage, each with a mic clipped to their clothing.

"Greetings," Roman said. "I'm sorry for the short notice, but we wanted to reach out to the community—worldwide.

Several weeks ago, we sent out a blast explaining we needed translators. We haven't received any resumes from anyone in the community, only humans."

"We have several dozen journals from the late Tothar king, Giuseppe Genovesi, who was an ancient Tothar. There is history that needs to be translated for our people. We implore you... if there are any translators among you, please come forward. This would be full-time employment for several people," Gage said.

"We have a translator here in Reading who will head up the project. We need your help in finding people to come on board for this project," Ari said. "Anyone with Chinese, Latin, Italian, and other languages should apply. You would need written and verbal skills, and the ability to translate the journals and books into English."

A woman in Lithuania who looked to be in her early thirties raised her hand.

"Yes... Janina?" Gage said, reading her name off the screen.

Janina curtsied. She appeared nervous and embarrassed. "My kings and queen... I don't have a formal education, but I speak, read and write Latin, Italian and English."

"Education doesn't matter, Janina," Roman stated. "All that matters are your skills. Please send us your full name, your email address and phone number as soon as possible—along with a note of your skills."

Janina looked about to burst with happiness. "Yes, but of course I will. Right now!"

The world watched as Janina worked her cell phone. "Everyone out there with these skills, please contact us as soon as possible. Today, preferably," Ari said.

They finished up the online world meeting and the screens turned dark.

Roman talked to the room of local attendees. "People, don't

be shy. If you have these skills, step up and let us know. We find it hard to believe no one here in Reading qualifies for one of these spots. And you heard me tell Janina that education and background don't matter. Skills matter."

Gage noticed a teenage boy nudging a middle-aged man with a beard. They had a whispered argument. "You there. Do either of you have something to say about this, or are you goofing off?"

The man gave the teenager a scowl, then faced Gage, Roman and Ari. He bowed. "Your majesties. My son wanted me to tell you about his brother, but he is disabled."

"What is your name?" Ari asked.

"Henry Shilds," the man said.

"Henry, tell us about your other son. What are his skills?" Ari asked.

"Alan has an ability with languages. He reads and writes several languages, but he is speech-impaired. He speaks through a voice recognition system," Henry said.

"What's wrong with him?" Gage asked.

"It's a disease called spasmodic dysphonia. Typically, it's something that people thirty and older get, but Alan is only twenty-two. They diagnosed him when he was eighteen. We noticed something was wrong when he was sixteen, but we assumed it was a normal voice change process. But it kept getting worse, and we could barely understand anything he said."

"Why isn't he here at the meeting?" Roman asked.

"He doesn't like to be around a lot of people because he can't talk right," his brother said.

"Henry, would you bring Alan here today or tomorrow? I want him to meet with Mr. Tran, our translator," Gage said. "Is he currently working?"

Henry looked embarrassed. "No, he's never worked. He takes college classes online."

"Get him here. We want to meet him," Gage said. The meeting wound down and people left.

Gage popped a leftover tartlet in his mouth. "These are good!"

Ari looked at the one remaining bite on the plate. "That looks like pecan pie." She grabbed the last one and took a bite. "Ooh, this is good."

Roman grabbed a mini quiche and bit into it. "Man, this is good stuff. Next time we need to grab some when they're delivered."

They boxed up the meager leftovers and set them aside to take to the front desk. The door clicked, and the cleaning crew entered.

CHAPTER SIXTEEN

AT FOUR-TWENTY, THE FRONT DESK CONTACTED GAGE. "There's a Henry and Alan Shilds here to see you," security announced.

"Send them up," Gage said. He rounded up Roman and Ari from their rooms.

"Don't stand by the elevator. We don't want to look like the enforcers or something," Ari said. "Go sit on the sofa, and I'll greet them."

Gage and Roman moved into the living room and sat down.

"Call Mr. Tran, Gage," Ari said.

Gage called and explained the informal interview with the young man and his father.

The elevator dinged the arrival of the Shilds. The door opened, and Ari noticed a young man who looked scared out of his wits.

"Hi Alan. Hi Henry. We're so happy to meet with you. I'm Ari. Come in."

Ari led them into the living room. "This is Roman and Gage."

The men stood and shook hands.

Alan clutched his phone in a death grip; he was so nervous.

"Your father and brother mentioned your incredible language skills," Roman said. "I want to see you at all our meetings. Don't hide because you're disabled, Alan."

Alan typed on his phone. A mechanical voice spoke. "It's difficult for me to be around some people because I can't talk."

The elevator dinged and Mr. Tran appeared with books in hand. He carried one of the Chinese books and the Tothar journal.

"Come in, Mr. Tran!" Gage said. "I'm so glad you could make it."

He introduced Mr. Tran to Alan and Henry.

"What languages are you studying?" Mr. Tran asked.

Alan typed. "All the old languages: Tamil, Latin, Armenian, Korean, Hebrew, Aramaic, Chinese, Greek, Egyptian and Sanskrit."

"That's quite a load, isn't it?" Roman asked.

"Not for me," Alan's mechanical voice said. "I've already mastered Latin, Hebrew, Greek, Chinese and Armenian."

Mr. Tran handed the journal to Alan. "Ah! You're a polyglot or even a hyperpolyglot! Can you read this?"

Alan opened the journal to the first flag and read the Italian words flawlessly. In Italian, then in English through his voice app.

Gage, Roman, Ari, and Mr. Tran grinned in delight. Next, Mr. Tran handed Alan the big Chinese book.

Alan ran his hand over the cover. He typed. "Wow, this looks old!" He opened the cover and carefully turned the pages, his fingers following the lines of Chinese characters. He typed.

"My life's work has been the study of animals and their human counterparts. My colleagues discredit my work, but I

will persevere and protect my research. They will value it one day."

Mr. Tran's eyes glistened. He was so happy at the young man's ability to interpret the Chinese symbols.

"Alan, you have a gift! An exquisite gift!" Mr. Tran said. "You are much better and faster than me."

Alan looked stunned, as if he could not believe anyone thought he was useful for anything at all.

"How would you like a permanent, full-time job with benefits?" Roman asked. "You'll need a passport because there will be times when you may have to go to Italy, where this room full of journals lives."

Gage pulled up the photo on his phone. "What I'm going to show you is highly sensitive information. You can't tell anyone about this, do you understand?"

Alan and his father swallowed, then nodded. The royals were putting their trust in them with critical information.

Gage showed Alan and his father the picture of the library. "This is probably the only library in the world that contains our historical information. The old Tothar king was approximately twelve-thousand years old. Evidently, he wrote in a journal every day of his life from the time he learned how to communicate in writing."

"Holy smokes! How many books are there?" Alan typed.

"We're not sure. There are approximately eight or nine-hundred years-worth of journals. We don't know if they are all in Italian or older languages," Ari said.

Alan remained wide-eyed. His fingers flew over the keyboard. "This is an opportunity of a lifetime."

Mr. Tran smiled widely and nodded. "That's how I felt when they interviewed me." He tapped the Chinese book. "I had been waiting my entire career for a project like this. We would work together if you were to accept the position. One of my colleagues is being interviewed Tuesday, so until more come on board, it will be just the three of us."

"There's a woman from Lithuania that we met this morning in our community online meeting, Mr. Tran. We're most likely going to ask you to be in on the interview to assess her skills," Ari said.

Mr. Tran rubbed his hands together. "The team is coming together. This is wonderful!"

Gage's eyes zeroed in on Alan. "I'm going to give you a bit of advice. Stop stating that you can't talk. You can communicate with your phone app. That's your voice. Be proud and thankful you can use this app."

Alan nodded and typed. "Thanks. I rarely feel like socializing because people make fun of me."

"I want you to think about this. Do they make fun of you, or are they curious?" Ari tilted her head.

Their newest employee and his father left, catching a ride down the elevator with Mr. Tran.

"We need to strengthen our people," Roman said. He snuggled up to Ari on the sofa. "I need to take a nap."

Ari grabbed his hand and lugged him off the sofa. "Come on, let's lie down." She snagged Gage on the way down the hall to Roman's room.

"I'm so glad the bed's fixed," Gage said. "Your bed is the most comfortable of all of ours."

ROMAN EXTRICATED HIMSELF FROM THE TANGLED LIMBS on his bed as his phone dinged an incoming text. He grabbed his cell from the bedside table and looked at the screen.

"We need to get dressed. Sherm will be here in less than ten minutes," he said.

"What time is it?" Gage asked, followed by a yawn. "Seven. I'm starving. As soon as Sherm leaves, we need to go out to eat," Roman said.

Ari hopped off the bed and grabbed her clothes from the floor. "Where's my panties?"

Gage dropped to his hands and knees and looked under the bed. He snagged them by the footboard. "Here."

They all dressed and wandered into the living room and turned on the lights. Roman and Gage flopped down on the sofa.

Ari went to the kitchen. "Anyone want coffee?"

"Yeah, I could use a cup. Make it strong," Gage said.

The elevator dinged Sherm's arrival.

"Hey, Sherm, want coffee?" Ari asked.

"Yeah. I don't sleep anyway, so coffee is good."

"You should talk to Mr. Tran. He can concoct something to help you sleep," Roman said. "The man is a genius."

"What's the news?" Gage asked.

Ari brought a tray with coffee, sugar, and a pitcher of milk. They all indulged.

"Tony called. Sal's in custody at the palazzo in the cell in the tower, Roman. He has six other guys and one woman in custody down in what he described as the dungeons."

"Dungeons?" Ari shrank into the sofa as memories resurfaced. Her abductor didn't have a dungeon, but the building was a torture chamber with a basement full of dead women.

Roman pulled her to his side and kissed the top of her head.

"Yeah, he said it reminded him of Medieval times. There are cells down there, and that's where he stuck the others."

"Jesus. Who knows what went on down there over the centuries," Gage said.

"The reason it took so long to bring these people in is that Sal had extracurricular activities going on. We're not sure if

Giuseppe sanctioned or ordered these or if Sal was freelancing his own deals," Sherm said.

"What do you mean?" Roman asked.

"Tony said they caught Sal and his people holding this family hostage. There were also two of his guys going around collecting protection money. They used the woman in sex blackmail situations."

"What did Tony find out about the family?" Gage asked.

"Seems like the daughter refused to marry Sal's younger brother, one of his thugs," Sherm said. "He threatened to turn her into a prostitute unless she married this creep."

"Oh, no!" Ari said.

"Do we know whether Giuseppe collected protection money from the village businesses?" Roman asked.

"I'm not sure. Tony wants to shoot everyone up with truth serum, but wants to know if he should wait until we arrive," Sherm said.

Roman glanced at his partners. "Everything's pretty much under control here, right?"

"We need to let Mr. Tran know when we're going so he can make any arrangements with his herbal business, or his kids," Ari said. "You should also take some of his tea and drops with you. Roman, you don't know how you will react to seeing that cell."

Roman dipped his head. "I know. That has been on my mind, but the sooner I face it, the quicker I can put it behind me."

"Okay. Sherm, tell Tony to check with Donatello or Marco to find out whether they know about these activities," Gage said. "We should be able to leave the day after tomorrow."

"We should ask Sandy to contact Janina and arrange for

her to be there. Mr. Tran can interview her. Hopefully, there will be a place for her," Ari said.

The Panther Industries jet landed at the private airport outside of Rome. Roman, Gage, Ari, Mr. Tran, Sherm, and everyone else retrieved their passports to present to the customs agent who came aboard. After the agent processed them, everyone left the jet and climbed into the waiting van.

They arrived at the palazzo, and the front door opened, and Jason, Tony, Donatello, and Marco piled out of the building.

Roman stared at the palazzo. This was the first time seeing the outside of the building where he had been held captive. When he had arrived months ago, they drugged him, and he didn't wake up until he was in a cell. When the team rescued him, he was still out cold. Today, he was meeting everyone for the first time in his human form. Until now, he had only talked to them via online meetings and phone calls.

Donatello shook Roman's hand. "I'm honored to meet you." He shook his head, his face covered with angst from the memories of months ago, and the role he played in the panther's near death.

"Stop." Roman said. "You and Marco put your lives on the line to get help. It was a bad situation, but it could have ended a lot worse for you, as we recently discovered. We'll talk."

Donatello nodded—at a loss for words.

Ari stepped forward, her hand on Mr. Tran's arm. "Donatello, Marco, this is Mr. Tran, our translator and historian."

The men shook hands.

"We have a lovely luncheon ready," Marco said. He guided everyone inside.

Lunch was a long affair where business discussions rambled on. Roman had enough of the trivial side of the business. He was eager to get to the more pressing issues of Sal and his troupe of thugs.

Donatello and Marco led Roman, Gage, Ari and Sherm up the tower stairs to the cell at the top, followed by Tony.

A big, burly man sat on the pile of straw that Roman's panther never used. He got to his feet and approached the bars. He sneered at the people on the other side of the bars and spat words at Roman in Italian. "The king was a fool to let you live. If it were up to me, I would have killed you back in the States."

Donatello translated.

In a flash, Roman shifted into his panther and was a snarling, growling mess pressing against the bars.

Sal jeered at Roman.

The panther could not reach him.

"Roman! Shift back," Ari shouted. Roman turned on her and lashed out.

Gage jumped in front of her and shoved Roman's panther back.

Roman leapt on Gage and he fell down.

Everyone backed away, yelling for the fighting to stop.

"Roman!" Sherm yelled. "Keep your head about you, man!"

Ari shifted into her gigantic liger. She roared. People scattered.

"What the fuck is that?" Sal yelled.

Roman's panther snarled at Ari.

Ari's liger grabbed Roman's panther by the scruff of his neck and shook him.

What do you think you're doing? Ari sent.

Gage got to his feet. "Listen, Roman. You're having a reaction to your time spent in the cell. Put that aside."

Roman's panther hissed and growled and fought the air. Ari shook him again.

Calm the fuck down, right now, Ari sent.

"Ari, bring him to our room. Someone find Mr. Tran and tell him we need his help," Gage said.

Donatello waved Ari toward the stairs. "I'll show you to your room."

Ari's liger followed Donatello down the stairs. The rest of the team followed at a distance. This brought back memories of Ari carrying a drugged panther down these same stairs months ago.

Marco was on his cell calling a helper to have Mr. Tran stand by.

They arrived at the bottom of the tower stairs. Donatello held the door to the palazzo for the liger and her captive to enter the main room. The Italian shifters gawked at the huge liger.

Donatello scooted around Ari and led her up the main staircase to the third floor where he showed her their room.

Mr. Tran stood in the hall outside the bedroom with Jason. He took in the sight of the enormous cat and the frantic panther. He stepped forward.

"Roman, I'm going to touch you to bring you relief from what your flashback apparently caused."

Ari's liger shook Roman's panther to calm him.

Roman! Mr. Tran is trying to help you. Be still! She sent.

Roman seemed to snap out of his rage and stopped lashing out. His angry eyes settled on the Asian herbalist.

Gage, Sherm, and Tony watched as Mr. Tran ran his hand along the top of the panther's head. Then he used both hands and started at the sides of the cat's nose and rubbed his hands across the cheeks to the sides of the neck. He tapped twice at the top of the panther's head and at each temple.

The panther finally relaxed.

Mr. Tran reached around and opened the door to the suite. "He needs to rest. I will prepare a potion for when he wakes up."

"I want someone outside of this room to alert us when Roman wakes," Gage said.

"I'll get someone," Jason said. He worked his phone texting someone.

ARI, GAGE, JASON, SHERM, AND TONY SAT IN JASON'S office and prepared a list of questions for Sal and a similar list for his people.

"I don't want to proceed until Roman can join us," Gage said.

"But..." Tony said.

Gage shook his head. "I don't care if these assholes rot in their cells. Roman needs to be involved in the questioning. This is not open for debate."

"I agree," Sherm said. "I feel confident he will be okay after Mr. Tran doses him with his herbal stuff."

"Tony, I understand your desire to move forward, but Roman is the head of Panther Industries. He's the one who built this organization from the ground up. Then, when Gage came on board, they pooled their resources and merged their businesses. The organization jumped from a multimillion-dollar company to a multi-billion-dollar company," Ari said.

"This has been a rough past few months for everyone—especially Roman. His demons have been at war throughout this entire experience. You were here. He was clinging to life when we rescued him. If it takes a little longer, then we'll wait. That's all there is to it."

Tony shook his head, upset. "I understand all that. What I'm concerned about are people who may be in dire circumstances we don't know about. These dickwads may have other people stashed somewhere."

Gage blew out a breath. "Fuck. This situation just keeps on giving and doesn't quit."

"Gage, we need all the journals for this entire year translated to see what Giuseppe had cooked up," Ari said.

Sherm looked over to Tony. "Did your people search Sal's place thoroughly for any paperwork, lists, books—anything that would show orders from the king, or Sal's own side business?"

"Why don't you and I tackle that?" Tony said. "We've gone over it, but maybe not as thoroughly as we should have."

"Ari, let's go see Mr. Tran. We can also contact Janina and get her here to help," Gage said.

CHAPTER SEVENTEEN

Tony and Sherm determined it would be prudent to have at least one shifter along when they searched Sal's house. They chose an Italian bear named Franny, since bears have the best scenting abilities.

Franny made a perimeter walk around the house with one of Tony's team in case of a surprise. As soon as they deemed the outside was safe to approach, Sherm made everyone glove up so as not to leave fingerprints. Franny led Sherm, Tony and the rest of the team into the house.

The bear silently walked through the front door and stopped. He took a deep breath through his nose. He turned, finger to his lips, and pointed to the right. Tony and Sherm moved around the bear and silently approached a partly ajar door. They heard sounds from inside the room.

Sherm held up a hand and finger-counted down from three. Tony flung the door open, and he and Sherm burst into the room.

A young woman in her twenties screamed and shot her hands into the air.

"Who are you and what are you doing here?" Tony asked in Italian.

"Don't shoot!" she burst into tears. "My name is Maria. I'm searching for my father's deed."

Tony translated for Sherm. The conversation bounced back and forth as Tony presented the whole story. Sal had been extorting money from Maria's father. When he could no longer pay, he had to turn over the deed to his house and property to Sal.

"Tell her we have Sal in custody and if we find the deed we'll contact her, but she needs to leave," Sherm said.

Franny stepped up, put an arm around Maria's shoulders and explained the situation. He walked her to the door, and they left the house.

"Okay, here's how we'll tackle this," Sherm said. "Roll up any rugs. Look for any hidden places. Take pictures off the walls. I want every surface searched. Look in containers, the freezer, mattresses, cushions—tear the place apart. We need to find Sal's orders, or his private business that his boss knew nothing about."

Sherm started at Sal's desk. He dug through every nook and cranny, looking for false bottoms and hollow spaces. Since there weren't any cardboard file boxes, he removed the file drawer from the desk and decided he could use it for any paperwork they discovered.

He moved the two chairs in front of the desk, then rolled up the rug. There weren't any floorboards that sounded hollow when he knocked on them.

"Hey, someone come in here and help me move this desk," Sherm yelled out.

Franny came into the room and grabbed one end of the desk. He and Sherm moved it several feet away and checked the floor. One board was loose.

Sherm got on his hands and knees and pressed on one end of the board. He lifted it up and found a cubbyhole that contained a ledger and a thick handful of papers. Sherm grabbed the ledger and the paper and put them on the desk, then returned to the floor. He felt around but didn't find any other possible hidden places.

"He could have kept everything in this room," Sherm said.

Tony entered the room. "Find something?"

Sherm showed him the board under the desk. "I have a feeling there's more."

Sherm, Franny, and Tony set to work on the walls and the bookcase. There was a bunch of junk on shelves that Sherm thought must have belonged to Sal's mother.

"He probably inherited the house from his mother," Sherm said.

They found nothing else in the house. One of Tony's crew hollered from the basement. "There's a chest-type freezer down here, but it's locked."

"That's never a good sign," Sherm said. "Come on. Let's find out who's in the freezer."

They traipsed down the stairs. The cellar was a catch-all for old broken furniture, canning jars with unrecognizable contents, boxes of old clothes and shoes—a lot of women's things.

Tony knelt in front of the freezer and dug a small black pouch out of his pocket. He worked on the lock and unlocked it. He stood and lifted the lid. An elderly woman, wire-rimmed glasses cockeyed on her frozen face, and strangulation marks on her neck, wasn't alone. There was someone beneath her.

"Sal's mother? Or his grandmother?" Sherm asked. He took a picture with his cell phone. "Let's carefully lift her and see who's down there."

A woman in her forties, neck at an unnatural angle, broken, rested on frozen packages of meat.

"You can see the family resemblance," Tony said. "Probably Sal's sister," Sherm said. "What a sick fuck."

He took a picture of the younger woman and sent both to Gage. "Have you searched all this stuff?" He pointed to all the boxes and castoffs.

"I just got down here," Tony's guy said.

"Let's get this over with." Sherm headed to a wall of jars on wooden shelves.

Sherm, carrying the file drawer, and Tony searched for Gage and Ari back at the palazzo. They found them, along with Roman, sipping hot tea in a meeting room on the ground floor. Sherm set the file drawer on the table.

Sherm walked up to Roman and placed a hand on his shoulder. "You doing okay?"

"Yeah. I wish I could turn this shit off. How the hell am I going to go through life not knowing when something will set me off?" Roman said.

"Got the pictures," Gage said. "You wiped the place down?"

"We went in gloved," Tony said.

"What'd you find?" Roman asked. He nodded at the file drawer.

"We searched through everything, and this is all I could find. The loose pages and that ledger were under the floorboards beneath the desk," Sherm said.

"Are we keeping this or looking at it and returning it?" Gage asked.

Everyone looked at each other.

"We don't want to leave fingerprints on the paper, so we should glove up," Gage said. He texted Jason. A few minutes later, Jason came in with a box of non-latex gloves from the library.

"Any luck?" Jason asked.

"We'll know soon," Gage said. He grabbed a pair of gloves, pulled them on and passed the box.

"Let me start with the ledger and those pages," Ari said. "Marco can help translate." She reached into the drawer and pulled out the loose pages and the ledger. If it involved numbers, she was the expert.

"We need to return that file drawer and call in the police," Tony said.

"Okay, let's go through the file drawer and see if there's anything we can use," Gage said. He reached in and grabbed the first couple of hanging folders and handed them to Donatello.

"What an ass," Donatello said. "He made notes of phone calls and printed emails. If the king weren't dead, he'd be swinging by his neck once the police got a hold of these files."

"Yeah, but Sal would have been swinging right beside him because he's the one who carried out all of these *chores*," Sherm said.

Marco was quiet as his eyes slowly scanned down the pages of the ledger. He glanced through each page until the end of the postings. Then he picked up the loose papers and studied them.

"Sal wasn't brilliant, that's for sure," Marco said. "Typically, crooks keep these two documents separated, so no one has all the information, which makes it more difficult for the authorities to connect the dots and place blame. The ledger shows lists of properties and other physical things in one section, and in another section the people extorted or elimi-

nated. There are initials beside each entry: GG or SDL. Easy
to guess who those two are."

Ari looked over Marco's shoulder as he continued to thumb
through the loose pages. "As far as I can tell by the dates on
these papers, they hadn't made it into the ledger yet."

"That makes sense," Sherm said. "They were sitting on top
of the ledger."

"Can we place the crimes on Sal, or is there backup to show
Giuseppe ordered Sal to do these things?" Roman asked.

"These files show the king ordered Sal to do specific things,
but it looks as if Sal started his own enterprise," Donatello said.

"Should we copy all of this and return it?" Ari asked. "I
wonder what the authorities will do with this? Can we trust
them to do the right thing, or are they all on the take?"

Roman pondered the situation as he sipped his now luke-
warm tea. "Make copies of everything and return the originals.
Then we should interview our guests. Once we have what we
need from them, we alert the authorities through a mysterious
phone call. Travis will route it thirty-six ways to nowhere so
they can't trace it. They'll find the bodies in the freezer and will
start a search for our guests. We'll lead them to the hidden
space under the desk."

"Okay," Gage said. "Jason, find someone who can make
copies. Have them wear the gloves. We need to sure that every
single scrap of paper is copied and legible."

"Sure thing," Jason said. He left the room and returned in a
few minutes with a librarian who took the box and left.

"Shall we?" Sherm asked.

They all left the room and walked over to the door to the
tower stairs.

SAL STOOD BACK FROM THE BARS WHEN THE GROUP gathered outside his cell. He stared at Ari. "What the fuck are you?"

"I'm the one who can snap you in half without effort," Ari said. "All you have to do is give me a reason and I'll send you to Hell."

Sherm unlocked the cell. He and Tony grabbed Sal and dragged him several yards down the hall to an old interrogation room. Rusted manacles and chains adorned the walls.

Ari stood out of the way while the four men fought Sal into the restraints.

"You fucking piece of shit. There's no point in fighting. You're going to answer questions," Gage snarled.

"You ain't gettin' nothing from me." Sal blustered as he yanked his arms against the fetters and chains.

"Don't worry, Sal, those old rusted chains and cuffs will not pull away from the wall," Sherm said.

"We found your mother and sister," Roman said. "Once we're done with you, we'll notify the authorities about your little family quarrel and everything you've been doing for the past twenty years. If you survive what we dish out, you can rest in the comfort of your local prison."

"I got nothin' to say to you." Sal looked smug in his restraints.

"We figured as much." Roman pulled a hypodermic needle out of his pocket, uncapped it, walked over to Sal and tapped the plunger. A tiny burst of liquid squirted out.

"Sing, little canary, sing." Roman jammed the needle into Sal's neck and pushed the plunger.

Sal screamed. Then he went quiet and his chin crashed to his chest. After several minutes, Roman prodded him.

"Hey, you awake?" Roman asked.

Sal lifted his head. His eyes couldn't focus as he tried to zero in on the voice. "Huuuuhhhh?"

"State your full name," Roman asked.

Sherm set a chair down in front of Sal with a recording device on it.

"Saalllvaaatorrrreee Duuuhhhh Luuucccaaaa." He laughed like a hyena.

"I think we gave him too much truth serum," Gage said. "We need him to answer questions coherently."

"It's okay, it'll level out—watch and see. We'll get what we need," Sherm said. "Sal! Hey, Sal... Stay with us."

Sal looked up with a goofy smile on his face. "Are you an only child?" Sherm asked.

"Naahh, I got a sissstteeerrr and twoooo brothhheerrss."

"You the oldest?" Sherm asked.

"Yeaaahhh."

"Who did you kill first, your mother or your sister?"

"Maarrtinaaa."

"Why did you kill Martina?"

"She was going to tell the police about me." Sal growled out the words.

"Why did you kill your mother?"

"I broke Martina's neck. My mother wouldn't stop screaming. She screamed and screamed—"

"Why did you kidnap the panther shifter?"

"Giuseppe wanted to teach him a lesson or something."

"Did Giuseppe have you collect protection money from people and businesses in Fiuggi?" Sherm asked. "Nah, Giuseppe didn't do that."

"So, you started a home-based business. Did your boss know you had this business on the side?" Sherm asked.

"Nah. He stayed out of my business."

The questioning continued for two hours. Sherm, Roman,

Gage and Tony mixed up the questions between Sal's business and Giuseppe's. They discovered there was one more member of Sal's gang who had a family under his thumb. Tony and his team immediately left and apprehended the guy and freed the family. They reunited the last scumbag with his friends down in the palazzo's cellar.

Through all the interrogations, they discovered the thugs had persuaded the mayor and police chief to turn a blind eye to the old king's business dealings. Giuseppe wined and dined both, and if someone disappeared, no one outside the palazzo noticed.

CHAPTER EIGHTEEN

"Open a new ream of paper," Sherm said. "Wear gloves so you don't leave fingerprints on the paper."

Ari edited the document on the screen one more time.

Salvatore DeLuca ~~has~~ *murdered his mother and sister. You will find* ~~them~~ *their bodies in the chest freezer in the basement. You will also find a ledger and papers under the floorboards beneath Sal's desk that outlines his criminal activities, along with that of the late Giuseppe Genovesi*

"I made two minor changes. It's ready to go," Ari said.

Donatello stuffed his hands into gloves, filled the printer paper tray, and shut the drawer. "All set."

Ari clicked the print icon, and the paper dropped into the print tray.

Donatello picked up the sheet of paper and looked it over. "Looks good." He held it as several pairs of eyes looked it over, then he folded it.

A young man stood in the room with Ari, Roman, Gage, Sherm, Tony, Donatello and Marco.

Jason entered the room with a clasp envelope. "I don't think we'll need that," Gage said.

"Claudio, do you have any questions?" Sherm asked.

Claudio shook his head. "No. I'll give the letter to the first cop I see."

"Whatever you do, don't let them get you inside the building," Roman said. "They'll keep you there. As soon as you hand off the letter, run as fast as you can—away from the palazzo."

"Leave through the kitchen door and go through the woods, then come around to the front of the police station," Tony said. "Stay in the shadows in the woods so no one will notice you. Your appearance has to be undetectable so you won't give away the direction you came from."

Claudio nodded. "I get it. I can do this."

"Okay," Roman said.

Claudio shifted into his border collie. He stood waiting.

Donatello held out the folded letter, and Claudio snapped it up in his mouth.

Tail wagging, Claudio and the procession of people walked through the palazzo to the kitchen. Donatello opened the kitchen door, and Claudio raced out, across the lawn, and disappeared into the woods.

"Now to wait and see if this plan works," Gage said. They all returned to the room to wait for Claudio to return.

The dog ran through the woods. He pulled up fast and listened. Children were playing up ahead. He made a large detour around the kids and continued on his assignment. The town square was up ahead. Claudio stopped at the edge of the trees and spied upon the local scenery.

He spotted a police car approaching the square and the police station. He clamped down on the paper in his mouth and shot out of the trees, running through the street to the sidewalk in front of the police station.

Two policemen got out of their cruiser.

Claudio sat and made eye contact with the cops. He went into a begging pose.

"What's that you've got there, boy?" an officer asked. He pinched the paper and gently tugged it until the dog opened its mouth.

Claudio took off running down the street through the town and disappeared.

"Huh," the cop grunted.

"Open it. Someone's probably pulling a prank," the second cop stated.

The policeman unfolded the sheet of paper and read the note. His eyes opened wide. "Find that dog!"

The second cop took off running but stopped and returned to his partner. "That dog is long gone." He snatched the paper out of the other cops' hands and read it.

The cops rushed inside.

Claudio returned to the palazzo kitchen door and shifted. Someone had folded his clothes and left them on the doorstep. He quickly dressed and returned to the room where the royals and his bosses were.

"Claudio! Any problems?" Gage asked.

"Nope, everything went as planned. I had to sit and beg so they would take the paper, but they finally did," Claudio said.

"Good job," Donatello said. "Now we wait," Roman said.

"No, now we call out to Raffaella, a tortoiseshell cat shifter who spends a lot of time between the mayor's office and the police station. They love her," Donatello said.

Raffaella?

Oh, Donatello! There's a lot of excitement here. I'm going into the big room to find out what's going on.

"She says there's something going on," Donatello said.

RAFFAELLA JUMPED ON ONE OF HER FAVORITE LAPS. THE policeman scratched her head as she settled in his lap.

The big screen on the wall showed a piece of paper with dog bites through the middle.

Donatello, they're looking at the piece of paper. The forensic woman said there're no fingerprints or identifying marks on the paper. Now the two cops who took the paper from the dog are explaining what happened, and that the dog took off. They want to put out a bulletin for the dog.

Oh, never mind. The chief said that's ridiculous—the dog can't answer questions. They're sending a team over to Sal's house. The meeting is breaking up.

DONATELLO REPORTED WHAT THE CAT TOLD HIM.

"Can you have her stay with the chief for a while? I'm wondering if he will contact the mayor and discuss their little problem of what might be in that ledger pertaining to them," Sherm said.

Donatello conveyed Sherm's suggestion. "She says the mayor's there. She's going to follow them into the chief's office."

RAFFAELLA BARELY SQUEEZED THROUGH THE DOOR WHEN the chief slammed it shut. She jumped up on his desk and groomed herself. The chief and the mayor faced each other in the middle of the room.

"Now, what are we going to do?" the mayor hissed.

"Whatever paperwork they find will go into evidence. The

only thing we can do is to be contrite—apologize for being under that bastard's thumb."

The chief walked around his desk and sank into his chair. He picked up the cat and settled her in his lap, and patted her.

"Just what we need, four months before the election," the mayor said. "I never should have listened to you."

"I don't recall you objecting to the money you received each month," the chief snarled. "Everyone hated Giuseppe. They saw how badly he treated his people at the palazzo. Every business in town that dealt with him feared doing something wrong to rile him. Hopefully, these new people—the Americans—will be easier to get along with."

"We knew it would end eventually," the mayor said. "I guess it's for the best—letting go of the guilt." He headed for the door. "Keep me informed about what your people find."

The chief grunted confirmation, and the mayor left.

DONATELLO TOLD THEM WHAT RAFFAELLA OVERHEARD.

"Maybe they aren't as rotten as we originally thought," Ari said.

"Anyone who had to deal with the late king really was shoved against a wall," Marco said. "He was cruel to everyone. Crushed as many people as he could who stood against something he believed in or wanted."

Roman glanced from Gage to Ari to Sherm. "Perhaps a little déjà vu is in order. Why don't we walk to the police station or the mayor's office and introduce ourselves? That should send a shiver up their spines."

Donatello led the group out of the palazzo, and they walked down the street to the mayor's office.

A woman in a navy pantsuit greeted them as they entered the office. "Buon pomeriggio!" (Good afternoon.)

Donatello introduced the Americans and asked if the mayor was in.

The woman picked up the phone and buzzed the mayor. "Mr. Mayor, the new owners of the palazzo are here to meet you." She listened a moment, then hung up.

An inner door opened, and the mayor greeted the group. "I hope you are settling into the palazzo with relative ease."

Introductions were made. The mayor's eyes made a tiny flinch when Sherm was introduced as the head of security for Panther Industries. Sherm made a mental note.

"My cousin was the type who over-documented everything six different ways," Roman said. "I've recently gleaned some very disturbing insights."

The mayor kept a straight face. "Oh? I hope nothing that can't be overcome. If I can help, please let me know."

"We're still going through all the paperwork and getting the palazzo up to modern standards with technology and equipment," Gage said. "Roman's cousin liked to do things the old-fashioned way."

Roman made eye contact with the mayor. "Did you and my cousin ever do business together?"

The mayor quickly shook his head in denial. "No, no. We never had any business ventures. I'm not even sure if the man ever voted in elections. He kept to himself pretty much."

Roman stuck his hand out. "It was nice to meet you. We'll be on our way now. I'd like to go meet the police chief."

They shook hands, and the group exited the building and crossed the street. A uniformed officer ushered them into the chief's office, where the cat was still curled up on the desk. He told Donatello that the chief would be in promptly.

Roman picked up the beautiful cat and stroked it.

Ari grabbed the cat and tossed it back on the desk. "What do you think you're doing?"

"What—?" Roman stared at her as if she'd lost her mind.

"That's a woman you're stroking," Gage said.

"Oh! Sorry!" Roman turned to the cat. "I apologize, Rafaella."

The cat hissed, jumped to the floor, tail high in the air, and strutted to the door. Sherm opened the door, and the cat left, indignant.

Moments later, the police chief entered, and introductions were made. The chief's eyes jumped all over the place.

Sherm was sure the chief had talked to the mayor.

As they chatted, an officer burst into the chief's office. Upon seeing the visitors, the officer calmed himself before he spoke. "Chief, I'm sorry for the interruption, but that errand we ran? We made some discoveries which require your immediate presence."

"I'm sorry, police business, you understand," the chief sputtered to Roman and the group.

"No, that's okay. We can visit another day," Roman said.

They all left the police station. Roman's group watched as the police chief and the officer made a beeline straight for Sal's house.

"Guess we know what they discovered," Sherm said.

Tony entered Giuseppe's old office, where Roman sat behind the desk studying pages in front of him. Gage and Donatello sat in front of the desk.

"There's a manhunt on for Sal," Tony said.

"Now that everyone is out from under Sal's thumb, how do you want to proceed, Roman?" Gage asked.

"Since Sal's friends don't know he's right upstairs, why don't we drop them on the police station's doorstep tonight?" Roman drummed his fingers on the desk. "They can sing like the canaries they are and tank their boss."

Tony nodded. "That would work. We'll hog-tie them together and leave them at the door. We can have someone go inside to let them know there are people tied up outside."

Donatello rubbed his hands together. "After this, there should not be any problems from Sal, or anything left over from Giuseppe!"

ARI AND MR. TRAN TALKED WITH JANINA IN A SMALL conference room. The woman did fluently speak, read and write Latin, English and Italian. Mr. Tran stood.

"Let's go take a look at the project," he said.

Janina and Ari stood. Ari could not help herself, but she tried hard to hide a smile. She couldn't wait to see Janina's reaction to *the project*.

Mr. Tran led them into the library. Janina's mouth flew open in disbelief.

"I can't believe it!" Janina said. "Are all of these in Latin and Italian?"

"We don't know yet," Mr. Tran said.

"We found a young man back in the States who has incredible early language skills such as Tamil, Armenian, Korean, Hebrew, Aramaic, Chinese, Greek, Egyptian, and Sanskrit," Ari said. "He will help out on the project. As you can see, we still need an army of translators."

"Would you be willing and able to relocate?" Mr. Tran asked.

"Oh, yes! This is such a wonderful opportunity. I'm not

married and my mother recently died, so I don't have any ties to my hometown or country," Janina said.

"Good! I'll speak with Donatello, Marco, and Jason to get your paperwork started," Mr. Tran said. "Panther Industries is a wonderful company to work for, and as you can see, the translation documents are very interesting."

Ari's eyes swept over Janina. "There are several non-disclosure documents you are required to sign. Some material is highly classified, as are some situations that may arise."

"I understand," Janina said. "I know Mr. Tran isn't a shifter —we talked. I recognize the scents of all the shifters and humans here at the palazzo."

Ari nodded. "That makes things a lot easier, but Donatello will go into greater detail."

CHAPTER NINETEEN

A YOUNG COUPLE TAKING A MIDNIGHT STROLL HAND IN hand down the main boulevard in Fiuggi, came upon a bundled group of people in front of the police station.

The young woman screamed in horror. The people appeared to be dead.

Her young man dragged her through the front door to the sergeant at the desk where Raffaella dozed, curled up in an inbox. Amid the sobs from his girlfriend, the man blurted: "There are dead people in front of your door!"

The sergeant rushed around the desk, followed by two policemen who had just come out of an office. They flung open the door.

They recognized the people as associates of Sal DeLuca.

The sergeant rushed back inside.

"I will be with you in just a moment," he said. "Please have a seat. We will have to take your statement." He called multiple people on the phone.

Within ten minutes, the mayor, the chief of police, detectives, and what looked like the entire police force were all over the place.

Someone escorted the young couple into a detective's office.

Raffaella also dashed all over the place, getting as many details as possible. The people were not dead; they were out cold. The cops hauled them into the jail and housed them in separate cells until they woke up. Then they would question the group before they processed and booked them on crimes too many to list. Sal was still at large.

SAL RATTLED THE BARS ON HIS CELL. "HEY! I'M HUNGRY! Where's breakfast?"

One man who refused to give up the brown robes came up the stairs. "You think this is a hotel or something?" He spat at Sal. "You can starve for all we care."

Sal scowled as the man disappeared down the stairs. He rattled the bars. "Hey! Hey! Get back here!" His stomach growled. An hour later he drank tepid water from the sink, trying to stave off hunger pains.

Several footsteps came up the stairs. Roman, Gage and Sherm stopped in front of the cell. Roman held a steaming plate of eggs, ham, toast, and a slice of melon. He set it on the floor outside the cell, against the wall of the hallway.

"If you can reach it, you can have it," Roman said.

"What the fuck?" Sal roared.

Roman stared at Sal. "That's how your boss treated me, except he drugged me and I couldn't move an inch for over two weeks. I'm being generous with you."

"You can't do that! I didn't do anything to you!" Sal yelled.

Gage reached into the cell, grabbed Sal's hair and slammed

his head into the bars. "You drugged him and flew him here. You're just as responsible."

"Come on, let's get breakfast," Sherm said. "I'm starving!"

They marched down the stairs and headed to the dining area where dozens of people shuffled through a buffet line. Roman noticed Ari, Mr. Tran, and Janina at a table with Marco and Donatello. After they filled their plates, they joined them.

Marco was reading the local paper. He held it up and read the headlines aloud. *Dangerous murderer at large.* They displayed a picture of Sal next to an article. Below that was a picture of Sal's crew in front of the police station. They divvied up the entire front page with articles about the ruthlessness of the criminals.

"Word's going to come out about your *cousin* and his involvement with the mayor and the chief of police," Donatello said. "I wonder how that will be handled."

"I expect them to admit their involvement," Marco said. "I also think they will want to embrace Panther Industries' new office here and do a photo op with all of you. It will lessen the sting of the situation."

Gage said, "You may be right." "The bad guy is dead. The new guy is an upstanding citizen with a successful business in the States. If Roman can't charm them, Ari will."

Jason entered the dining room and headed for the buffet line. After he got his food, he joined the group at the table. "Morning, everyone." He kissed Ari on the cheek.

"What are you going to do with that piece of shit in the tower?" Jason asked. He blushed when he realized that Mr. Tran and Janina were listening to his big mouth.

"I apologize, Mr. Tran. And to you. I don't think we've met."

Janina sipped water to cool her burning face.

"Jason, this is Janina," Ari said. "Janina, Jason is my oldest son. You'll have to excuse him for his manners. But I should warn you, we are a cursing group of people, so you'd better toughen up if you're going to be within hearing distance of us."

"It's okay. I use cuss words sometimes when I'm mad," Janina said.

"To answer your question," Sherm said, "I thought it would be fun to hogtie him and slip him into a patrol car."

"What a great idea," Roman said. "Tonight?"

"No point in taking up space here," Sherm said. "We've found everyone he had under his thumb. I'm hoping more people come forward after he's in custody and they've read the newspaper. They'll feel safe and will tell their stories so they can testify against him and his gang."

"I think it would be handy if we introduced Ari using her professional title so she can offer her services with those ledgers," Gage said.

"Marco created a spreadsheet for me," Ari said. "They weren't that clever in their attempt to hide their identities. Everything's there—people they extorted, dates, times, and places of murders. It's mind-boggling how anyone could be so sloppy."

Donatello's cellphone chirped a text from the new front desk. The large entryway had two employees at the desk: a greeter who answered the phones, and a security person.

"Speak of the devil," Donatello said. "The mayor and the chief would like a meeting with Panther Industries ASAP."

"Have them come here in forty-five minutes," Roman said. "We can meet with them in a conference room." He turned his interest to Janina and Mr. Tran. "I wanted to welcome you to the company personally, Janina. Mr. Tran is the head of the translations department, and you report to him. When he returns to the United States, you will have access to him through phone, email, and video calls."

"Use the World Clock Meeting Planner," Ari said. "That way you will determine the best time to call."

"You will be the only translator here at this office until we hire more people. Our preference is to hire shifters, but so far we're not having much luck finding anyone with language skills," Roman said.

"I'll order a set of clocks for the library for times around the world," Marco said.

"The first thing I would like to do is to label the shelves with datelines," Mr. Tran said. He looked from Marco to Jason. "Would you order a label maker with extra tape? Each section of shelves may contain decades of journals. If we label the shelves, we'll be able to find what we want much easier."

"We can start today, if you'd like," Janina said. "We can tape the dates on the shelves until the label maker arrives."

Roman stood, followed by Gage, Ari, and Sherm. He nodded to Donatello. "Let's get ready for our guests. They should arrive shortly."

Donatello escorted the mayor and the police chief, with a briefcase, to the conference room. "I know you met the other day, but why don't we go around the table and introduce ourselves."

Sherm set the newspaper aside on the conference table.

"That's a good idea. I'll start," Roman said. "I'm Roman Davenport. I started Panther Industries as an electronics company a few decades ago. When Gage and I merged our companies, we decided we shared the same ideas regarding security, so we branched out. Today, our security division has teams across the globe." He nodded to Gage.

"Gage Stryker. I'm the other half of Panther Industries. We have manufacturing in the States and some overseas locations. Our security detail protects private individuals and corporations, governments—we rarely turn anyone away. If you look at our website, you will find much more information about the company."

"Ari Davis. I'm a forensic accountant. My job is to sift out crooked books," she said.

Sherm chuckled. "Sherman Foo. Don't let Ari fool you. Her professional codename is *The Sifter*. I'm the head of Panther Industries' Security Division. We go in, do the job they hired us to do, and we are never compromised or caught. I hire only the most highly skilled people. Not only do our clients rely on us to get the job done, but also with the greatest discretion."

The police chief and mayor shared a nod.

"I've looked into your backgrounds and your company, and I'm quite impressed." The chief squirmed. "We have this situation —I'm sure you've heard about our troubles." He nodded to the newspaper with Sal's face above the fold. "We are just now finding out about the filth this man was involved in."

The mayor jumped in. "We need your help. The detectives found a ledger and papers that most likely outline all the criminal activities of this Sal and his people."

The chief lifted his briefcase onto the table and opened it. He pulled out the ledger and papers that Ari already had in her possession. He slid them across the table toward her.

"We would like to hire you to unravel this information so the prosecutor can use it in court." The chief displayed a grim expression as he looked at the mayor. They both sighed. "We were not honest with you when we met the other day. Giuseppe had been paying us to look the other way. We're not proud of it, and we plan to go public with the information. We wanted you to know that we are aware you will find our names in that paperwork."

The mayor jumped to his feet. "That bastard—thank God he's dead. Everyone hated and feared him. He was not a man to disagree with. People disappeared or had accidents if they didn't smile his way and jump when he said jump. I'm so ashamed of my participation. But the flip side was if I did not agree to do what he said, they threatened to dismember my daughter and rape my wife in front of me."

The chief stared at the table. "I know there are a couple of bad eggs in my organization. But now that Giuseppe's dead and we have rounded up Sal's people, all we need is Sal to close that door. I'm going to be cleaning house. Anyone who was not being forced to work for those bastards—anyone who enjoyed that type of cruelty—will be fired immediately. I want to start with a fresh slate." The room became quiet.

The chief cleared his throat. "Just so you know, we will not investigate how Sal's people landed on our doorstep."

Sherm quirked up a tiny smile.

Ari flipped open the ledger. She was already familiar with the entries. She slid her fingers down the columns and turned the pages. Ari looked at their guests. "I can help you with this. I'd be happy to testify as a professional witness if you require my presence in court."

"I'll have my team search for DeLuca. We'll deliver him as soon as we find him," Sherm said. "Have you alerted airports and other transportation modes?"

"Yes, we have his picture with every agency. He's not getting out of Italy," the chief growled.

Roman tapped the table. "Okay. It looks like we have a plan."

At two-thirty in the morning, Officer Giordano left the service station with a fresh cup of coffee and a cannoli. He got into his police car and barely missed scalding himself when muffled urgent noises sounded from the back seat.

He looked in the back and was surprised to discover Salvatore DeLuca trussed like a pig for market. His mouth was duct-taped and his arms were bound behind his back with zip handcuffs. A rope connected his arms to his legs, bent at the knees, ankles zipped together.

Giordano came out of his stupor after a moment and engaged his radio to call the police dispatcher. Within ten minutes the parking lot was lit up with official vehicles and a news truck screeching to a halt.

The chief barked out orders. "Get these people out of the way so they don't contaminate any evidence."

Cameras flashed off the windows of the back seat of the cruiser as everyone strained to get the perfect shot. The police pushed back reporters and onlookers.

The CSI team took their pictures before they cut Sal free and hauled him out of the back seat. They removed the tape from his mouth and bagged it, along with everything that bound him.

"Get this cruiser back to the lab and go over it from top to bottom," The chief said.

Cameras flashed as Sal was promptly shoved into the back seat of a different police cruiser. Reporters yelled questions at Sal, all unanswered.

The chief, a detective, and one of the CSI team went into the store.

"We need access to your camera tapes," the chief said.

The clerk escorted them to the back room where the equipment was located.

Catherina, the CSI lady, looked over the controls for the two outside cameras and the two inside cameras.

"Let's see if there's footage of whoever dumped Sal in the cruiser. Had to be more than one person," Catherina said.

They huddled around the equipment as she went through each tape. One by one, they discovered someone had looped the tapes to show nothing other than the empty store and parking area.

"Someone with skills," Catherina said. "You're looking at a professional who pulled this off."

The chief didn't even blink. He knew exactly who had delivered Sal. He also knew they could spray the entire vehicle with Fluorescein, and would pick up no evidence of those special ops people who delivered the murderer. Everything he had read across the Internet about Panther Industries Security Division described their ghostlike ops. He was seeing it first-hand. He never wanted to be on the wrong side of that group.

They left the back room of the store. News camera flashes and video lights blinded the clerk at the counter.

The police tow truck hauled the patrol car aboard the flatbed.

"Chief! Can you verify the identity of the man in the back seat? Was it Salvatore DeLuca?" a reporter asked.

The chief stood before a news team. "Yes, that was Sal DeLuca. We will have more information to give you later in the day. He is on the way to the police station where he will be booked and charged."

With that, the chief and his entourage got into vehicles and left the scene.

CHAPTER TWENTY

Roman and Gage's cellphones dinged a text in the middle of the night. Sherm supplied pictures of the discovery of Sal, the media circus, and the thug being hauled away.

Ari woke, rubbed her eyes and stared in the dark at the lit cellphones. "What's going on?"

"Closing another chapter," Gage said. "Sherm must be on a roof somewhere." He showed her the pictures.

"That boy! He seems to have fun no matter what," Ari said.

Roman set his phone on the side table and flopped back onto the bed. He rolled over and locked his lips on Ari's mouth.

Gage looked on to determine if they were engaging in sex or just kissing. He didn't want to miss out. It had been way too long and infrequent since Roman's ordeal.

Don't you want to make love? Roman sent.

Of course. I wasn't sure if we were going to Gage sent. Everything seemed back to normal. Roman wasn't aggressive. The three of them interacted as they always did, sharing their love.

Gage flipped Ari onto her hands and knees. He rode her

from behind while Roman received a blowjob that rolled his eyes back. They switched places and positions, then showered and fell back into bed to sleep a few more hours.

"WE HAVE ALL LOOSE ENDS TIED UP," ROMAN SAID, AS HE ate from two breakfast plates piled with food. "I miss our bed."

"I'm going to meet with the police chief and mayor today," Ari said. "I made a short video to make it easier for them."

"Did Sherm help?" Gage asked.

"He was the one who suggested the video. May save me a trip back for the trial," Ari said.

Sherm wandered into the dining hall and shuffled through the buffet line. He looked tired as he joined them at the table.

"Get any sleep?" Roman asked. "There's nothing going on here today. Why don't you sleep awhile?"

"Can't sleep," Sherm said. He was groggy from lack of sleep.

Mr. Tran joined them at the table with a cup of tea and a plate of food. He looked Sherm over. "After you eat, come see me in the library. I'll give you something for your insomnia. How long has this been going on?"

"Since I was about seventeen," Sherm said.

"Hhhmm," Mr. Tran said. "We will talk later."

"Mr. Tran, how long do you want to stay here to get Janina situated?" Gage asked. "We're thinking about going home tomorrow."

"I have Janina and three additional people labeling the shelves," Mr. Tran said. "I would like to box up a few of the older journals and bring them back to Alan. I wish we had more people on board."

"Why don't you have Sandy contact the universities?" Ari asked. "There may even be people who can work in between classes. Possibly even people here in Italy or Europe. We can ask Donatello and Marco to make inquiries."

ARI, MARCO, THE MAYOR, THE POLICE CHIEF, AND THE prosecutor sat in a conference room at the police station. She passed out stapled pages to the authorities. Marco translated for Ari.

"This is the key to understanding and unlocking the coding on the ledger pages. Whoever created this wasn't very sophisticated, so it was easy for me to break and decipher all their secrets," Ari explained.

"This spreadsheet you put together," the prosecutor asked, "what exactly does it contain?"

The mayor and the police chief studied the pages. "Extortion, murder, assault and battery—Vic, just read the pages," the chief said. He sounded irritated.

"Okay. I didn't want to waste my time," the prosecutor said.

Ari stared him down with venom in her eyes. "Evidently you know nothing about me or my background; otherwise you wouldn't act like such an ass."

The prosecutor gave a veiled dirty look Ari's way. "And what exactly is your background?"

"I'm a forensic accountant with decades of experience. I've worked with law enforcement agencies across the United States and a few foreign countries, corporations, the US government, security companies like Panther Industries—want my resume?" Ari dripped sarcasm with every word. "Perhaps you should research me online. I've prepared a video for evidence gathering, and possibly as professional testimony in court."

Ari stood. "I'm done here." She left the conference room. She could hear angry yelling from the conference room all the way to the front door.

ARI STOMPED INTO THE PALAZZO WITH ANGER WAFTING out around her.

Roman, Gage, where are you?

In the small conference room. What's wrong? Gage sent. Ari joined them with a huff.

"They didn't like what you presented?" Roman asked.

"The mayor and chief appreciated what I put together, but..."

Donatello held up his hand. "Let me guess. The prosecutor was all uppity?"

"He talked down to me as if I were a little woman who had no business in that meeting," Ari stewed. She was furious.

"Send them an invoice and wash your hands of their mess. We'll see what happens when the prosecutor finds familiar names on your spreadsheet," Gage said.

"I want to go home." Ari patted Donatello's arm. "It's not like I don't like the palazzo, Donatello. I'd like to get back to our bed and apartment."

"No offense taken. All of you have been through a lot," Donatello said.

"Where's Sherm?" Ari asked.

"Mr. Tran gave him one of his herbal teas and sent him to bed," Roman said. "We'll make arrangements to leave tomorrow."

They dragged into the penthouse in Reading two days later at three in the morning. They dumped their luggage in the foyer, changed into pajamas and dropped into Roman's large bed.

The elevator pinged a visitor at eight-thirty in the morning. Kevin stepped into the apartment and noticed how quiet it was. "Mom? Roman? Gage? Anybody here?"

Gage stumbled down the hall in pajama pants.

"Crap," Kevin said. "I didn't know you were still sleeping. You're usually up so early."

"We got in a couple of hours ago," Gage said. "Everything okay?"

"Yeah. I just wanted to say hi. I'll be here for a few days," Kevin said. "Go back to bed. Tell Mom to call me when she's rested."

Gage stumbled back down the hall as Kevin left.

Margaret, the youngest of the Rustan coyote clan, was driving back to Reading, singing her heart out to the radio in her hot red Toyota Tundra. As she passed the private road to the Tothars' house and cabins in the woods, she slammed on the brakes. The truck screeched to a halt, leaving rubber on the blacktop, trying to avoid a little naked blonde-haired girl who darted out into the road.

Margaret threw the truck into park, jumped out of the vehicle and rushed up to the child. "Oh my God! Honey, where's your mommy or daddy? I almost ran you down!"

The little girl's chest was heaving as she sobbed uncontrollably. Margaret lifted her up into her arms.

"Shh, shh. It's okay. Where's your mommy?"

The little girl pointed back to the forest. "A wolf pack hurt mommy. I tried to help her." She shivered.

Margaret brought the child to her truck and opened the passenger door. "Let me find something I can wrap around you." She settled the girl on the seat, opened the back door and rummaged through a gym bag. She brought out a bath towel and wrapped it around the tiny girl. "Stay here, okay? I'll go find your mommy."

The little girl nodded as she clutched the towel to her chest.

Margaret headed in the direction the child had pointed.

She came upon a grisly scene. The woman was dead. Mauled by several wolves. She saw the child's clothes and shoes nearby. Margaret tried to control her emotions, but tears ran down her cheeks as she retrieved her cellphone from her jeans. She thumbed through her contacts and placed a call.

"King Roman?" Margaret lost it when she retold the details. There were instances where she knew she was not understandable at all. She finally pulled herself together to relay what happened.

Thirty minutes later, two helicopters approached and landed a distance away. Sherm, Roman, Gage, and Ari disembarked from one, and Lonnie and his team rushed from the other to the red truck. Margaret curtsied as she held the little girl.

"Where?" Sherm asked.

Margaret pointed. The men took off in that direction. The little girl held her arms out to Ari.

"Oh, honey. What's your name?" Ari asked as she hugged the child to her.

"Edris. But you can call me Eddie," the little imp said. "I'm three!" She held up three tiny fingers.

"My goodness. You sure are a big girl!" Ari said. "Eddie, where's your daddy?"

"I don't have a daddy." Eddie sniffled, then choked out a sob. "Mommy screamed. The wolves hurt her. She told me to go, but I shifted and tried to help her." Eddie pantomimed hissing and clawing.

"What a brave little girl! I'm so glad you're not hurt," Ari said. "Have you ever flown in a helicopter?"

Eddie's eyes widened as she looked at the helicopter.

She shook her head.

"Well, you're in for a treat. Not many little girls ever get a chance to ride in one, but you're special and today you're going to ride in one with me!"

Eddie's teary face brightened into a smile.

SHERM, GAGE AND ROMAN RETURNED TO WHERE ARI, Margaret and Eddie were. Sherm held the shredded clothing and child's shoes.

"Actual wolves, not shifters," Roman said. "That's a relief, in one sense. It worried me that we had a worse situation than what we have with this woman being killed."

"We've avoided the wolf tracks. They haven't been trampled by footprints," Gage said. "Sherm and Lonnie's team kept the scene viable for when the police get here."

"Okay, this may be delicate," Sherm said. "The police can't question her. They can't know she's a shifter."

Eddie reached out her arms to Sherm. He shoved the clothing into Gage's hands and latched onto Eddie.

"Well hello, princess," he said.

Eddie patted his face. "You're cute. I'm going to marry you!"

Sherm chuckled along with the others. "I'll be an old grandpa by the time you're old enough to get married, honey."

He handed Eddie back to Ari and got down to business.

"We found a car parked on the private road. Looks like they were packed up. I don't know if they were heading to town or leaving. I've got Travis and Kevin tracking down information from the woman's ID in her purse, plus the license plate. Her driver's license was expired, but shows a Reading address. Only had seven dollars in her wallet."

"She said she doesn't have a father, so he probably abandoned the woman when she told him she was pregnant," Ari said.

"What should we do? How do we proceed?" Roman asked.

"We need to call the police," Sherm said.

"Should we call Valk?" Gage asked.

"When they go through the car, they'll discover there's a child, and they'll want to question her, Margaret, and us," Sherm said.

"Mommy told me I can't talk about my kitten," Eddie said. "It's a big secret."

Ari turned to Margaret. "Can you get her a change of clothes from the car?"

Sherm texted Lonnie: *Woman coming your way. Get her some gloves. Need clothes for the kid from the car.*

"Sure." Margaret walked toward three team members. One of the guys brought her over to the dead woman's car, hidden in the trees on the private road.

"I wonder what she was doing on your private road?" Ari asked.

"Maybe she was heading to one of the cabins? Doesn't look like they had squat," Roman said.

Eddie's head rested on Ari's shoulder, and she sucked her thumb, eyes closing.

"We can't let this child go into the system," Ari said. "CPS isn't the place for a shifter child."

Gage ran his fingers through Eddie's blond curls. "We could get temporary custody until we find the father."

"Put in a call to Valk. We'll talk to him when he gets here. Just make sure he understands we're not turning her over to CPS," Roman said.

Sherm nodded and stepped away from them to place the call.

"Shit! I just realized there may be shifters on the property—maybe even wolf shifters," Gage said. He called out to anyone in the cabins and surrounding two thousand acres on the visitor side of the property.

This is your king. A woman was killed by wolves—not shifters. If there are any wolf shifters here on the property, shift back to your human form and return to your cabin or vehicle. The authorities will be here shortly and they will hunt wolves.

There were three responses. *We'll leave to be on the safe side.*

Have you seen any wolves? Roman sent.

No, just the three of us.

Roman retrieved his cellphone. "Lonnie, check the cameras and see if you can find the wild wolves. We had three wolf shifters, but they're leaving now."

Margaret came back with a plastic bag of clothes for Eddie. "There wasn't any luggage, just a bunch of garbage bags stuffed with clothes, bathroom things, and some toys. This bag must have been Eddie's. There're clothes and shoes and a couple of stuffed animals in here."

Ari kneeled on the ground, and Margaret joined her. They rummaged through the bag and put together an outfit for Eddie. Ari dressed her, then fished out one of the stuffed animals and held it out to her.

Eddie grabbed the little stuffed tiger. She held it out to Ari. "This is me! Mommy said I look just like this little tiger!"

"You're a little tiger?" Ari asked.

Eddie crushed the tiger to her chest and nodded.

"I'm a big cat!" Ari said.

"You're a kitty?" Eddie asked with wonder.

"Uh huh."

Margaret looked at her watch. "I'd better call my family. They're most likely wondering where I am."

Gage got out his cellphone. "I'll call Leander and find out what he knows about the big cats. If this little girl is a tiger, her mother must have been a cat. He can start asking questions."

"Good idea," Roman said. He held his arms out to Eddie. "Why don't I hold her for a while?"

Ari's lips quirked up. "I never took you for the father type, Roman. She's a sweet little girl."

"See, after all this time I can still surprise you," he quipped. He called to one of the team members. "Take this bag back to the car."

Ari gave him a questioning look.

"It would be a little strange for her clothing to be missing," Roman explained.

"Ah." Ari nodded.

Two hours later, a line of flashing lights coming down the highway brought the police, Valk, the coroner's office and a flock of news trucks. Doors opened and slammed shut, and people hurried or ran over to where Ari, Roman, Gage and the rest stood.

Valk had the cops hold back the reporters. He walked up to

the group. "This child's mother is the victim who was attacked and killed?"

"Yes," Roman said.

Valk stared at him, then glanced over to Ari, Gage, then Margaret. "Why is it that you are here, Mr. Davenport?"

"Ms. Rustan called. This land is adjacent to our property. The woman parked her car on our private road. Roman's eyes never wavered off Valk.

Valk turned his attention to Margaret. "Tell me what happened."

Margaret dabbed her eyes and gave details about how she almost hit the child running out into the road.

"Berks County CPS will have to process the child," Valk said.

Ari practically got in his face. "That's not happening. If Roman has to get our legal team involved to get temporary custody until someone can locate her father, that's what we'll do. And Valk, you know we'll sling money into this and the city won't be able to afford to fight us." Gage looked from Ari to Roman.

Roman shook his head. *Not yet, Gage. I'll handle it for now. If we need to get legal involved, we will. I'll talk to Judge Dillhunt as soon as we get away from here.*

"Berks County will still want you to sign something," Valk said.

"That's fine. My license to practice law is still in effect," Roman said. "They won't be able to pull a fast one on us."

A man walked over to Valk. "Looks like there were four wolves. Tracks are distinct. After the attack, they ran into the woods. I'm shocked they didn't attack the little girl."

Valk turned to the group. "This is Suarez with Animal Control." He nodded to the group. "This is Sherman Foo with

Panther Industries Security, Roman Davenport and Gage Stryker of Panther Industries, and Ari Davis."

They nodded to the man.

"Lonnie is checking the camera feeds on the property to see if the wolves passed through Mr. Davenport's land," Sherm said.

"You have cameras out here, Roman?" Valk asked.

"Yes. We've had trespassers and hunters. Didn't want to take any chances," Roman said.

"How much land do you have?" Valk asked.

"Just under five thousand acres," Roman said.

Suarez let out a whistle. "Must be nice."

"I'm sure the city appreciates the taxes it collects from my properties and businesses." Roman tried to keep his tone civil. He didn't like the animal control man.

"You can leave. I'll catch up with you and take statements later," Valk said.

They headed to the two helicopters. Camera flashes blinded Eddie as the news crews swarmed the group. Questions were shouted. Microphones shoved toward Roman, Gage, Ari and Sherm.

Lonnie and his team held back the reporters while Roman, Gage and Ari boarded the helicopter. Eddie's eyes widened, and she smiled brightly. "We're going to fly?"

"Yes! You'll be able to see all the cars, trees, houses—everything!" Gage said.

Sherm got in the front and began safety checks. Gage sat in the front while Roman and Ari got in the back and buckled in. Eddie sat on Ari's lap. She looked out the glass sides.

Lonnie and his team boarded the second helicopter, and they lifted off.

When Sherm's helicopter lifted off, Eddie squealed with

excitement, making everyone laugh. She watched the ground shrink as the bird rose into the sky. As they flew over the highway toward the city, she pointed to the ground.

"Toy cars!" Eddie squealed.

"Those are big cars, but we are way, way up in the air, so they appear little," Roman said.

Eddie climbed into his lap and put her arms around his neck and hugged him. "Will you be my daddy?"

Roman glanced at Ari. Gage turned in his seat to stare at him.

How do I answer that?

However you choose, Ari sent.

If her father doesn't show up, or releases rights to her, we can adopt, Gage sent.

I think you two have fallen in love with a little blond girl, Ari sent. She chuckled.

"Eddie, first we need to find your father. If he can't take care of you, Gage and I will be your new daddies and Ari will be your new mommy. Would you like that?" Roman asked.

Eddie kissed Roman on the cheek. "Oh, yes! And Sherm and I will get married!"

"I think you have to wait a few years," Gage said. "First, you have to go to school and grow up."

Eddie thought about it. "Okay!"

The helicopter landed on the roof of the Panther Industries high-rise. They took the stairs down to the penthouse, and Roman set Eddie on the floor in the living room.

"Eddie, are you hungry?" Ari asked.

"Yes!" Eddie said.

"I'll call Judge Dillhunt," Roman said. He disappeared down the hall to his suite.

Ari led Eddie to the bathroom. "Let's get washed up first,

okay?" Ari ran a washcloth under warm water, wrung it out, and washed Eddie's face, then washed her hands. They went to the kitchen. "Let's have a good breakfast, shall we? Do you like eggs, bacon and toast?"

"I love bacon! Toast, too. And eggs!" Eddie said, in her slightly loud, excited child's voice.

Gage was beside Ari. "What do you want me to do?"

"Can you start the bacon? I'll do the rest." Ari picked up Eddie and sat her at the kitchen table. "Why don't you stay here and watch? The stove is hot, and I don't want you to get burned."

"Okay. I'm going to eat everything!" Eddie said.

When everything was ready, Ari called out to Roman. *Roman, breakfast is ready.*

Be right there, he sent.

A few minutes later, Roman entered the kitchen and kissed Ari on the cheek. He grabbed their coffee cups and poured coffee.

"Eddie, would you like orange juice?" Roman asked.

"Yes. Mommy adds water so it will last longer," she said.

"We don't do that here. Only good, thick orange juice with pulp will go in your tummy," Ari said.

They all sat at the table.

"Eddie, you'll have to eat on your knees until we get a booster chair for you. Is that okay?" Ari asked.

"I'm okay." Eddie picked up a piece of bacon and crunched.

"What did the judge have to say?" Gage asked.

"Everything's okay. We have temporary custody until they find the father. We'll see what happens at that point. We're going to get a home visit from a caseworker to inspect the house and make sure we are suitable foster parents," Roman said.

"Let's go to Target after we eat and get a few things. Eddie needs clothes, a booster seat and a lot of other things," Ari said.

"We should go furniture shopping," Gage said. "She needs a different bed and furniture for a child."

CHAPTER TWENTY-ONE

EDDIE CHOSE A PRINCESS COMFORTER SET IN A RAINBOW of pink and purple at Target. Three overstuffed shopping carts later, they left the store with most likely the biggest purchase for the store that week.

At Reading Furniture, they bought an exquisite white French-style poster bed with a padded headboard and footboard, a dresser, a mirror, and a nightstand. For the sitting room, they found a toy box, bookcases, a desk and chair, a child-sized wing-back chair and sofa, and a round table with four chairs.

Gage called someone in the shifter community from the stuffed SUV. "Emilio, are you available for a small job today?" He listened. "First, we need all the furniture in the spare room and sitting room moved to the warehouse. Then we need those two rooms painted for a little girl. Probably white with a hint of pale pink." Gage looked to Ari for confirmation.

Ari nodded.

"We should be home within the next ten minutes." Gage

pocketed his phone. "All set. Eddie should sleep in your room tonight, Ari."

Roman pulled the SUV into the parking garage and stopped by the door to the lobby. "Let's unload everything here and I'll park."

The men got out and unloaded the large shopping bags and boxes. Ari grabbed smaller bags and led Eddie by the hand through the door to the lobby. They approached the elevator.

"Need help, Ms. Davis?" the security guard asked.

"Yes! There's a ton of things for our new little girl here," Ari said.

The guard stooped. "Well, hello, princess. What's your name?"

"Edris, but you can call me Eddie," she said.

"It's nice to meet you, Edris Eddie," he said.

Eddie giggled.

The guard slid the penthouse card in the slot.

Roman and Gage came through the door from the garage. "Hold the door. We've got a ton of stuff to bring in," Gage said.

The guard relieved Gage of his bags and placed them in the elevator. After a few minutes, everything was loaded into the elevator, and the family rode up to the penthouse.

Within ten minutes, Emilio and a crew of three men arrived. He studied the walls, woodwork, and ceiling. "Doesn't look like I need to do any prep work. Your walls and trim are in excellent shape, so all I need is tape and the wall paint. I'll pick it up on the way back from the warehouse."

They dismantled the furniture, wrapped it in moving blankets, loaded it on dollies and hauled it away.

Ari rummaged through the bags and found Eddie's new toothbrush, hairbrush and other bathroom supplies. She placed them on the bathroom counter, along with the shower curtain that matched the bedding, and the hooks.

She brought the bags of clothes to the laundry room.

Eddie picked up a dress with tulle on the bottom, like a tutu. "Can I wear this?"

"We have to wash all these clothes before you can wear them," Ari said.

"Why?"

"Because a lot of people touched these things while they were in the store and they probably had dirty hands. Who knows, maybe they picked their nose or didn't wash their hands after they went to the bathroom." Ari made a scary face.

Eddie giggled.

"And before the clothes got to the store, they were in the dusty warehouse."

"Eww!" Eddie said.

Ari snipped tags and loaded the washer. "Let's go hang your shower curtain."

They went back to the spare room bathroom, where they found Roman hanging the shower curtain.

Eddie clapped. "It's beautiful!"

The elevator dinged a visitor. Eddie ran to the foyer and into Jason and Kevin.

"Whoa! Who's this?" Jason asked. He reached down and picked up Eddie.

"Edris! But Mommy calls me Eddie. Who are you?"

"I'm Jason, and this is my brother, Kevin. Where's your mommy?"

"The wolves hurt mommy. Ari is going to be my new mommy," Eddie said. Her bottom lip pouted out, and she rubbed her eyes as tears fell.

Jason and Kevin shared a questioning look.

"Mom?" Kevin called out.

Ari came down the hallway, followed by Roman and Gage.

"What's going on?" Jason asked.

"Come sit down. Do you want a sandwich? I was just going to make lunch," Ari said.

Gage grabbed napkins and put them on the table. He took drink orders.

"Get Eddie a glass of milk," Ari said.

The boys sat at the table. Eddie's new booster seat was on a chair and Jason placed her on it.

Roman joined them at the table and explained the situation. "The court granted us temporary custody."

Jason looked at Ari at the kitchen counter. "Are you seriously thinking of raising another kid, Mom?"

"Why not? Are you suggesting I'm too old?" Ari glared at her son.

"No! I just didn't think you'd want to be tied down for another fifteen or twenty years, that's all." Jason backpedaled.

Three hostile faces glared at him.

"She needs a home. It appeared they were living in their vehicle, but we're not sure of the circumstances. Leander and Travis are checking into the situation and trying to find her father. In the meantime, she's going to live here, and we hope to adopt her." Ari glared at Jason.

Kevin raised a hand. "I'm staying out of this. I don't have any problem with you raising one or a dozen kids."

The elevator dinged Sherm's arrival.

"Sherm's here!" Eddie screamed out. She crawled out of her booster chair and ran to Sherm.

He reached down and picked her up. "Hi munchkin. Are you being a good girl?"

"Yes! Jason and Kevin are here. Do you want to eat lunch with us?" Eddie invited.

Ari looked to Sherm. "Mustard and mayo, right?"

"You know what I like," Sherm said. He pulled out a chair

and sat with Eddie on his lap. "Okay, here's what we've got. Her father's name is Edmund Dovensky. Her mother was Clariss Sullivan. I'm assuming they combined their names and came up with the name Edris. I couldn't find a marriage certificate, and he wasn't paying child support. Found a DNA test claiming him as the father. He's out there somewhere. We're looking for a current address."

"Do you know where they were living?" Roman asked.

"The last rental information Travis found was an eviction notice from a low rent complex a month ago. No current employer. No bank accounts. She was on the edge," Sherm said.

Ari brought plates to the table. She placed a small plate in front of Eddie with a sandwich cut into four pieces, along with some potato chips and sliced kiwi fruit. After everyone had a plate in front of them she sat.

"How could she have fallen through the cracks? What about the shifter community? What group did she belong to? I don't understand why no one reached out to us!" Ari nibbled on a chip.

"I didn't recognize her," Roman said. "I don't think she's been to any of the meetings."

"We should hear from Leander soon," Gage said. "I wonder why she didn't shift when the wolves attacked."

"The bigger question is, why did the wolves leave Eddie alone?" Sherm said.

"Those bad wolves were afraid of my kitten." Eddie made growling sounds and clawed the air with her little hands.

An hour later, Emilio and his crew returned with paint, supplies, and ladders. They spread drop cloths on the floors in the bedroom and the sitting room and taped the ceiling and woodwork.

AFTER LUNCH, JASON AND KEVIN RETURNED TO WORK. Leander arrived. Like everyone else, he fawned over Eddie. Ari ducked into the butler's pantry and tossed Eddie's new clothes from the washer to the dryer.

"Well, look at this little princess!" Leander squatted beside her kitchen chair. "I'm Leander. You're Edris, right?" He poked her in the side.

Eddie giggled and squirmed. "Hi Leander."

He stood and walked to a vacant kitchen chair. "I've talked with the leaders and no one recognized Eddie or her mother. She must not have been involved with the community, or she came here from somewhere else."

"We can blast an email across the country with a picture of the mother's driver's license, along with a picture of Eddie," Roman said. He turned his focus to Sherm. "Can you find out how long that lease was for, and if there's anything previous to that?"

Sherm worked his phone. "I'm on it. Should hear from either Travis or Kevin in a little while. What I want to know is if the mother wasn't involved in the shifter community, how did she end up on your private road?"

Roman, Gage, and Ari shared thoughtful looks.

"Just doesn't make sense," Gage said. "How would she know to go there? She must have talked with SOMEONE in the community to know there were cabins out there."

"Why did those wolves attack her? Are we one-hundred percent sure they were wild wolves and not shifters?" Roman asked. "Why wouldn't they attack a defenseless child?"

"We should ask the bears to go out there and scent the scene and follow the trail into the forest," Ari suggested.

Roman grabbed his phone. "Bradley? We've got a problem and we need your clan's help." Roman delved into details about the attack and the big question about the wolves. He ended the call. "They're on it. We probably won't hear anything for a while, since it takes a couple of hours to get there."

"Do you think her father was a wolf?" Ari asked.

"That's the only thing that makes any sense," Gage said.

Ari looked at Eddie across the table. "Eddie, did your mommy ever talk about your daddy?"

Eddie's happy face turned sad. "Mommy said Daddy didn't like trick or treat."

Eyes bounced off each other around the table, trying to make sense of that information.

"Maybe he thought she tricked him with the pregnancy?" Leander asked.

"What else did your Mommy say about your Daddy?" Ari asked. "Did your mommy say what your daddy's animal was?"

Eddie kept her eyes averted as she shook her head. She clearly didn't want to talk about it.

"Why don't we go to my room and you can take a nice nap?" Ari suggested. "What a long morning we've had! You must be very tired."

Ari got up and picked up Eddie. She walked down the hall to the third hallway where Eddie's room was and settled Eddie on her bed. She covered her with a soft throw and kissed her cheek. "Have a good nap. We'll be in the kitchen or living room, okay?"

"Okay," Eddie said. She snuggled into the comforter, stuck her thumb into her mouth and closed her eyes.

Ari returned to the kitchen, disturbed. She sat and drummed the table with her fingers. "Something doesn't add up. Wild wolves would attack the easiest prey first. If they were shifters, why would they leave a helpless child to fend for herself?"

Roman, Gage and Sherm looked ferocious for a minute.

Leander was downcast.

"If we discover those were shifters, they will pay for their crimes," Roman growled out.

CHAPTER TWENTY-TWO

Bradley Parsons and Big Bear Muchisky seemed to fill all the space in the penthouse living room. Their massive bulk was intimidating to most people, but seemed no threat to a tiny blond-headed little girl.

Eddie sat on one of Big Bear's knees and giggled as he bounced his toes.

Roman, Gage, Sherm, Leander and Ari listened as Bradley told them what the bears discovered.

"We tracked them for seven or eight miles in a wide loop back to the highway," Bradley said. "They shifted and got into a vehicle."

Roman was livid.

Sherm worked his phone, texting his team. "I'm having Travis and Kevin check the cameras to see if we can get images of their human forms and that vehicle."

Roman turned to Ari. "That was a good suggestion for the bears to scent the scene. They smelled like wild wolves. I didn't detect any human scent."

Gage shook his head. "I can't believe Roman and I didn't detect their humanity under that fur."

"Probably used something to mask their human scent," Big Bear said. "I've heard of it being done before, but I don't know what product does it."

"They're not getting away with this. While the authorities consider this an animal mauling death, we know it was murder," Roman said. "As soon as the guys find visuals, we can blast out the details and find these fuckers."

Language! Ari sent.

All the shifters grimaced at Roman's word choice.

Oops! Guess our pet words need to be reined in, Roman sent.

Can she hear us in her head? Gage asked.

The shifters looked from one to another and shrugged. "I feel left out," Sherm said.

"I'm sorry. I often forget you can't hear us," Ari said. "I told the guys to watch their language."

Sherm snickered. "Oh, yeah. This ought to be great."

"Don't you have work to do?" Gage said.

"Keeping you guys out of trouble is a full-time job," Sherm said.

Leander stood. "I've got to run. Trisha Anderson and I are going out to eat."

Ari gave a thumbs up. "Is this a date?"

Leander blushed. "Oh, no. Nothing like that. We're going over some protocols. Figured we'd grab food at the same time."

"You're both single..." Ari said. "Why not order wine and mix in some personal stuff?"

"I don't think she likes me like that," Leander said. His face was red.

"Leander, she's agreed to go to dinner with you over some

flimsy excuse to talk shop," Gage said. "There's plenty of time for that during the day. I think she likes you."

Leander seemed unsure.

"Just get a nice bottle of wine, and after your meal, share a nice dessert," Roman said.

"Okay, I'll give it a try," Leander said.

Right after the elevator door closed, Sherm's phone dinged three times. He opened the pictures included in the text.

"Three white guys and one black guy got into a gray Ford pickup, registered to one Edmund Dovensky of Springfield, Massachusetts," Sherm said.

"Her father?" Ari bellowed.

"Travis sent progressive pictures showing them at the edge of the forest in their wolf forms and coming out of the forest as humans. Appears they left their clothes and dressed after they shifted," Sherm said.

"Why wouldn't he take his daughter with him?" Ari practically yelled. "Why would he leave her like that? Near her dead mother and a dangerous road?"

Roman was quiet in thought. "I believe it's time for our worldwide community to form a task force. Perhaps one for the US and one for overseas, where the team would gather and apprehend people like these scumbags and bring them to justice."

Gage, the bears and Sherm nodded. Ari was too livid to talk.

"That's a good idea," Sherm said. "You can't be the ones to always go Charles Bronson on the bad guys. Take these men into custody, bring them here—maybe to the warehouse instead of this building, and conduct a trial. They could even be assigned legal counsel from the community."

Everyone nodded. "Excellent," Bradley said.

Ari pulled herself together with a deep breath. "Let's put something together to send to the leaders. We should appoint representatives from across the states, and they don't have to be the leaders themselves, but others of high moral standing in their community."

"We need to be specific about what these positions entail and how their power should be used," Gage said. "We sure don't want a vigilante attitude. We, as shifters, are not outside the law. Shifters need to understand they are accountable for their actions just like humans."

"There have been instances I monitored over the years where a shifter was arrested by human law enforcement. They either served time in a local jail or state prison," Roman said. "I'm not sure whether they served their sentence, or managed to shift unnoticed and escaped as their animal. This task force needs to be formed immediately to take care of this."

After everyone left, Ari and Eddie wandered down the hall to Eddie's new room.

"Look at your pretty walls!" Ari exclaimed.

"It's beautiful!" Eddie said. She held her tiny hands to her heart.

Roman and Gage came into the room.

"Oh, wow, the paint looks great," Roman said.

"Look, they lowered the closet poles," Gage said.

Ari crossed the room and looked into the closet. "I hadn't thought of that. Emilio was one step ahead of us."

"It's so pretty!" Eddie said.

"Your furniture will be here tomorrow. Are you excited?" Ari asked.

"I've never had my own bed!" Eddie said. "Mommy and I slept on the sofa."

"Mommy didn't have a bed?" Roman asked.

Eddie shook her head. "Our sofa was stinky."

"Did you and your mother sleep in the car?" Gage asked.

Eddie's eyes opened wide. "Yes! Mommy said it was like camping! I didn't like it very much, and I was hungry."

"I'm going to fold clothes. Why don't you two keep Eddie company?" Ari sent, *Be gentle with your questions, okay?*

We understand, Gage sent.

After I put her to bed, we can work on the task force and get that email sent.

Do you think we should put the members to a vote—like a ballot? Roman asked.

That sounds better. We'll contact all the leaders to put this into action immediately. Should this be done by region or by state? Ari asked.

Region. We don't want one from each state. That would be way too many members, and the task force would probably develop infighting, Gage said.

Okay, we have a plan. You two can work on this while I fold clothes. I'll take Eddie with me, Ari sent. *This needs to be put in place immediately, so we can apprehend those bastards.*

"Eddie, would you like to help me fold and hang your clothes?" Ari asked. "Gage and Roman have work to do right now."

"Okay," Eddie said. "I love my new clothes!"

THE HOUSE PHONE RANG. ARI GOT UP AND GRABBED THE cordless phone. "Hello?" She listened. "Send them up!"

She turned to Eddie. "Guess what? Your furniture's here!" Eddie got out of her booster seat and rushed to the elevator, squealing all the way.

245

A**FTER THE FURNITURE DELIVERY PEOPLE LEFT,** E**DDIE** settled into her sitting room to explore her new furniture and play with her new toys, while Ari focused on shifter business. The lobby called to announce Ms. Moore of CPS.

Ari called out to Roman and Gage in somewhat of a panic. *They're here! CPS!*

Don't panic, Gage sent.

Be right there, Roman sent.

Gage met Ari at the elevator as the door opened. A woman in her late thirties or early forties with shoulder-length, wavy brown hair appeared stunned as she took in the penthouse. She wore a below-the-knee pencil skirt, a button-down blouse and a little jacket, along with practical two-inch heels.

Roman came down the hall and joined his partners.

"Hello, Mr. Davenport?" She looked from Gage to Roman.

"That would be me. And you are?"

"Angie Moore with CPS," she said. She was still in the elevator.

"Please come in," Ari said. She motioned their guest to the living room where they all sat.

"I'm sure the court informed you that I would do a home inspection, and to meet the child to determine if this is the best place for her," Ms. Moore said.

"We understand," Roman said. "Detective Valk mentioned it as well as Judge Dillhunt. How would you like to proceed? With an interview or a tour?"

"Why don't you show me around and let me meet Edris," Ms. Moore said.

They all stood. Roman waved a hand toward the kitchen. "As you can see, this is the kitchen, with a butler's pantry where the laundry facilities are, the dining room, and this is the living area. Each of us has his own suite, including Eddie."

They walked down the main hall and stopped at Roman's suite. "This is my suite, with my home office beyond in the sitting room."

"My goodness! I have never seen such an enormous bed before," Ms. Moore said.

"It's custom," Roman said.

He guided the social worker back to the main hallway, and they looked at Gage's suite. Then they arrived at Eddie's domain.

"Did you take custody of the child yesterday?" Ms. Moore asked.

"Yes, that's correct," Roman said.

"Was there another child living here previously?" Ms. Moore asked.

"No, why do you ask?" Roman asked.

"It seems this space was set up awfully fast," Ms. Moore said.

"Why would that even be an issue?" Ari asked.

"It seems unusual," Ms. Moore said.

"Ms. Moore, we were extremely fortunate to find a crew who could put this together for us so quickly," Roman said.

"Are we the first wealthy people you have interviewed?" Gage asked.

Her eyes ground into Gage's. "Yes, but that's irrelevant."

Don't say anything else, Gage. She seems to be fishing for excuses, Roman sent.

Gage's jaw was tight as he curbed wanting to speak his mind. *I can sense she has a problem with money.*

Roman's eyes shifted to Ari. She appeared livid.

Ari, you need to look calm. We'll talk about this later.

Ari took a deep breath and relaxed her face.

Roman guided the woman into the sitting room where Eddie was playing. "Eddie, we have company. Can you come say hello to Ms. Moore?"

Eddie jumped up and ran up to them. "Hello, Ms. Moore. Do you want to play with my dollhouse?"

"I would love to!" she turned to Roman, Gage and Ari. "I won't be long. I'll ask Edris to bring me back to the living room."

"No problem," Roman said. He closed the bedroom door on their way out.

Eddie took Ms. Moore's hand and led her to the table. "Would you like to sit down?"

"I'd love to. What a beautiful room, Edris. Do you like living here?"

"You can call me Eddie. That's what Mommy called me," Eddie said. "I love my new room." She jumped up and ran to the bedroom. "I've never had a bed before! Isn't it beautiful?"

Ms. Moore followed Eddie to the bedroom. "Your mother didn't have a bed for you to sleep in?"

"No, we slept on the lumpy sofa or in the car," Eddie said.

"Where's your father?" Ms. Moore asked.

"I never had a daddy, but Roman and Gage will be my new daddies and Ari will be my mommy! I love them!" Eddie exclaimed. "I have two big brothers! Know what their names are?"

"No. Tell me," Ms. Moore said.

"Kevin and Jason. They're real big." Eddie jumped, hand over her head.

"Why don't you take me back to the living room now so I can talk to your new family," Ms. Moore said.

"Okay," Eddie said. She took hold of Ms. Moore's hand and led her out of the room and down the hall to the living room.

Eddie dropped Ms. Moore's hand and ran to Ari and crawled into her lap and hugged her.

"Everything seems in order," Ms. Moore said, as she looked over at the group on the sofa.

"Can we answer any questions?" Gage asked.

"I don't have any questions at this time. All that's left for me to do is complete the paperwork," Ms. Moore said.

They all stood, Ari with Eddie in her arms. They walked Ms. Moore to the elevator, and she left.

Eddie squirmed to get down. "I'm going back to my room now."

"Okay. I know where to find you," Ari said, poking Eddie in the side to tickle her.

Eddie ran back to her room.

"Well?" Ari grilled Roman with a questioning look. "Did you pick up on anything?"

"She seemed fixated on my bed—I don't mean about getting in it with me, but it bothered her."

"What would that have to do with anything?" Ari felt a wave of possessiveness toward Roman.

He placed his hand on her arm. "There's nothing to worry about. You shouldn't feel threatened by that woman. The only woman who will ever be in this bed, or in my heart, is you."

They returned to the living room and sat, the mood definitely touchy.

"Don't you think this visit was rather quick?" Gage asked. "I expected her to interview us thoroughly to determine our worthiness as parents."

"She wasn't here long," Ari said. "I thought she would spend a good amount of time with Eddie."

"It seems rather strange," Roman said. "She also seemed fixated on our wealth. I'd think that would be a bonus for adoption. We can provide a wonderful home environment, education and security."

Ari fretted.

"Don't worry, honey," Gage said. "We've got this custody thing."

"Jason has set up accounts for the new shifter task force. We're flying them in soon, and we'll go over the details. Then Sherm or Lonnie will fly with them to Springfield, Massachusetts, to get those bastards into custody," Roman said.

"How many representatives are there?" Gage asked.

"Six. Jason's set up overnight accommodations for them in the building. We can wine and dine them," Roman said.

"Jason is a fast worker," Ari said. "That boy and his brother have changed so much I hardly recognize them."

Gage moved in for a kiss. Roman wrapped his arms around Ari.

Don't start anything! We have a child here, remember? Ari sent.

Roman and Gage sprang away from Ari.

No more spontaneous sex in the living room! Gage sent.

Do we need to lock the door when we're in bed together? Roman asked.

"Let's go to Pomodoro's for dinner, then stop at Target," Ari said.

They gathered up Eddie and rode the elevator down to the lobby, then stepped out to the garage. Roman buckled Eddie into her new car seat and tugged on it to make sure it was secure. He was taking his parenting responsibilities seriously.

They rode to the restaurant two streets over and piled inside.

"Well, who might this little Goldilocks be?" the maître d' asked.

"This is our new charge, Edris," Roman said. "She likes to be called Eddie."

The maître d' reached out his hand. "It is a pleasure to meet you, Ms. Eddie."

Eddie giggled as she shook his hand. "We're very hungry."

"Let us get you started right away then!" the maître d' said with a smirk. He snapped his fingers, and one of the staff produced a booster chair. He led them to a table and let them settle in.

"Eddie, let's go over the menu, shall we?" Ari perused the child's portion of the menu. "There's macaroni and cheese, spaghetti and meatballs, a hamburger patty with French fries, or chicken noodle soup."

"Mac and cheese!" Eddie said.

"Okay. Will you eat a little salad as well?" Ari asked. Eddie scrunched up her nose.

"Salad is an important part of the meal," Ari said. "Your body needs fresh greens every day."

"Oh, okay."

"How about honey mustard salad dressing? It's yummy," Ari said.

Eddie nodded.

The server brought a bread basket and took their orders.

He supplied Eddie with a placemat and crayons.

They ate their meal, then drove to Target. Ari steered them to the baby department, where they picked up a child monitor for each room of the house. Then she hunted for chimes. They found them in the garden department, and Ari chose a delicate, small set to place on the doorknob in Roman's room.

"Should we get one for each of our bedrooms?" Gage asked.

"We've never ventured into your bedroom, Gage," Ari said. "But that's not a bad idea." She snatched two more sets from the stand.

251

Roman read the boxes with the baby monitors. "We need batteries."

They returned home, and Roman and Gage worked on setting up the baby monitors for each room. Ari slipped the chimes out of their packages and hung one on the inside of their bedroom doors.

Two days later, Roman and Gage's phones dinged messages as they ate breakfast at the kitchen table.

"Our people acted fast on this committee project. They understood the importance, acted immediately and communicated with their people," Gage said.

"Now we need to send the details about this situation. Everyone can fly into Philly and gather here," Roman said.

"Tell Jason to set up an account for the travel. Remember, some of these people don't have the funds to pay for travel expenses, and this would be a shifter expense, not a Panther Industries expense," Ari said.

"You're right. Need to separate the two," Roman said.

CHAPTER TWENTY-THREE

THE LIMO DELIVERED THE TASK FORCE MEMBERS TO THE high-rise. They stopped at the front desk where Leander met them. He secured their badges, which also allowed them entry into their accommodation.

They rode the elevator up to the twenty-eighth floor to the Panther Securities domain. Leander led them to a large conference room and got them settled. Sherm, Roman, and Gage joined them. Leander made introductions.

Ari joined them after a few minutes. "Vanessa, Dr. Tanner's wife, is watching Eddie for a little while."

She looked around the table. Four men and two women. She was happy to see that the communities did not choose all men. Especially under the circumstances. She hoped these people were parents who could understand and appreciate the gravity of the situation.

Roman jumped in. "We thought it prudent to establish a non-biased task force to conduct investigations and act as a court of law when the need arose."

"A few days ago, four wolves killed a woman close to my private property. They were all shifters," Roman explained.

"They killed a woman?" a man asked. He was shocked to hear such a thing.

"As bad as that is, it's not the worst," Sherm said. "They abandoned a three-year-old child by her dead mother, close to a highway."

The six visitors gasped.

"It gets worse," Ari said. "One of those wolves was the child's father."

One man jumped up. "How could he do should a thing?" He settled into his chair and raked his hair with one hand.

"We don't know," Gage said. "He wasn't involved with his child. She was unaware she had a father, and her mother never mentioned him or his animal."

Sherm queued up the camera pictures he had shared with Roman, Gage and Ari, along with new pictures of the attack.

When Ari saw the pictures of the wolves attacking the woman, and of Eddie shifting to her tiger kitten, she slammed a fist on the table. "I'll tear that bastard apart!"

"Stand in line," a woman growled.

"My team has located the father, Edmund Dovensky, in Springfield, Massachusetts, and we have identified the other participants," Sherm said. "We can do this one of two ways. I can send in my team to apprehend these men and bring them back, or your task force can travel with us. My team members are not shifters, but I have a special ops team that works with the shifter community."

"Since this task force is new, we need to determine how we will handle this. In the past, Roman and I were judge, jury, punisher and executioner," Gage said. "We feel we need a little distance."

"That's understandable, Your Majesty," a man said. "We discussed our roles among ourselves, and we take our positions seriously."

"We would be happy to accompany you to Springfield," the other woman said, "because we are more than capable of handling these wolves ourselves. But we will have to keep our emotions under control. So, it's best for Sherm's team to do the extraction of these loathsome bastards. Otherwise, they may not make it back to Reading."

They discussed the mother, Clariss Sullivan, the DNA test, and the absentee father. Sherm showed pictures of the deplorable condition of the vehicle and everything his people had discovered over the course of the past couple of days.

ARI SUGGESTED TO GAGE AND ROMAN THAT THEY HOST A dinner party so the task force could meet Eddie, and everyone could get to know each other. Leander, Sherm, Jason, and Kevin attended as well.

They learned that Agatha was a gray wolf from Michigan. She was in the marijuana business and went from eking out an existence two years ago to earning a six-figure salary.

Mr. Dundy was a duck from Florida. He wanted people to call him Mr. Dundy. He was an attorney for senior citizens and had spent the past forty years defending them against unjust fights, sometimes against their own greedy families.

Jules was a bear from San Francisco who owned an art gallery. He dressed artistically chic in a French way.

Susan was a janitor at a middle school in Colorado, and spent time at the school as a calico cat.

Kyle was a spotted mongrel dog from Mississippi. He played the trumpet in a jazz band and thought of himself as a Louis Armstrong type of man.

And Francis was a stag from Upstate New York who plowed driveways for a living in the winter and mowed yards in the spring and summer.

None of them had ever seen a king cobra or a liger before, and stories floated around the dining room table.

"It shocked me when I shifted into my liger," Ari said. "Everyone had told me that my Tothar line was so weak that I didn't have an animal. Same with my sons." Ari turned to her life partners. "I really need to go see my aunt before it's too late."

"Make the arrangements. Let's go after this is all settled." Roman nodded with determination.

"There was nothing more awe-inspiring than my mother carrying Roman down the tower stairs in his panther form," Kevin told the group. "I'll never forget it. She's huge, and the most beautiful animal I've ever seen."

Eddie liked Susan, the calico. "I'm a kitten!" She dashed off to her room and returned with her stuffed tiger. "This is what I look like!"

"You're a tiger kitten?" Susan asked. "I'll bet you'll grow up to be a beautiful tiger!"

Eddie said matter-of-factly. "I'm going to marry Sherm!"

Sherm shrugged. "What can I say? All the ladies love me."

Roman, Gage and Lender delivered the task force members to their apartments when they called it a night. They agreed to meet in the lobby at eight the next morning for a quick trip to get breakfast. From there, they would drive to Reading Regional Airport to take on the grueling task of rounding up the wolves.

Sherm headed up Bruce's team instead of Lonnie, who was

out of the country on a mission. Sherm's team was in full commando gear and armed with tranq guns in case things got touchy.

Jason had to engage Travis and Kevin to line up a second vehicle in Springfield to haul the wolves to the jet. They figured the wolves would be unruly, so they required a reinforced van similar to one that hauls prisoners. When everything was in place, they began their extractions.

Edmund Dovensky was the first wolf they approached. He was a welder, and they found him on a job site, behind a welder's mask wielding his torch, cutting through metal.

Sherm approached the supervisor with a fifty-dollar bill for no interference or explanation. They hauled Dovensky outside, where he was thrust in front of the task force.

Mr. Dundy read him his shifter rights, and Dovensky was handcuffed with zip cuffs and placed in the reinforced van.

Next stop was for Gerald Ford Oatham, who lived in a project and didn't think very much of hygiene.

"You are a disgrace to your name," Mr. Dundy snarled to the wasted specimen of a shifter.

They collected the last two wolves without any problems. Bruce drove the criminals in the van with two members of his team, while Sherm drove the rest of their party back to the jet. They returned to Reading and brought the wolves to a warehouse that looked like a jail in a western movie.

Roman, Gage, Sherm and the task force members inspected the work Wendel Smith had done constructing the ten cells.

"Damn, this looks just like the cells over at the Reading jail," Gage said.

"If we're going to be the capital of the shifter world in the US, we will need this facility to handle situations that come up," Roman said.

"This is much nicer than some jails I've seen in Florida," Mr. Dundy said.

The task force met Larry, the Kodiak bear that Roman had appointed as jailer. Everyone in the community knew how intimidating he was, so he was the perfect jailer. He wouldn't tolerate nonsense.

Larry took his new job seriously. He stood in front of the cells. "Listen up. I'm only saying this once, and you'd better not have your ears stopped up with wax," Larry bellowed.

"My name is Larry, and I'll be your jailer during the day. My animal is a Kodiak bear. Kodiaks are second largest to polar bears. While in my animal form, I weigh around fourteen-hundred pounds, and when I stand on my hind legs, I reach around nine-feet eight inches tall. You cannot overtake me, not even all four of you together, so don't even contemplate the notion."

"Until your trial, you will receive three meals a day. As you can see, besides your cots, your cells are fitted with a sink, a plastic cup for drinking, a toilet and a shower head. You will receive a clean towel every morning. I suggest you hang it up if you plan to shower again at night."

"An attorney will be assigned to defend you. I will award you one phone call per day for good behavior. If you require medical attention, Dr. Tanner will take care of you. This is not a luxury jail. You will not have Netflix or Amazon Prime. There is no TV here. If you wanted entertainment, you should have thought of that before you committed your crime."

"My wife will prepare your meals. She's also a very large bear, and she doesn't like wolves, so don't tempt her. Your nighttime jailer will be Big Bear Muchisky. Don't make him mad. He can pry the bars apart with his bare hands and may forget to keep you alive until your trial."

Naomi, Larry's wife, entered the warehouse with arms

loaded with linens. She curtsied to Roman and Gage, approached her husband, smooched him, then went directly to the cells. She passed sheets and blankets through the bars of each cell. "I'll return with pillows."

Moments later, she came back with child-sized pillows and handed them out.

"I need to know if any of you have any food allergies," she said.

"I'm allergic to tomatoes," Gerald said.

Naomi nodded. "Anyone else? No? Okay, then. I'll see you at suppertime."

"What about lunch?" Edmund asked.

Naomi looked at her husband, then turned to the large group.

"Can you make them sandwiches, Naomi?" Gage asked.

"Sure," she turned to face the cells. "Your choices are ham and cheese or bologna and cheese. Mayo and mustard, or one or the other alone."

"You're treating them too nice," Mr. Dundy said. "They get what they get, no asking them their preferences."

"I can do that," Naomi said as she left the warehouse.

The task force, Sherm, Roman, and Gage, left the warehouse and returned to the Panther Industries building. Roman led them into the ground-floor meeting area and texted Jason to arrange for food.

"Should we have a worldwide tribunal?" Roman asked the group.

"We need to set precedence's," Mr. Dundy said. "Our kind has been loosely formed, at best, until you two became our kings. I like the organization and the chain of command you've established."

"The people in my region feel more comfortable now that you have taken the guesswork out of what Mr. Dundy said—the chain of command," Agatha said. "If we can't settle something locally, we can petition you to hear us."

"Who will represent these cretins?" Mr. Dundy asked.

Sherm worked his phone. "I'm having Jason look at the list to see if there are any local criminal attorneys. If not, we will have to go to the regions and fly someone in. Should they each have an attorney, or one for all of them?"

"Ideally, it would be one attorney per client, but if we have to, we could use one for the four of them," Roman said.

"Also, who will pay the attorneys?" Jules asked.

Roman and Gage shared a look, weighing the subject.

"We've set up a special account for any shifter-related expenses," Gage said. "The fund will pay the attorney fees and their travel expenses."

The task force members shared nods.

"I'd say we should move forward. Find attorneys, allow them time to question and prepare, see the evidence," Mr. Dundy said. "Who will be the prosecutor?"

"The tribunal—the entire shifter community will have an opportunity to cross-examine these men, then pronounce or recommend their fate. If there are several suggestions, then we vote on the final outcome," Roman said.

"For now, we should be able to go home, right?" Susan asked. "This sounds like a long process."

"I think you're right. We should be able to conduct any of our business online with video calls," Gage said.

IT WAS A LENGTHY PROCESS FINDING ATTORNEYS WHO were in-between cases. The warehouse had modifications to include a glassed-in room with a TV, phone, and internet to conduct attorney/client meetings. The glass was shatterproof.

There was also a wall constructed of wood and sheetrock that hid the jail from any outside visitors. Sophisticated security coding kept the jail and the inmates safe.

Mostly, the inmates were not a lot of trouble. They were escorted once a day to the secured glass room to make their allotted ten-minute phone call. They scrambled the first week in captivity to contact their people. It was obvious they would lose their lodgings because they were incarcerated. If they wanted to save their belongings, they had to find someone willing to pack up and store them.

Sherm installed a sophisticated intercom system on the outside of the jail wall that recorded visitors by way of voice and visuals. When anyone visited the inmates, they were frisked and gone over with a metal detector wand. The jail had also bought Snoozy, a dog trained in weapons detection.

Edmund Dovensky received visitors two weeks after being incarcerated. A young woman with two small children arrived at the jail. She and her children were documented and vetted as safe. They were escorted into the glass room, and Edmund was brought in.

The woman cried when she wrapped her arms around him. "Mundy, why are you in jail? What happened?"

"Daddy! Daddy!" the kids cried out.

"You shouldn't be here, Virginia," Dovensky said. He kissed her and the children.

"Please tell me what kind of trouble you're in," Virginia said.

"You need to move on, find someone else to take care of you and the kids," he said. "I won't be able to come home—ever again."

She stared at him in disbelief. "Mundy, what am I supposed to do? Our kids need their father. I need you. I can't work and take care of the kids at the same time."

"Look, I did something terrible. You need to go and not come back."

"Do you have a lawyer? Maybe he can help you?" she asked.

"No one can help me. I was stupid. Get in touch with my parents. Tell them you need help. I can't help you from here," he said.

He looked through the glass at Larry, who was standing facing the room. "She needs to leave."

"But Mundy, we still have the rest of our visitation hour," Virginia exclaimed.

"There's nothing left for us, Virginia. When you find out what I did, you'll hate me, and I deserve that."

Larry opened the door. He pointed to Edmund. "Move back." He escorted the woman and children out of the glass room and out of the jailed area, then he returned to bring Edmund to his cell.

"How could you possibly have done what you did? Kill the mother of your child, then abandon your little girl near a highway?" Larry asked.

"She contacted me for money, and I couldn't let my wife find out I had another family," Edmund said.

"Now none of your kids have a father," Larry said as he locked Edmund in his cell.

CHAPTER TWENTY-FOUR

SEVERAL WEEKS PASSED. AN ALERT WAS SENT TO THE worldwide shifter community announcing the tribunal. It was the first ever of its kind. Not only did shifters have to obey human laws, but now there was a system in place for their kind.

The day of the tribunal arrived. They brought the four criminals into the Panther Industries meeting rooms on the ground floor, via the back door by the loading dock. They wore chains and handcuffs.

The attorneys were present, and the local community had a presence. The regions across the US and territories, Europe, Australia, New Zealand, the Middle and Far East, and Russia were present via online meeting venues.

A loud buzz arose in the room from the local participants and the viewers.

"Settle down," Roman demanded.

Gage, Ari, Roman, and others noticed how packed the Italian palazzo looked on the screen.

Alaska was having difficulty connecting, as was New Zealand, but after several minutes the proceedings began.

Mr. Dundy presented the case. He spoke directly to the camera. "Please hold your comments until this proceeding is over." He queued up the camera footage showing the attack and slaughter. Everyone saw how Eddie had shifted and tried to help her mother. Margaret testified.

Edmund's wife, Virginia, her parents, and Edmund's parents cried in disbelief as they watched in horror from the newsfeed. They were shocked beyond belief when the heinous crime was revealed.

Next up were the attorneys and their clients. The three wolves followed Edmund Dovensky, their pack alpha. They were guilty of allowing the alpha to go forward with the plan instead of contacting the Tothar kings.

Mundy had no defense. His actions were premeditated, as he had discussed what to do with his pack of wolves a week before the event. He killed the mother of his child and abandoned the child in a dangerous location.

Mr. Dundy announced that it was time for the tribunal to assess the crime and determine punishment. He reminded world viewers that shifters lived a very long time, and that this fact should be taken into consideration when determining sentences. The trial would resume the next day.

After the video feed was offline, Mr. Dundy announced that the prisoners would be returned to jail. The Reading shifter community would compile suggestions as to the fate of the guilty. The worldwide votes would be gathered and merged with the US votes. From there, they would sentence the four criminals.

The next day, the suggested sentences were discussed and listed.

1. Burn them alive

2. Hang them upside down with throats slit to drain out
3. Twenty years for every bite mark on the woman's body
4. Twenty lashes with a whip, then jailed for life
5. Hang by the neck in the forest and left to rot
6. Branded as murderers and set free after a specified amount of time
7. Branded as murderers and jailed for life
8. Electrocution
9. Tortured and beaten for one solid decade
10. Lethal injection
11. Walled up in a cave and left to starve

After they posted the suggestions for all to see, discussions started. They threw out numbers one, nine, and eleven. Who exactly would be the people to carry out that sentence?

Everyone thought numbers eight and ten were too easy a way out for these criminals. They were either going to hang from a tree, be beaten, branded, or jailed for life.

Arguments ranged throughout the US and the world. Numbers three, four, and seven were debated heavily. The general consensus was why should the prisoners receive three meals a day for the rest of their lives if they received life sentences? Jail was too comfortable.

If they were hung, who would be responsible for the bodies? Where would they be hung so as not to be discovered by humans?

All that remained of the suggested sentences was branding and release. No one was thrilled with that, because the wolves could easily return to their previous lives if they were welcomed back within their communities.

One final suggestion that came from the African continent was *an eye for an eye* type of punishment.

Gowon, a shifter from Nigeria offered a solution. "If these criminals are branded and released, they should also run through a gauntlet of shifters, where they would receive punishment from the community."

That suggestion received unanimous approval.

"If anyone from around the world would like to take part in the gauntlet, you have a week to plan and fly into Philadelphia," Mr. Dundy announced.

EDDIE WAS IN HER ROOM PLAYING WITH HER ANIMAL TOYS. Gage was napping on the sofa in the living room. Roman was downstairs taking care of Panther Industries business, and Ari was reading in her suite when the house phone rang.

"Hello?" Ari answered. "I'll be right down." She peeked in on Eddie and saw Gage sprawled on the sofa, lost in dreams. She took the elevator down to the lobby.

"Hi, guys. How's it going?" she asked the guards and the receptionist.

"Busy day," the receptionist said.

One of the guards handed Ari the envelope. It was from the court. She frowned as she headed back to the elevator. As the car journeyed back up to the penthouse, she opened the envelope. Her jaw dropped. Anger flushed her face.

She stormed out of the elevator and called out to Roman to get back upstairs immediately. Gage jerked awake from her silent call.

"What's going on? What's wrong?" Gage said, as he sat up on the sofa.

The elevator dinged Roman's arrival. "What happened?"

"CPS has denied our temporary custody of Eddie," Ari railed.

"What?" Roman snatched the letter out of Ari's hand. "Let me see that." He read in silence, anger building as his eyes wandered over the lines. "This is bullshit. No one is going to remove that child from this apartment."

He pulled out his phone and made a call. "Judge Dillhunt. Ask her to call Roman Davenport. Tell her CPS has denied our custody application, and I'd appreciate it if she could check into this for me."

"What is it that's inappropriate for us or this apartment?" Ari asked.

"That Moore woman was hung up on the bed," Gage said.

"If that's what she's basing her report on, I have news for her," Roman said. "That won't stand up in court."

Eddie came out of her room. She felt the tension in the room. "What's the matter? I felt your anger in my room."

Roman, Gage and Ari sat down on the floor around Eddie.

"It's just adult business, honey," Gage said.

"There's nothing to worry about. Adults sometimes have discussions that get a little heated," Roman said.

"Don't worry, these things happen all the time, and no one is mad at you," Ari said.

"Okay," Eddie said. "Can I have some hot chocolate?"

"That sounds like a good idea. Who wants some?" Ari said.

"Do we have marshmallow cream?" Roman asked.

They sat at the kitchen table drinking hot chocolate with a dollop of marshmallow cream and nibbling on cookies.

Roman got up and put his cup in the sink. "I've got to go back downstairs. I'll let you know when I hear from the judge." He kissed Ari, then bent and placed a kiss on Eddie's cheek.

"How come you didn't kiss Gage?" Eddie asked.

"Gage and I don't kiss. We kiss Ari," Roman said.

Gage tried to hold back a laugh, but he ended up snorting.

"Do you kiss Jason and Kevin?" Eddie asked.

"No, we shake hands or hug," Roman said.

"Oh," Eddie said.

"I'll be back in a little while," Roman said. He entered the elevator and rode down to Jason's office.

"Sorry, there's a delicate issue I'm trying to take care of," Roman said.

"What's going on?" Jason asked.

"This CPS woman doesn't think we're a good choice for temporary custody of Eddie," Roman said.

"What the fuck's that all about? What could she possibly have a problem with?" Jason asked.

"My bed," Roman said. "Your mom practically went off about that."

"Your bed? What does that have to do with anything?" Jason asked.

Roman's phone buzzed with an incoming call. "I've got to take this. Hello, Judge Dillhunt." He listened. "Donna, what the hell does my bed have to do with our ability to raise a child? I've had that bed for a very long time and paid a lot of money for it and the custom sheets. To begin with, Ms. Moore had an issue because we furnished Eddie's room with a little girl's furniture overnight." He listened.

"Oh, okay. I'm sorry, but I've been riled up about this. Ms. Moore must have personal issues, but I won't stand by and let her take those issues out on me. Are we good then?" Roman nodded while he listened. "Thanks, Donna. I appreciate it. Will there be any problem for us to proceed with applying for adoption?"

When the call ended, Roman let loose a loud sigh.

"Why did that woman give you a hard time about the furniture?" Jason asked.

"She probably has money issues. Rich people can make things happen at the snap of their fingers. She had a difficult time digesting that the furniture was bought and delivered almost immediately. Thank God she never asked about the room being painted so fast," Roman said. "Let me text Ari and Gage."

He worked his phone and put it away.

"So, where did we leave off with the shifter community funds?" Roman asked.

"I've transferred a million dollars from one of the Italian accounts," Jason said. "We will pay all the task force and jail expenses from that account."

"This year, I'd like to set up a Christmas and other holiday fund." Roman said. "I thought each community could have funds to throw a party with a full holiday meal. We could create a fund for the US, and Donatello and Marco could set something up for overseas."

"I'll need to know who specifically to send money to for each of these locations," Jason said.

"Work with your mom on this," Roman said. "She has this huge database and has talked to a lot of different people."

"Will do," Jason said.

"I'd better go," Roman said. He clasped Jason on the shoulder.

ARI CARRIED EDDIE TO SANDY'S OFFICE. SHE KNOCKED ON the open door frame to get Sandy's attention.

"Hi, Sandy, do you have a minute?" Ari asked.

Sandy scooted around her desk. "Who is this little angel?" She tickled Eddie.

"This is Edris, but we call her Eddie. She's going to be our little girl," Ari said. "Should we wait until the adoption papers come through to add her to our benefits?"

PEOPLE ARRIVED FROM ACROSS THE COUNTRY, AND SOME came from across the ocean to take part in the gauntlet run for the criminals. Wendel Smith prepared branding irons—an M for the forehead and the word Murderer for the back at the shoulder blade area.

Gowon, the man from Nigeria, arrived at the Panther Industries building at six-forty-five in the morning. The thirty-year-old was dressed in traditional clothing, including a gold and white fila (cap) and a gold and white three-piece agbada. The agbada consisting of a long-sleeved white shirt with gold embroidery, a pair of white pants called sokoto, and a white wide-sleeved robe with intricate gold embroidery.

The guard stared at the man for several seconds, then came to his senses. "May I help you?"

Gowon spoke in a beautiful, lilting voice in English. "Good day to you, sir. I am here to see my king, Roman Davenport."

The guard continued to stare at Gowon. "Is he expecting you?"

"Most definitely!" Gowon said.

The guard picked up the phone and called the penthouse. "I'm sorry to disturb you, but there's a gentleman here to see you." He looked at Gowon. "What's your name, and where are you from?"

"I am Gowon Adebayo from Nigeria," Gowon said.

The guard repeated the information over the phone. "I'll send him right up." He came around the reception desk. "The elevator will take you to the penthouse, where you will be met."

He led Gowon to the elevator, inserted his card for the penthouse and stood back while the man entered the car.

Gowan, whose animal was a brush-tailed porcupine, was greeted by his kings and queen as soon as the elevator door opened.

"Welcome to the United States, Gowon," Roman said. He shook the man's hand.

"King Roman!" Gowon bowed low.

Gage shook Gowon's hand, then introduced Ari. They settled in the living room.

"Would you like to join us for breakfast, Gowon?" Ari asked.

"I do not want you to go to any trouble for me," he said.

"It's breakfast," Gage said. "Do you eat bacon, eggs and toast?"

"Yes, I eat all those foods," Gowon said.

"How about coffee?" Ari asked. "We drink café mocha, but we can prepare anything."

"I would like to join you for a traditional American breakfast." Gowon smiled widely. Excitement wafted off him.

"Were you the one who suggested the gauntlet?" Roman asked.

"Yes. I have taught many cultures the correct use of the gauntlet for punishment," Gowon said.

Eddie came down the hall in her princess pajamas, rubbing sleep from her eyes. She perked up when she saw their company.

"Who are you?" She gently touched his robe. "You're beautiful!" She climbed onto her booster seat.

"Thank you! I'm Gowan from Africa. What is your name?"

"My name is Edris."

Ari raised an eyebrow. She turned back to the stove.

Gage was beside her. He shrugged.

"It is so nice to meet you, Edris," Gowon said.

They prepared breakfast, and they all sat at the table to eat.

"Tell us about your experience with the gauntlet," Roman said.

"The people can be in their human or animal forms—they can decide," he said. "There should be enough people so that there is no space between them. You don't want the punished to be able to slip through and try to run away."

"That makes sense. I'm sure there will be a lot of participants," Gage said.

"Sometimes, the ones being punished don't make it to the end of the gauntlet. That is a just punishment," Gowon said. "If they successfully make it to the end, they may not survive for long because of their injuries."

"Are those bad wolves going to be punished for hurting mommy?" Eddie asked.

Ari got up and came around to Eddie's chair. "Why don't we get you dressed, young lady. Roman and Gage can talk to Gowon like grownups."

"Okay. Can I wear my white dress with the pink tutu?" Eddie asked.

"That's a great choice," Ari said. "It's all clean and hanging up in your closet."

Roman, I'll let you explain the circumstances to Gowon.

Will do, he sent.

As soon as Ari had Eddie out of hearing range, Roman and Gage explained the whole scenario to their guest.

When Ari entered Eddie's room, she went to the closet and removed the dress from the hanger. She set Eddie down, pulled open a drawer, and retrieved underpants. She helped Eddie to dress.

"Why didn't you ask Gowon to call you, Eddie?"

"He's a king!" Eddie said.

Roman, Eddie said Gowon was a king.

Where'd she get that from? Gage asked.

"How do you know he's a king?" Ari asked.

Eddie shrugged. "I don't know."

She said she doesn't know. Wait until we come back out there.

"Look in your mirror! You're dressed like a princess!" Ari said.

Eddie opened the closet door and stood in front of the full-length mirror. "This dress is beautiful!" She threw her arms around Ari's legs and hugged her. "Thank you for being my new mommy. I love you!"

"I love you, too! Let's go show Roman, Gage and Gowon how pretty you look."

They held hands and walked down the hall to the living room.

"There's a princess in the room!" Gage boasted.

Eddie's face was alight with a huge smile. She twirled in her bare feet.

Roman got up and grabbed Eddie in a hug. He kissed her cheek. "What a pretty dress!"

"So, Gowon, Eddie said you were a king. Is that true?" Ari asked.

Gowon started. He looked from Eddie to the others in the room. "I have not been a king for hundreds of years. How did she know?"

"She said she didn't know," Ari said.

"We'll have to explore that," Gage said. "Might be an interesting skill that will develop as she grows up."

"Did the reception desk assign you accommodations in the building?" Roman asked.

"No, I checked into the hotel down the street," Gowon said.

"Please, let us put you up here in the building. We have

several suites, and you would be very comfortable," Roman said.

"That is very kind of you. I will check out of my hotel this morning."

"Stop at the front desk. They'll assign you a suite and give you a cardkey for the elevator and your room," Roman said. "Do you need help?"

"I should be fine," Gowon said. "I only brought two pieces of luggage."

CHAPTER TWENTY-FIVE

INCLUDING THE LOCALS WHO WANTED TO TAKE PART, TWO-hundred three people arrived for the branding and the gauntlet. Ari made people double up in the vacant suites in the high-rise, and they filled a nearby hotel.

Roman, Gage, Leander, Sherm and Gowon worked out the logistics for the day before the event. A fire pit was created at the end of Roman's private road to the house in the woods.

People lined up on both sides of the road. A prisoner van was parked on the grass with the rear door facing the gauntlet. Edmund Dovensky, Gerald Ford Oatham, Robby Keene and Cezar Ramirez, all shackled and handcuffed, peered out the reinforced window at the long line of shifters.

"Jesus, Mundy! How the fuck we going to survive this?" Gerry was spitting mad.

"They're going to brand us then beat the shit out of us!" Robby wanted to pound Mundy into the ground for talking him into his plan.

"You're the worst alpha on the planet," Cezar stated. "If I make it through this, I never want to see your stupid ass again."

Gage and Wendel checked the branding irons in the fire. They were red hot.

The task force members, along with Roman, Sherm, Atsa and Leander huddled close by discussing the best way to move forward.

"Haul them out one at a time," Atsa suggested. "They need to shift into their wolf for the branding, then they can shift back to human to run the gauntlet."

"We can't make them shift," Mr. Dundy said.

"If we brand them as humans, the brands won't show up in their wolf form," Leander said. "Remember Lisa?"

"We're not going to wait all day for them to cooperate," Roman said. "We need to get started."

"You guys go get in the line where you want to be. Lonnie, Bruce and the team will handle this," Sherm said.

Roman positioned himself at the far end of the line opposite Gowon. Kevin and Jason were opposite each other at the midpoint in the gauntlet. They were antsy to take their aggression out on the lowlife wolf shifters.

Ari and Gage were the last in line.

"Ari, you need to be at the end in case you shift into your liger. You're too dangerous to be in the middle of the group," Atsa said.

Lonnie and Bruce hauled Gerry out of the van and brought him before Sherm.

"It would be best for you to shift into your wolf for branding, then shift back to human to run the gauntlet," Sherm said. "It's up to you."

"What am I supposed to do after? How am I going to survive? I won't have any money or clothes or anything," Gerry asked.

"You should have thought about that a long time ago,"

Lonnie said. "You're a wolf. You'll have to be self-sufficient, catch your own food or starve and die if you survive today."

"Fucking Mundy." Gerry shifted to his wolf form.

Lonnie and Bruce removed the shackles and handcuffs, and they hauled Gerry to where Sherm and Wendel manned the brands at the fire pit. Lonnie had a firm hold of the wolf's scruff.

Two of Bruce's team stood at the back of the wolf and held him down. Sherm walked to the wolf and inserted a tracking chip into Gerry's scruff while Wendel pressed the M brand to the wolf's forehead.

The wolf screeched and howled in pain.

Wendel grabbed the other brand and pressed it across the wolf's shoulders.

They released the wolf. He lay on the ground panting, his eyes darting everywhere.

The crowd taunted him.

Guards were between him and the gauntlet—there was no escaping his punishment. Gerry pulled himself up onto all fours and stumbled for a minute. He knew he had to run fast to avoid as much pain as possible. He trembled as he stood ten feet from the start of the gauntlet.

Gerry whined as he faced his fate. He looked back at the van. He saw his pack-mates staring out the rear window. Gerry showed his teeth and snarled at them, turned and found his strength. He ran for all it was worth.

Teeth and claws came forth from the shifters. They mauled Gerald Ford Oatham through and through. He was a stumbling, bloody mess by the time he exited the gauntlet and disappeared into the woods.

Robby was next, then Cezar.

They finally hauled Edmund Dovensky out of the van and dealt with him. Whereas his pack put on a brave face as they contended with their brutal punishment, Mundy proved to be nothing but a big coward. He couldn't handle his fate. He didn't think he deserved what the tribunal handed out.

When the tribunal decided there would be no lengthy jail sentence, Mundy practically begged his attorney to help him out of the dire consequences. That's when he learned that his legal representative washed his hands of the case.

After surviving the branding, Edmund "Mundy" Dovensky stood on trembling legs and stared at the people lining the road. It shocked him to see his own father opposite his father-in-law in line, anxiously waiting for his turn. That's when everything dawned on him. He no longer had a family. He would not find comfort there.

He shifted to his human form and shot forward. A little past the midpoint, he fell down.

Gowon yelled to the members. "Pick him up. Don't leave him on the ground to catch his breath!"

The shifters grabbed Mundy and roughly hauled him to his feet and thrust him forward.

At the end of the gauntlet, Gowon stepped away from people. "Move away!"

Roman, Gage, Atsa and Ari stepped back and away.

As Mundy stumbled down the rest of the gauntlet, Gowon disrobed. His brush-tailed porcupine let loose of his quills into Mundy. The shifter screamed as quills covered him, head to toe. He dropped to all fours as he shifted into his wolf form and took off into the trees.

Sherm pulled out his laptop and brought up the tracking program Travis had created. He found the four dots on the map. Three together heading in one direction, and the fourth nowhere near the others. He was sure Edmund wouldn't be welcome in that circle ever again.

Ari yelled out to the people. "The buses will bring you back to Panther Industries. We have a nice meal set up in the event room downstairs. If you didn't bring your badge, get a temporary badge from the reception desk. No one is allowed past reception without a badge."

Roman joined Wendel, Sherm, Lonnie, and the team at the fire pit. Sherm poured a bucket of water over the hot coals. He stirred them to make sure there were no embers left.

"Wendel, can you hang on to the brands?" Roman asked.

"Sure. They'll be hanging on the wall in the forge. Hopefully, we'll never have to use them again." Wendel gathered the brands and his gear and stowed them in his pickup truck.

The buses headed out, followed by Wendel, the security team, and the royal family. As is typical, Leander brought up the rear. The cobra shifter took his responsibilities seriously.

They combined two event rooms with the doors slid open to hold the crowd. Ari, ever the gracious hostess, visited as many people, as possible while the army of servers delivered food and drinks to the tables.

Roman and Jason were in discussion with Gowon when Gage joined them.

"How did you do that with your quills?" Gage asked.

"It's like flexing a muscle," Gowon said. "I discovered this talent many decades ago. Few animals will approach a porcupine unless they are starving or sick. It's too much of a risk."

Ari wandered up to Roman and Gage. "I need to go pick up Eddie."

Roman hugged her to his side and kissed her forehead. "We'll leave in just a minute. Do you want to bring her here to meet people?"

"No. I don't want to take a chance that someone will mention her father," Ari said. "She's too young to understand what he did to her and her mother."

Roman nodded. "You're right. People would offer sympathies; she would never understand the tragedy."

SHERM AND LONNIE RETURNED TO THEIR DOMAIN ON THE twenty-eighth floor and headed directly to Travis' cubicle. Their eyes immediately zeroed-in on the surveillance monitor, where Lisa's and the wolves' tracking chips blinked on the screen. Lisa was still in Montana. Three of the wolves were just outside Roman's property boundaries. They appeared to be running for their lives.

The lone wolf was miles away in the opposite direction. It appeared that Edmund Dovensky would not join his pack.

"Keep an eye on this one," Sherm instructed Travis. "What about the other three?" Travis tapped the dots that depicted the three wolves.

"I feel strongly we don't have to worry about them," Sherm said.

"K." Travis returned to his current project. He was triangulating data for a team over in Siberia.

Two days later, Travis tapped on Sherm's office door. "What's up?" Sherm stretched.

"That one dot hasn't moved," Travis said. "Do you think that wolf is dead?"

Sherm hit the speakerphone and placed a call. "Gage, would you be able to fly a reconnaissance mission? The tracking device for Edmund Dovensky hasn't moved in two days." Sherm listened. "Okay."

He disconnected the call. "He's on his way down so you can show him where to fly."

The elevator dinged Gage's arrival. He walked into Sherm's office. "Could he be dead?"

"Can't think of any other reason he wouldn't have traveled any further than where he stopped a couple of days ago," Sherm said.

"Show me," Gage said.

They all returned to Travis' cubicle and looked at the monitor. Travis showed where the wolf was in relation to where the house in the woods stood.

"Okay. I'll fly out there and look around," Gage said. He rode the elevator back upstairs and searched for Roman. He found him in his sitting room at his desk.

"I'm going to fly out and check on Dovensky," Gage said. He explained what was going on. "Shut the sliders after me so Eddie doesn't go on the balcony."

Roman followed Gage to the living room. Gage kicked off his shoes, removed his socks and the rest of his clothes. He strode out to the patio and shifted into his eagle, leaped off the railing and soared into the air. He headed towards the mountains.

Roman shut the sliding glass doors and locked them. *I locked the doors, so holler when you return.*

Good idea, Gage sent.

GAGE'S GIGANTIC BALD EAGLE FLEW OVER THE CITY, HIGH in the sky. At this height, he would be mistaken for a regular bird, or perhaps a hawk, by onlookers on the ground. He headed to the mountains and circled the house in the woods to make sure everything was as it should be. Then he floated over the property across the private road to the cabins. Three vehicles were parked in front of the cabins, and he caught a woman shifting into a deer.

He continued on and veered to the East. When he figured

he was within the right area, he circled in the air, eyes on the ground. He made several fly-bys looking for the wolf or the human, whichever form he was in.

Gage spotted something on the ground and flew in for a closer look. He landed in a large oak tree and watched.

Dovensky sat naked on a patch of grass in a clearing. He appeared to be pulling quills out of his body. The murder brand across his back appeared to be scabbing over. Shifters healed quickly.

Gage waited for the man to lift his head. He recognized the M on his forehead, which was also scabbing over. He noticed small bones on the ground close by. The wolf must have caught small game and fed. Satisfied, Gage took to the sky and flew back to the penthouse.

I'm back!

Roman hurried to the sliding doors and unlocked them. Gage came in and dressed. "Let's go downstairs."

They went to Sherm's office.

"It appears he's made a camp." Gage reported what he had discovered. "I'm not comfortable with him being so close to the property."

"We've got cameras near the cabins and on the perimeter of the back acreage," Sherm said.

"Why wouldn't he move on?" Roman pondered aloud. "If it were me, I'd want to be hundreds of miles away from the place where I met my fate."

"Maybe he went as far as he could and stopped to heal?" Sherm offered.

Gage nodded. "Yeah, that could be what's going on."

Sherm hit speaker on his desk phone. "Travis, I want you to put an alert on that lone wolf. Let me know when he's on the move—if he leaves that location and doesn't just go out to hunt and return."

"Okay, I'm on it." Travis started work on the alert.

Sherm disconnected the call. He stared at Roman. "No more episodes?"

Roman shrugged. "Knock on wood. There's no telling what could trigger something. Mr. Tran's stuff has helped me tremendously."

"What about that social worker?" Sherm asked.

"That's been handled. We're going to move toward adoption," Roman said.

"Don't think in twenty years you're going to become our son-in-law!" Gage playfully slugged Sherm on the biceps.

"That was so cute," Sherm said.

Roman and Gage returned to the penthouse. Eddie was taking a nap. They found Ari in her suite at the computer, working on a spreadsheet.

"What are you working on?" Gage asked.

"A global shifter database. I'm combining the US database and the one Donatello and Marco created manually, of all the organizations they knew about," she explained. "I'm trying to determine the educational level of each shifter to determine how they can be uplifted in some way. Where did you two go?"

Gage explained his reconnaissance flight.

"You don't suppose he's going to backtrack and move into one of the cabins, do you?" Ari asked.

Roman pondered. "Surely, he's not stupid enough to do that, but Travis has an alert on him, so we'll know when he's on the move."

"That fucker better not even think of setting a toe on our property!" Gage fumed.

Ari made a face. "Language!"

"Eddie's napping. We can do and say anything while she's sleeping. I can't stop my bad language. I like cussing," Roman said.

"I'm setting up a bad language jar. Every time either of you is caught saying bad words, you put a dollar in the jar," Ari said. She got up and went to the kitchen, and entered the butler's pantry. She grabbed a canning jar and plunked it on the kitchen counter. "You can start, Gage. You owe the jar one dollar."

Gage grumbled, dug into the pocket of his jeans and pulled out crumpled bills. "Here's a five. I'm paying ahead."

Roman snorted and slugged Gage in the arm.

CHAPTER TWENTY-SIX

Two months passed quickly. Roman had no further episodes of aggression.

Ari had to get a larger hard drive and more memory for her computer to work her huge databases of shifters that included photos.

Gage was learning Italian.

Eddie settled into her new life.

The three wolves had crossed over into Canada, and Edmund Dovensky was last tracked in Colorado.

Jason seemed awfully interested in everything regarding the Panther Industries Italian headquarters and had made two trips. Ari bribed Donatello into spying on her son. He sent her a picture of Jason and Janina in a lip-lock, which she shared with Roman and Gage.

"Whoa! That's a pretty steamy kiss," Gage said. He nuzzled Ari's neck.

"Ah ha! That's why he gets twitchy whenever I go to his office. Bet he's shutting down FaceTime." Roman smirked.

"She seems like a nice girl," Ari said. "Do you think he's going to want to move there?"

"It's not like Janina can move here. The library is there in Fiuggi," Roman said. He placed his hands on Ari's shoulders.

"It's too soon to fret over this."

"Can't help it. It's the mother in me, and even if he were eighty, I'd still fret over him." Ari snuggled into Roman's chest. "Why's Kevin spending so much time traveling? Ever since he broke up with Amanda, he's been adrift."

"He's not adrift, Ari," Roman said. "He likes his work."

"What exactly does his work entail?" Ari had asked dozens of times and was always side-stepped from the answer.

"Look, he works with Sherm's division." Gage searched for something he could offer her that would not upset her. He came up empty-handed.

Ari pouted. "You two are hiding something from me."

Don't you dare tell her what he does, Roman sent.

I'm not going to step in the line of fire, but we have to come up with something. She doesn't need to know about his new skill sets, Gage sent.

"He helps the teams with wiring, setting up cameras—things like that," Roman said.

Ari studied him, then turned her focus on Gage. She huffed as she returned to her desk and her work. She wasn't falling for Roman's description of Kevin's work, and she knew they'd had a private discussion excluding her.

I heard you! Eddie called out to everyone.

The three of them were stunned. They stampeded to Eddie's sitting room where she was playing with her dolls. They sat on the surrounding floor.

"Okay, Eddie, there are important rules about mind-talk," Roman said.

"Never eavesdrop on someone's silent conversation," Gage said.

Ari glared at the men. "What your daddies mean is that mind-talk is our way of having private, silent conversations we don't want other people to hear—especially humans. Eavesdropping is like spying on people. We don't do that."

"Over time, you will learn how to talk to one person only and shut others out," Gage said.

"If you want to send me a private message and you didn't want to include Mommy or Gage, you could focus on me and they won't hear it," Roman said. "Want to try?"

Eddie looked wide-eyed with surprise. She nodded and thought really hard. *I'm going to talk to Daddy Roman.*

Roman smiled. He looked at Gage and Ari. "Did you receive Eddie's message just now?"

"Nope," Gage said.

"You did it!" Ari told Eddie. "What a big girl!"

Eddie thought really hard. *I won't tell mommy what you said about Kevin.*

Gage and Roman squirmed.

That's good. Sometimes it's better for mommy not to know something that would make her upset, Roman sent.

Thank you, princess, Gage sent.

I love you, Mommy!

I love you, too, Edris!

GAGE NAPPED ON HIS FAVORITE SOFA IN THE LIVING ROOM when his cell dinged. He stirred, reached over and snagged his phone off the coffee table, and looked at the screen. The eagle shifter chuckled, then sat up and slipped his shoes on. He went in search of Ari.

"Honey, I'm going over to Leander's store. Those shoes I ordered for Eddie came in." He opened his text and showed her the picture.

"Oh, those are so cute. She's going to love them." Ari kissed him on the cheek. "Be back for dinner."

"I'll only be gone for a half hour," Gage said.

"Uh huh. When you and Leander get talking, time flies," she said.

"Okay—I'll be back in an hour." Gage took off.

ARI WAS IN THE KITCHEN FINISHING UP MAKING A SALAD when her phone rang. She noticed it was Leander. "Hi. Did Gage forget something?"

He hasn't been here. I was calling you because he hasn't answered my calls or texts, and I'm about to close shop for the day, Leander said.

Ari looked confused. "He left here hours ago to pick up the shoes. Let me check with Roman. Maybe he caught up with Gage. I'll call you right back, but go home. Don't wait any longer."

Let me know what's going on, Leander said, and disconnected the call.

Roman! Is Gage with you?

No. I'm down here with Sherm. What's wrong?

He left here hours ago to go to Leander's store, and he never got there. I'm worried.

Five minutes later the elevator sounded. Roman and Sherm arrived in the penthouse and headed to the kitchen.

"We've both sent him texts and called his phone, but he doesn't answer either," Roman said.

Ari stiffened. She looked alarmed. "You don't think

someone has kidnapped him, do you?" She was on the verge of freaking out completely.

"Lonnie and Travis are looking at the cameras between here and Leander's shop," Sherm said. "It's not far. Three streets over and several blocks down."

Sherm's phone rang. "Find something?" He put his phone on speaker.

"Found the Mercedes on the way to Leander's place. Looks like it was in an accident. The driver's side door is open, but Gage isn't there," Lonnie said. "I'm headed over there."

"Let's go!" Ari said. She turned off the stove. "Eddie!"

Eddie came into the kitchen. She felt and saw the worry on everyone's faces. "What's wrong? Where's Daddy Gage?"

"Gage was in an accident in the car. We're heading over there to see if we can find him," Roman said. "Let's get your shoes on." He took Eddie's hand, walked her back to her room, and helped her with her tiny shoes.

They all went to the garage and got in the big SUV. Roman settled Eddie into her car seat and buckled her in. Sherm got behind the wheel, and they took off.

They arrived at Gage's car. Lonnie and his team were going over the Mercedes.

"There's blood on the driver's window. The airbag deployed," Lonnie said.

"White paint on the side here," one of his guys yelled out.

Roman looked at the passenger side of the car. "Can you get a scraping and identify the paint?"

"Do you think the other driver took Gage to the hospital or to a doctor?" Ari asked Sherm.

"That's a possibility," Sherm said. "I'll have people call hospitals and emergency clinics." He worked his phone.

Leander's car pulled up and parked. He got out of his car and joined them at the Mercedes. "Gage was in an accident?"

He looked in the car, then in the two SUVs, but didn't see Gage.

"He's not here," Ari said. She shifted Eddie on her hip.

Sherm's phone dinged multiple times. "He hasn't been in any of the emergency rooms or clinics."

Roman blasted out to the community. *King Gage has been in an accident. We don't know where he is. He may have a head injury. Please contact us immediately if you see him.*

Roman's cell rang. Caller ID showed an incoming call from Atsa, and Roman put the call on speaker.

"Are you sure this wasn't a staged accident?" Atsa asked.

To Be Continued...

Tilted, Book #3

Where is Gage?

The Panther Industries Security Division scours storefront cameras and satellite data, hoping to get a fix on his location.

Gage's bank account pings when he withdraws a large amount of cash, but the Division still can't find him. They speculate that his ongoing silence has something to do with his recent head injury.

Four days after his disappearance, a shifter recognizes Gage in a biker bar in Arkansas and reports back to Roman. Soon, Gage's closest friends and a team of commandos fly to Arkansas to retrieve him. Gage doesn't recognize anyone. He finds himself being hauled out of the bar, shoved into an SUV, and loaded onto a jet.

Dr. Tanner determines Gage has TBI: Traumatic Brain Injury caused by a concussion. Dr. Tanner and Mr. Tran begin treatment immediately. Gage is less than cooperative with everyone except Eddie. He adores her. She talks to him about his eagle—he scoffs at the notion that he is anything other than human.

Ari receives a special delivery letter from an attorney. She meets with the attorney and discovers that her Uncle Charles— whom she never knew existed—has passed away. Her uncle left his entire estate to Ari.

Sherm reaches out to the royals in a panic. His mother and grandmother are coming to visit. They bring news that shocks Sherm and everyone else. His entire life tilts.

The translations of the journals and big books continue. The shifter world is growing more organized and unified.

ABOUT THE AUTHOR

Dawn Greenfield Ireland (DG Ireland), the award-winning author, has written 22 published novels, including 5 series (cozy mystery, sci-fi/fantasy, billionaire shapeshifters, and dystopian), a stand-alone sci-fi romantic adventure, and 7 nonfiction books. Dawn has adapted 4 of her 15 screenplays into book format. She has also created over 50 themed notebooks

Two of her screenplays were optioned, and she worked on a screenwriter-for-hire project. Dawn has a certificate from the Professional Program in Screenwriting from UCLA (2002) and ScreenwritingU (2023).

Dawn's business, Artistic Origins, has been around since 1995. Besides writing, she coaches writers, edits books, formats and publishes clients' books.

Her former day job as an award-winning technical writer played a major role in her fiction writing. She is detail-oriented, the organizational queen of the known universe, and never misses a deadline.

If you buy her books and products, she'll love you forever.

TO ALL MY READERS... if you discover bloopers in this book (or any of my books), PLEASE send me an email and tell me what the blooper is so I can fix it! dawn@degreenfield.com

 facebook.com/dawn.ireland.18

 x.com/dawnireland

 instagram.com/dawngreenfieldIreland

 goodreads.com/dawnireland

 linkedin.com/in/dawnireland

www.ingramcontent.com/pod-product-compliance
Lightning Source LLC
Chambersburg PA
CBHW021210250626
47155CB00008B/2760